ORDINARY MIRACLES

MARTYN CAREY

Matador
9 Priory Business Park,
Wistow Road, Kibworth Beauchamp,
Leicestershire. LE8 0RX
Tel: 0116 279 2299
Email: books@troubador.co.uk
Web: www.troubador.co.uk/matador
Twitter: @matadorbooks

ISBN 978 1838594 602

British Library Cataloguing in Publication Data.
A catalogue record for this book is available from the British Library.

Printed and bound in Great Britain by 4edge Limited
Typeset in 11pt Palatino by Troubador Publishing Ltd, Leicester, UK

Matador is an imprint of Troubador Publishing Ltd

For Anna, for letting me do this
and
Jane, for not letting me stop

1

With no more than a whisper of sound the steam train hurtled into Paddington Station and crashed through the buffers. The noise was huge, shocking, a blow to the ears, even in that vast, high space. It ploughed through the concourse, blasting debris around like a bomb exploding. There had been people sitting on the banks of chairs, idly looking at the departure screens, but I lost sight of them when the mass of steam and steel gouged its way through the station. It crashed into the back wall, almost reached the lobby of the Hilton Hotel on Praed Street. The screaming started before the echoes had died.

I'd been trudging across the station, muffled against the bitter midnight wind and feeling unsettled, probably from a hasty kebab, when it happened. I dropped my bag and ran towards the crash, grabbing shocked and confused people and urging them away. One man was standing rigid, staring at a fragment of something embedded in his arm and screaming in an oddly high-pitched voice. *Part of a bone from someone else's leg*, I thought, feeling a lurch of nausea. The woman next to him appeared to be uninjured, but was immobile with shock, wide-eyed and trembling.

I grabbed a bruised and limping teenager and used her

to guide them both away from the area. Two men in high-vis jackets, stumbling on the debris that littered the ground, had made a cross-hand seat for a man with a badly broken leg. A mute and limp child, its face a mask of blood, was being rushed away by a distraught looking man, a palely-ineffectual woman trailing behind them weeping.

It was a blur of images, soaked in adrenaline and fear; glimpses and moments as victims fled the scene. The trail of blood behind some of them should have made me feel sick, but I felt nothing.

Once they were clear I started searching for the injured amongst the crushed and scattered benches. My mind was numb, no emotions edging in, despite the evident danger, and yet there was a tremor in my hands that I couldn't stop. 'Cope at the time, shake afterwards' – what psychologists call 'deliberate calm' – has always been my way in an emergency.

I could see others rushing to the rescue elsewhere in the cavernous station, but that didn't concern me. These were my people to save, to heal, although I am not a Healer. The hiss of the train's boiler was getting worryingly loud when I discovered a man in a Crossrail jacket, clutching the back of his head and crawling in the wrong direction. I turned him towards rescue and tried to get him to walk, but the way he tracked my voice told me that he was blind. A member of the station staff darted forward to help him.

As they stumbled away I turned back to the traces of life that I could detect under the rubble, twisted steel and crushed displays. A few seconds later, and a few feet closer to the trembling metalwork, I found a child of perhaps four beneath some seats that had been thrown over by the impact. He stared up at me with wide, blank eyes and gripped his mother's hand. She was unconscious, her hair bloody, her clothes torn. I pushed the benches away without touching them.

"Don't worry, everything will be fine," I said. I wasn't certain who I was trying to reassure. "Let's wake mummy up, shall we?" My voice felt weak, but the child nodded, his face serious but oddly not frightened. Shock, I suspect. Now I did feel sick.

I bent over the mother, fighting a horrified vision of trying to drag this child away from a corpse, but it wasn't necessary. I placed my hands gently on the mother's head and did my best to help her. She slowly woke, blinked at me, felt her son's hand in her own and squeezed it gently. I helped her to sit up.

"Come on, we need to get you away from here," I said, easing her to her feet. A younger man, his obviously broken arm supported inside his jacket, appeared from nowhere and guided them to where the blue flashing lights chasing around the walls showed that ambulances and the police were arriving. I should have been relieved that they were there, that I could escape and leave this to the professionals, but I wasn't. I knew that there were three more people under my bit of the smashed train and I knew that I couldn't leave them.

By now I was right up under the lee of the first carriage, with the engine and tender almost out of sight across the platform. It was leaning heavily towards me, supported by only the sagging departures board. From the way it was trembling it was obvious the inevitable collapse was only briefly delayed. The metal groaned as I edged closer. I suppose I should have been too frightened to go near it in case it finished falling over and landed on me.

I wasn't scared because I wasn't anything. There were people that needed help, so I had to help them. The tremor in my fingers was worse; I tried to pretend it was the cold.

A hand pushed aside some fractured and jagged metal, and I saw a face. A man, a man I'd never seen before, trying to pull himself out from under the mass of razor-sharp steel and broken stone. He reached out, a gesture of supplication, a wordless cry for help. I dashed forward, and his face changed from despair to hope to relief. I had just touched his hand, felt the cold sweat and recognised the copper smell of fresh blood, when the departure board finally gave up the unequal struggle and collapsed.

The noise, the shock, the blast of air was violent, terrifying. Everyone in the station turned to look. Except me. The falling steel had missed me by bare inches, but had landed squarely on the man I was trying to help. I felt his hand jerk, tighten and then fall slack as the life went out of his eyes. Something powerful rushed through me then, driving me to my knees, leaving me dizzy and disorientated for a moment. I gashed my shin on some broken glass as I fell, but I didn't feel it. "I'm sorry," I whispered, then finally let go of his hand.

I was numb again. There should have been fear, rage, fury, sadness, sickness... there should have been *something*, but there was just nothing. The twisting collapse, the fall of the huge departures board, had exposed the other two people I had known were there. One was far beyond help, and I looked stony-eyed at the ruin of the man and didn't even try. The other was a dark-haired slip of a girl, barely into her teens, just conscious, with a long bloody gash down one thigh, bone and muscle exposed. I couldn't see or feel any other injuries, but I knew that she was in danger of bleeding to death.

I ran over to her, pushing back the teetering metal that was almost brushing her face. I used so much force that one of the departure board stanchions snapped as it fell away and shattered, and the fragments fell around me like lethal iron hail. I wrapped my hands around the gash and tried to stop the bleeding.

I could feel the blood slick and throbbing as her pulse raced her towards her own death, but I didn't stop. I tried not to think about what I was doing, the closeness of the dead man and the groan of the metal as it started to sink towards me again. The bleeding had slowed when the paramedics arrived.

"We'll take over now." With kindly force they moved me out of the way, flushed the wound, strapped it up and had the girl on a stretcher within half a minute. I just stood and watched. "You'd best get back," said one of the paramedics. "That don't look too safe to me." I took his advice, moving back away from the train. I didn't know who the girl was, or if she would survive.

Then the most astonishing, most terrifying thing of all happened. The train re-formed into its undamaged state, in exactly the reverse order of its disintegration, and then disappeared.

The engine vanishing made everyone in the huge space stop and stare. They were surprised; so was I, but it frightened me more than anything else that had happened. Because that meant this wasn't terrorism, a tragic accident or a spectacular suicide. This could only be magic, and because I am a mage, a wizard if you like, that meant that when they went looking for someone to blame, they might well come looking for me.

2

I kept my head down and went on doing what I could to save lives, limbs and sanity until there was no more that I could do. I stumbled into a corner with the other people who'd been helping and was given coffee – which was awful – and then, huddled in my coat, fell into a shallow, troubled sleep, despite the noise, at around two in the morning. Nobody asked us to leave, or seemed to pay us much attention at all. They were far too busy with people who needed immediate assistance.

The damage didn't look any better when I woke up about three hours later, but by then all the bodies were gone and a bloody catastrophe had become an exercise in civil engineering. Without the train itself the destruction seemed less, as if removing the cause had somehow diminished it.

All the civilians who had helped gave their details to the police and were officially thanked by the emergency services. I was taken into the station staff changing room, where they let me have a shower and put on some clothes that weren't soaked in blood. After some rudimentary first aid to my hands and leg they found me a taxi to take me to St Pancras for the first train home.

I picked up the early editions of the newspapers when I got there. Information was scarce, so they said little beyond a basic description of what had happened. As I rode the escalator up to the platform I realised that none of the people reading the newspaper had any idea that the ordinary looking twenty-something man in the background of some of the photographs, exhausted, haggard and bloodstained, was me. For some obscure reason I felt cheated by that. The newspapers were calling us heroes, but I couldn't accept it. I didn't feel like a hero for having done it, but I would have felt like a coward if I hadn't.

The journey home took the usual hour and a half, and it passed with the speed of a tranquilised sloth. My thoughts were incoherent, racing then sluggish. I felt detached and, now, scared. I knew I had Healed people but I didn't know how, because Healing is not a Talent I possess. Had I made any mistakes?

If I'd gone to help the man under the stanchion first, would he have survived? But if I had, would I have been able to save the mother and her little boy as well? Would the teenage girl have bled to death in the meantime? There were no answers, just an acid parade of 'what ifs'. I spilled my coffee because my hands were shaking so much.

*

The fuss when I got to the college in Nottingham that afternoon was, unsurprisingly, huge. When I got to the common room, all worn chairs, chipped tables and scattered papers, I had expected to see the usual collection of people drinking coffee, staring at their mobiles and treating the laws of physics as a matter of opinion. Instead, everyone in the room was facing the front where Professor Wicks, the head of the college, was about to speak. She looked grim.

"What…?" I began, but my friend Amy, serious water Talent and trainee psychopath, grabbed me by the arm and pulled me into a seat next to her wheelchair. Clara, her magical partner, nodded from the other side of her, but didn't speak.

"Mike, sit down and shut up," said Amy quietly, then ignored me, which is fairly typical. Professor Wicks didn't glare, because it's hard to glare and look that disturbed at the same time.

"You're aware of the incident in London," she said. She's short, blonde and from Texas or Arizona or somewhere else that's hot and American. "People ain't happy. We gotta become acclimated to being under suspicion. What we do ain't exactly secret, and most folk can't recognise us with a flashlight and a mugshot, but who we are is gonna leak out."

"Like sewage from a broken drain," muttered a dark brown voice behind me. It just had to be Ambrose. He's a pure-blood Ghanaian and as usual he was dressed in the traditional clothes of his homeland; jeans and a sweatshirt with something rude on it – he comes from Bethnal Green.

"What can we do?" The man speaking from the front row had shoulder-length ice-white hair, with suspiciously dark roots, and a taste for flowing black and emerald clothes. Unfortunately his name is Brian, which rather spoils the effect.

"Do?" Professor Wicks snorted. "What do ya think? Keep your fool heads down, don't mention magic, don't let anyone see your books and focus on your normal degree work."

"But surely there is something that we can do to track down this dastard?" Brian said. He can't spell sententious but, boy, does he know how to do it.

"No. Somebody capable of doing this would eat most of you for breakfast. You'd end up with brains like kitty litter, those of you that ain't like that already. The Central College is putting together a team. None of you will be on it." She paused. "You understood all that?" None of the two dozen or so people in the room spoke. "Good. Now push off – I'm busy." She strode away without another glance.

Terry-Anne Wicks would, I suspect, be happier if there were no students getting in the way of her research.

"Who in hell would want to wreck a railway station?" Ambrose asked the room.

"Who the hell would want to wreck a railway station in the middle of the night?" Amy replied. "Would have been much more effective if it was full of people."

Psycho under construction, yeah?

"What I don't get is how they did it," I said tentatively. Already the abstract, intellectual discussion in this drably familiar space had begun to soften the impact. It felt like it might not have even been me that was there, but some alternate version of me.

I had been able to tell my parents something of what had happened when I got home, but not all of it. They knew that there was very little that they could say, so mum had just given me a hug, put me in the shower, fed me breakfast and let me sleep for a few hours.

"That's because you don't have any magic bone in your body," said a light voice behind me.

"Hello, Sam." Sam is my magical partner and a stupendously powerful air Talent. She draped her arm around my shoulders and leant heavily on my back. I'm no more than averagely big, if fairly heavily muscled, but Sam is short and slight and fragile looking. I can just about claim to be five-foot ten – that's 1.77m for the metrically inclined – and she barely comes up to my chin.

Her magic is amazingly powerful, but that means that she tires quickly when doing big spells. Her leaning on me might have seemed like an affectionate gesture, but I could feel her drawing *Indar* (strength) from me. I winced – the back of my left shoulder was quite sore. Some unfelt impact at the station, probably. My shin was certainly still painful.

"Aah, sweet," said Amy, pulling her strawberry-blonde hair back into a metallic tie. She does have a powered wheelchair, but only uses it occasionally, so her arms and shoulders are shapely with muscle.

"Stick it," I said with a tight smile, although I felt sweat touch my forehead.

"You want to try sticking something near me?"

"In your dreams, buddy."

She laughed, made a half-hearted attempt to run me over and headed for the college coffee shop. I swear she would put blades on the wheels if she were allowed.

"The technique that appears to have been employed in this case – although making such a swingeing assumption on such scant evidence is barely defensible – was a variation of *Irmo Argi*."

"Damn," said Ambrose, which earned him a disapproving glare from the cadaverous Professor Weaver, who had been standing, unnoticed, at the back of the common room.

"Indeed," said Weaver and coughed. I don't know if it's a nervous habit or a persistent respiratory infection, but he seems to punctuate almost everything with a cough. "Creating 'hard-light' objects, although the term is no more than approximately accurate, is very advanced and requires intense focus and concentration. Other than in truly exceptional cases, one would have to be *Jaun* 4 to create such a thing." Weaver had a faint trace of a West Country burr, but it was mostly overlain by the more dominant accent of desiccated academia.

Even Ambrose was silenced by that. *Jaun* means 'master', like a black belt in karate or something. There is only one person above *Jaun* 6 in the whole college – Professor Wicks, who is *Jaun* 8. Weaver and the other professors are all *Jaun*

5 at least. As students, we are *Iksale* (er... student), graded 10 to 1. Ambrose is *Iksale* 5, which is typical for a third year, despite being a year or so older than me. Amy is *Iksale* 3, as is her magical partner, Clara. Sam and I have been grade 2 for a while now. Just one more grade, then several years as *Ikasberri* (apprentice) and then we can try for *Jaun*. A lot of mages never make it to *Jaun* at all. Not all of them even make it to *Ikasberri*.

But whatever flavour of mage you were, whichever of the Talents you specialised in, we all knew that the magical world was in serious trouble.

*

You probably don't know that there are Colleges of Magic. We very much do not advertise, and even the stubborn and ubiquitous Google has trouble pinning us down. Magic has been around since pretty much forever, but it didn't get properly organised until we gave up burning witches. The first proper magical college in the UK (in the world in fact), a centre dedicated solely to the study of magic, was opened in Cirencester in the 1650s. It was shut down, and then burnt down, by the professional killjoys of the Catholic church less than ten years later.

Most of the current colleges were founded in the mid to late eighteen-somethings. The two dozen or so are scattered across the country, in places like Southampton, Wrexham, Newcastle and Bristol. Oxford and Cambridge were offered colleges, but they thought that they were special enough already and both declined to house one.

Most colleges are within universities, and we even have our equivalent of the Russell Group, which consists of Chester, Swansea, Nottingham, Glasgow, Norwich, Larne and Falmouth. I know that all seems very professional and properly regulated, but don't be fooled – the organisation of the colleges is mostly held together by good will, bloody-mindedness and gaffer tape. This was going to put a severe strain on everyone.

3

The nature of the crash, and my level of involvement in it, meant that I had no choice but to tell my family that I was a mage. It was inevitable that the police would want to ask me some more questions, and it would come out then, so...

I had tried to do it before, of course, but however often I dropped the hint, nobody had ever caught it. So after I got home from college that afternoon I simply said it straight out.

"You're doing what? I thought you said you were doing a theology course." Mum stopped tidying the supper table to stare at me, which is a millennial event in itself. She didn't sound very pleased.

"Thaumaturgy, mum, not theology. The study of magic."

She tried to be understanding and accepting and all that stuff, but horrified smells the same whatever label you put on it. People like us just aren't mages. People from boring middle-class homes in boring middle-class suburbs of Nottingham aren't mages. Or goths. Or *Daily Mail* readers, for that matter – I mean, there are limits.

"What, with spells and wands and... that kind of thing? Isn't it a bit, you know, I mean, do your friends know? What do they think about you being... like that?"

"Billy, Amin and a few others from karate know, and

they're mostly fine about it. They don't mind provided I don't start doing... stuff. Some people are curious, but mostly... we just don't talk about it. It's my thing and they're OK with it, as long as I don't try to recruit them to the college." Not that I could – you're either born a mage or you aren't, but it's a typical reaction.

Finding out that you can cause minor earth tremors just by getting cross does come as a bit of a shock, but fortunately the college detects emerging Talents very quickly. When they contacted me I asked them not to tell my parents, and because I was sixteen, they didn't. Instead, Professor Weaver rather huffily taught me enough to keep my magic under control until I got to college, when my proper training started. That kind of culture shock, and the realisation that you actually *are* different, can be quite a thing for an impressionable young mind.

It isn't difficult getting to be a mage; you're born like that. Getting to be good at it – that's another matter. The training is confusing, difficult and occasionally bloody dangerous, as is trying to hide it when you've done something wrong. I've had lots of practice at that. Of course, I didn't explain any of this to the parents. I don't like to hide stuff from them, but sometimes you do have to... shade things a bit.

Then there's the matter of your partner. All mages work with a partner, otherwise it's like trying to chase a rainbow with your hand tied to a tree. Mages never operate alone. Well, they do, of course, when they're making tea or changing their socks, but they rarely do when there are really serious spells to be done.

Mage pairs are normally the same gender, within two years of each other in age, never the same Talent, and uniformly very bright. A stupid mage is generally referred to as an 'unexplained death'. The subtitle 'police baffled' appears to be compulsory, as is laying the blame at the door of the government, the CIA, the Russians, UFOs, the Freemasons or immigrants, depending on which newspaper you read.

You don't get to choose your partner either, the magic does that, but nobody has been able to work out how. The first thing you do – Day One, Freshers' Week at college – is to find out who it is. Well no, the first thing you do is find where the bar and the toilets are, but you get the idea. And before you ask, no, we don't use a bloody Sorting Hat. The professors do a spell and it's like fireworks in your head and you just find yourself standing with them. Unnerving would be a good word.

I told my parents that my partner's name was Sam, which is true, in an abbreviated sort of way. I am mostly British, wearily middle-class, educated to the point of boredom and twenty-three years old. Sam – which is short for Samantha, even though her real name is Yu Ying Lee – is Hong Kong Chinese, part of the rump of their nobility and nineteen. Her name means 'Jade Eagle' (I suspect mine would be 'Jaded Englishman') and she already has better university grades than I do. If she were any brighter I'd be standing her in front of solar panels.

"Yes, mum, I'm training to be a mage, a wizard."

"Oh warlocks," said Simon. He's my kid brother, a brat of the first water with the magical potential of a lightly stunned beagle. "You know, that might be the first cool thing you've ever done," he said. I ignored him.

"But why do you want to do it?" Mum asked, sounding bemused, the same tone that she used when I enthused about my favourite pop groups when I was a kid.

"Well, it isn't a choice – you're either a mage or you aren't. You can't choose any more than you can choose the colour of your eyes."

"Couldn't you, I don't know, just not do it?"

"No. I have to learn how to control it, otherwise I

might accidentally burn the house down, turn dad into a newt or explode."

"Don't let me stop you," muttered Simon. He's nearly eighteen and a collection of elbows and knees held together with acne and hair gel.

Dad, magisterial in zipped cardigan and tartan slippers, stirred slightly. "If Michael has alighted upon a path, why shouldn't he be able to pursue it?"

"That's what you said when he told us that he was going to be an astronaut," replied mum drily.

I was about twelve, OK, space shuttles were bouncing up and down like a hyperactive toddler on a pogo stick, and it seemed like a really cool job.

"Well," said dad, "I for one have no desire to be turned into a frog. Let him be."

"So what do we call you then?" Simon asked as he edged towards the door. "The Amazing Bunko and Doris?"

"I'll bloody Bunko you in a minute," I warned, but he ignored it, just like he ignores everything I say apart from 'do you fancy a pint?'. Talking about this was uncomfortable, but I couldn't just leave it.

"I know you finish uni next summer," said mum, loading the dishwasher distractedly, "but when do you stop doing the... other thing?"

"I'll finish my training about the same time as I get my degree, but you never really stop – I'll be a member of the Nottingham... group... forever, wherever I am. This stuff doesn't wear off; it just gets stronger."

"Really?"

"Well, it is possible to lose your... abilities, but it's unusual."

Dad flexed his paper back in front of his face, which signalled that the discussion was over. I was still really weary, so I went to my room and tried to read, but images of the crash kept getting in between me and the words. Mum woke me an hour or so later, tactfully not mentioning that I'd been crying in my sleep.

*

So as soon as it reached beer o'clock I went to the pub; it's called the Slug & Botulism or something and the food is legendarily dodgy. The wood on the bar has a shiny veneer, like the smiles of the staff, but it does serve decent ales and they don't turn the music up so loud that you have to shout to order a drink.

Most of the senior grades from my karate class were there, as normal. Billy, Josh and Amin were at our usual table and arguing about something – well, bickering really, the kind of circular discussion that rattles around and around as the pints vanish until you realise everyone is talking utter bollocks. Its familiarity was a reassuring return to my ordinary, not very exciting, life.

It was Amin who read my expression right. "Oh, you've told the parents then?" I nodded. "I take it that it wasn't a positive experience?"

"Could have been worse, I suppose," I shrugged. "I mean, the room could have been full of snakes as well."

"Told you that you shouldn't tell them," said Billy, taking a long, slightly unsteady pull on his drink and putting the glass back on the table with a definite, if rather wobbly, gesture. So probably his third pint that evening.

"Bloody did not, you tosser – it was you that said I should." I made a tiny wedge of power and pushed his glass towards him.

Josh lifted it off the table and glared down at me – he looks like an emaciated Viking; blond, six-foot-lots tall and built like chopsticks, with a fearsome roundhouse kick and the IQ of a gibbon.

"I wish you wouldn't do that," he said. "It's just unnatural."

"I don't get it," I said. "Why have you suddenly got a problem with this?" I gritted my teeth – the last thing I needed today was to be challenged about anything more serious than what sort of crisps I wanted.

"You know why. You shouldn't be doing that in public. You shouldn't be doing it at all." He made a conciliatory gesture. "I know you can't help yourself but… it's people like… I mean, it's this sort of thing that's behind those girls dying in Scotland – magic going wrong. If they hadn't been doing that stuff in the first place it wouldn't have killed them. And now that business in London." He made it sound as remote as Venus.

I knew nothing about any girls. "Well, sort of. But then you could equally say that dear old Agnes in her Honda Grey-Mobile is behind some moronic boy racer stuffing his Impreza into a motorway bridge at a hundred miles an hour."

"No I couldn't," said Josh sharply. "That's basic idiocy; what you do is a violation of the natural order of things."

"How can it be a violation? Nobody did anything to me to make this happen." I was getting cross and uncomfortable with this now, which is not something that usually happens. I took a deep breath, releasing the tension in my muscles, and ran my hand over my face. Still needed a shave.

I didn't want to tell them what I had done at Paddington, because I was afraid they would think I was boasting or fishing for compliments if I did. Maybe I should have. They would have understood, I'm fairly sure. I was amazed that they couldn't see the blood on my hands, but then I blinked and realised that there wasn't any.

"I'm not so sure about that," said Josh, looking away. I've known him through thick and thin, and his other girlfriends, but he's never been comfortable with even the idea of magic.

It's a common enough attitude, but that doesn't make it any easier to live with.

Amin sniggered. "Will you two stop it? It's like listening to an old married couple arguing about what they're having for dinner."

Josh glared at him. "Why aren't you bothered by this?"

"Why would I be?" He shrugged, his dark eyes serious. "He's no more able to stop this than you are to stop being ridiculously tall."

Josh fell silent, taking a long pull on his pint. He looked very uncomfortable. "I'm sure you use it to cheat in competitions."

"I don't need to cheat to beat you, you great streak of piss."

"Bloody do, short arse."

"Bugger off."

Amin shook his head. "Now, now, children, let's try to play nicely."

"Drink your orange juice and shut up."

Amin laughed and threw a beer mat at me. I almost stopped it in mid-air but thought better of it and ducked.

"Oi, you lot," came a voice from behind the bar. "Pack it in or you're out."

"Yes, mum," said Billy, grinning at the girl. When it was time for us to go home I couldn't help noticing that while Josh was happy to ride in the front of the car with Amin, he wouldn't look at me.

He had only understood about real magic for a few months – before that he thought I did it for kids' parties – and I wasn't sure he would be around much in the future because of it. That made me sad – I'd known him since school, but I wasn't going to give up something like this just for him, even if I could.

*

19

Breakfast was unusually muted; I'd got home late and slept badly, so everything, especially getting up, had been a struggle. Even my normally reliable basic magical skills seemed rough and no longer effortless. I felt old and creaky; although I'm only in my twenties, people say I act and think much older; I always have. No idea why. Sam calls me an 'old soul' and suggested that I could be a reincarnation. Most people just think I'm a boring old fart. Even Simon was quiet, which either meant another hangover or trouble with his boyfriend, Idris (as in Elba, but any resemblance beyond that is entirely wishful thinking).

"Bad business, this crash," said dad. I didn't have much idea of the details – I hadn't wanted to find out – so he showed me the front of his paper. The police had released all the information, and it was horrifying.

"Bloody hell."

Contrary to normal practice I took my toast into the front room and turned on the TV. The breakfast presenters were looking grim about what had happened, but pleased to have something of substance to talk about.

I watched the reporters standing far enough away to be safe, but close enough that everyone could see the rubble. They were talking about how the train seemed to vanish, and speculating about what had happened. Even though the damage was extensive, they said that, fortunately, the casualty list was small.

It doesn't seem like a small list when you've got someone else's blood in your eyes and you can't hear the tannoy for the screaming.

They had got as far as asking random passers-by what they thought had happened when I turned it off, my toast cold and forgotten. "This has got to be something to do with you," said dad heavily.

"Not me personally," I protested absently, glancing up

20

at him. "I just happened to be there." I blinked rapidly. "I tried to help. I used everything I could." My hands weren't steady. "I really did." The dying man looked up at me until I blinked him away.

"But this was magic…"

"What we do is just a set of skills, dad – it doesn't make us devils or angels. Some people who can paint really well create images of uplifting beauty; some of them do heavy metal album art. It's like that."

"Were you involved in making this happen?" This was very blunt, and marked how disturbed dad was.

"No, not at all."

"It's just that you were there, weren't you?"

"Yes I was. I'm sure I was also near several car crashes, at least one assault and several instances of being drunk and disorderly. I can crash cars, hit people and drink heavily, but that doesn't mean I'm responsible for it every time it happens." I may have been a little irritated at this point. I wanted to scream 'just leave me alone', but habit and circumstances told me that this was not an appropriate reaction.

Dad was silent for a moment. "Fair comment."

"I need coffee," I said. I thought dad was looking at me darkly, but it might have been dyspepsia. We headed back into the kitchen.

"So," said mum, trying to restore normal life by being relentlessly domestic. "What are you up to today?"

"Back to classes," I replied carefully. "I've got an essay on the ecological impact of the Industrial Revolution to finish." I'm reading Environmental Sciences, which isn't nearly as much fun as it sounds.

Silence, until Simon stirred. "So when are we going to meet Doris?"

"Who," said dad, eyes on his truncated egg, "is Doris?"

"The Amazing Bunko's charming assistant."

"Oh yes. Sam, isn't it?" I shouldn't have been amazed but I still was – dad doesn't seem to listen to anything but he still hears everything, even when he isn't in the room. "Sam…?" He let the question hang.

"Lee. Sam Lee."

He nodded. "Where's he from?"

"Parents live in Hong Kong, but I don't think that's where they're from originally."

He nodded again. "Same age as you?"

"A little younger, and very bright."

"He does the same sort of things as you?"

"Yes, but specialising in meteorology." I didn't discuss the whole mage pairs thing at that point – if you get too far into it, it can sound like a dating agency for the terminally deluded. The conversation lapsed, so I decided to leave.

"Essay," I said, and poured myself more coffee. Dad nodded; mum smiled; Simon ignored me. I left. It still felt uncomfortable in the house.

*

Mum and dad were a bit less inclined to blame me for the train crash by the next day. I'd tactfully spent the night at a friend's house in Leicester to try to lower the temperature. I'd worked steadily once they'd gone to work, but by mid-morning the essay I was writing made no sense, even to me, so I decided to go for a walk; walking and drinking coffee are things I do a lot.

The streets around us are leafy, quiet and full of Volvos for the poor people and Audis for the rich ones. It's about as exciting as a paint catalogue, and as it was late November it was also bloody freezing. I'd only got as far as the coffee shop on the main road, the Cosy Café, or the Costly Café as most people call it, when Sam mentally nudged me. I'd nearly dropped my mobile calling her back because my hands were so cold, so I decided to go in there for a bit of a warm.

"What have I done now?" I asked as my coffee arrived, slopped into a saucer that smelled of washing-up liquid. I was the only person in there.

"Nothing," she replied, "as usual."

"So what…?"

"Professor Wicks want us all in college now. Been another one."

"What, now?" I sipped my drink and set it aside without regret.

"*Shì.*"

"OK."

*

"There has been another incident," said Professor Wicks. The room looked just the same as last time, but now Amy was gripping my hand, her face a mask of concern. I don't know if she was holding my hand or I was holding hers, but I couldn't help but notice the warmth and the hard patches from pushing her wheelchair. I don't know if she noticed the tremor in mine.

"But…," Brian started.

"Shaddap," said the professor, cutting him off with an abrupt gesture. "Last time it was a train in London. This time it was a large vehicle, truck sized, damn near demolished a multi-storey parking garage in the centre of Leicester."

"When?" The voice was Ambrose, but the thought belonged to all of us.

"Last night. The police department thought it was just an RTC, even though they couldn't find the driver, right up to the moment when the vehicle just ups and vanishes right in front of them." Despite the excellent heating system, the room suddenly felt cold.

"Injuries?"

"It was three o'clock in the AM, so not so many, although one person is reported dead. Half the building fell into the underpass next to it, and they still haven't managed to clear the highway." She smiled with bleak humour. "This is now officially fucking serious," she said. "Things are going to get real difficult for all of us 'less this gets sorted out real quick."

She left, in her abrupt sort of way, and the room fell into a shocked muttering. At least one person was crying.

Amy looked at me. "Why didn't you tell us you were at Paddington?"

"I'd been staying with a friend near Windsor." I shrugged. "So I... was just there, so... I helped. I couldn't walk away." I was embarrassed at the idea this was somehow noteworthy. I mean, it was what anyone would have done, wasn't it?

Ambrose sighed. "Typical. Why is it always you that *happens* to get involved when something goes off? And when you chuck yourself into the middle of something real big you just forget to mention that you're a bleedin' hero." A few other people were listening now, which was embarrassing, so I tried to make light of it.

"I'm not a hero. I just wanted to help." I tried to get up, to leave, but Amy wouldn't let me.

"They screened the CCTV footage on the TV, Mike," she said, looking at me intently. "Pulling people out from under a gantry just before it collapses? That's trip to Buck House-level bravery that is."

I shrugged again. I didn't know what to say. "Um... thanks." I may have blushed.

Ambrose laughed. "Come on, Superman, I'll get you a coffee." We walked away and I noticed Amy smiling and shaking her head.

Sam came into the coffee shop a little while later, when the crowd had thinned from a throng to a scattering; she was vibrating strongly – not literally, I mean you couldn't have used her to mix a Martini, for example – but in the way you do when you've just cast a really big spell. The power to cast spells comes from the person casting them, so big spells use a lot of energy. "What have you been doing?"

"Professor Weaver ask me to do locator spell with him. All professors are looking for who sent vehicles." She sat down heavily next to me and sighed.

I nodded, refusing to be more impressed than necessary. Mind you, that's still a lot of impressed. 'Track and trace' spells are easier, but they can only give you the general direction that somebody is in. A full power locator spell, properly called *Maparen*, can pinpoint anything, even inanimate objects. Unsurprisingly, locator spells are bloody hard to do, and as an air Talent, it isn't something that Sam specialises in. "You all right?"

"Tired." I reached out and took her hand. She had so little strength I was amazed that she was upright, so I channelled a lot of *Indar* into her. She breathed very slowly as her colour improved, and after a few minutes she seemed much more her usual self. She squeezed my hand and I let go.

"*Xiè Xiè.*" Sam often uses Mandarin for short phrases like 'thank you'. I knew that she would do the same for me – had done in fact – it's just part of how it works with mages. She smiled as the coffee shop bustled around us, although the clatter of cups and bright, brittle speculations seemed unnaturally intrusive.

"Who were you trying to locate?"

"I said, person who send train. Professor got faint *esku*." The word *esku* literally means 'hand', but it signifies a recognisable way of spell-casting, the same way Morse operators can identify who is sending a message just by the way they tap out the letters.

"Enough for an identification?"

She shook her head and looked at her watch. "I go. I have lunch with Jerry, Ambrose and others people. *Huítóu jiàn.*"

"Yeah, see you later." In case you were wondering, I don't speak Mandarin, but because the link between us is so strong, I usually know pretty much what she's saying, except some of the really rude words. 'Son of a water buffalo' is one of her favourite curses, and she has a number of insults that involve eggs, for some reason.

The rest of the room emptied. With the events of the previous days catching up with me, I moved off the table and onto the vaguely comfortable chairs by the window. I wasn't really thinking anything, idly flicking fragments of light into the air and watching them fade slowly away. The spell is *Zirta*, which means 'spark', but we usually call them 'sprites'. Professor Gowan, my tutor, calls it 'messing about', so of course it was her that found me, half an hour later, still communing with them. I couldn't stir myself to do anything, and I kept wiping my hands on my trousers like they were sticky.

"Michael."

I looked up. "Hello." All my sprites stopped moving. "Did Professor Weaver find anything?"

"A little," she replied, sinking gracefully into the chair next to me. She's quite tall and elegant, with cropped brown hair and grey eyes, but she pays very little attention to her appearance. If she had been from a council estate she would have lived in a shiny tracksuit.

"Has it given you a clue about why this is happening, or who's doing it?"

"No. Well, not much anyway." She didn't seem disposed to say any more, so I started the sprites moving again.

She watched them with a faint smile, then raised several of her own that swerved and swooped around mine, leaving varicoloured contrails like a very expensive neon advertising sign.

I added contrails to mine as well, and they danced around each other for a little. Several people came over to watch, but nobody spoke. This kind of genial competition is quite commonplace, and is often used to settle disputes like whose round it is or who's going to tidy up the mess *this* time.

Professor Gowan upped the stakes by broadening her contrails into ribbons and sustaining them for longer as they passed. I took a deep breath and split mine, so each of my contrails became two, then three, which wove around each other in a scintillating sky dance. I changed the colours and added more sprites, but she matched me with ease – she is *Jaun* 6 after all.

I added noises, whooshing mine around like jet aeroplanes, so she added smoke, then set her sprites going around and around at high speed to create a sphere that contained all of mine. It must have been six feet across by the time it settled, and attempting to break through it was like trying to punch a hole through concrete with a kipper.

She was looking relaxed, so I left my sprites zooming around inside the sphere and created another, like the King Kong of fireflies. I shot it straight up into the sphere of light and shattered it into a million fragments, like smashing a huge glass Christmas bauble, but without the swearing and sweeping up afterwards. All the sprites dissipated in one silent, varicoloured moment.

The professor gave a delighted laugh and clapped her hands. The assembled throng applauded, including, I was startled to see, Professor Wicks. For once she didn't look like she was sucking lemons.

She looked at Gowan. "Catriona, was that *Dantza* 2?"

"No. 5."

Her eyebrows crept up slightly. "So he's...?"

"Aye." Sometimes she sounds very Scottish.

"Come to my office," Wicks said to me. "Get Sam here too." Mystified, I nudged Sam and, to a hum of speculation, followed the two most powerful mages in the college out of the common room.

*

"What you done now?"

These were, typically, Sam's first words when she came into the office. I shrugged, looking confused, mostly because I was.

Wicks leant back in her creaky swivel chair and ignored the papers scattered all over the battered wooden desk. "Right, well, I'm going to do something real unusual now," she said. "Catriona?"

"Sam, the locator spell you did," said Gowan, looking serious but pleased, "was a *Jaun*-level casting. We already know that you're powerful but the level of control and stamina that you displayed was... remarkable." She looked at me. "And your little game just now..." She shook her head.

"I was just flying sprites," I said in a small voice. For some reason I felt tearful, convinced I'd done something wrong, but I had no idea what.

"Not that," said Wicks, "when you broke up the sphere. As an *Iksale* 2 you shouldn't have been able to do that. How did you?"

"Um, I just put a lot of energy into the last sprite and then released it all in one go when it was right in the middle."

Wicks nodded. "While controlling all the other, what, two dozen sprites and their weaving contrails? And then safely dispersing all that energy – apparently with no effort at all."

I looked at Professor Gowan. "I thought you…"

She shook her head. "I withdrew all direct control the moment you broke in; I wanted to see what you would do."

"What you actually did," Wicks went on, "was a counter spell, a neutraliser, which you haven't been taught yet. I'm not at all sure where you even got it from. It's a *Jaun* 2 spell."

I did wonder, briefly, if being there when the train vanished might have had some sort of effect on me; some sort of backlash, but what that could be and how it could affect this I had no idea.

The levels in magic are symbolised by wearing a coloured tag, which can be a pendant, an earring, a bracelet or a ring. Sam and I both favoured the bracelet option. *Iksale* are supposed to wear them all the time but nobody bothers with them much, other than on formal occasions.

Wicks made a gesture over a small box on one side of her desk, and the cold winter sunlight that was flooding the room went hazy for a moment. Then she opened the box and pulled out two bracelets.

Iksale grades range up through the spectrum in the blues, starting with white at level 10 and going to deep navy at level 1. The *Jaun* levels are silver, tinted for your specialisation and darkening as you become more senior. These bracelets were a lustrous, metallic green. We'd just been promoted to *Ikasberri*.

"Son of a water buffalo," I muttered.

Gowan grinned delightedly, and ushered us from the office where Wicks was actually smiling. "Congratulations. Now go out there and be smug."

4

I suppose now would be a good time for The Lecture. It should really be called 'Yes, But How The Bloody Hell Does It Work?'

It has long been known that the world is pervaded by electromagnetic radiation, from both natural and artificial sources. Mankind has been interacting with this for its own benefit – using magnetism to operate compasses for example – for a long time, and the natural world even longer.

Magic works by practitioners using thoughts, gestures and occasionally words to change the electromagnetic field, gravity and similar fundamental forces to create the desired physical effect. They learn how to achieve this from existing practitioners and by their own research.

A pigeon's brain has magneto-receptors made of magnetite crystals that are associated with the trigeminal nerve. These allow them to sense the Earth's magnetic field directly. Human beings have the same crystals in the bones of their noses, but in most people they don't do anything. They do in mages, so they could be considered as a kind of super-pigeon, able to both perceive and manipulate the field, but hopefully with a slightly higher IQ and better toilet training.

Some highly unethical experiments in the 19th century established that it's largely to do with how a person's brain is wired. It doesn't reliably run in families, although there is a statistical correlation, and its appearance seems to be otherwise random, so much so that even if one twin has it, there is no guarantee that the other will.

There are foci in magical forces that roughly correspond to the classical four elements. Mages focus on spells associated with Fire, Water, Earth and Air. There are two further 'Talents' – Healing and *kemen*. This last literally means 'energy', but refers to the direct control and manipulation of the electromagnetic spectrum, rather than the specific spells it can be used to create. Mages use parts of all of the Talents but focus strongly on one, at least when they start their training.

What Healers do is self-evident, and they study the broadest range of subjects within the discipline. All mages are encouraged to learn as many of these skills as possible. Fire Talents control heat and all forms of combustion. Water Talents control water and ice and have a particular skill with lower temperatures. Earth Talents work in the environment and with growing things. Air Talents deal with the weather and *kemen* specialists work on the control of pure energy. A mage normally works strongly in one Talent and slightly in another. More unusually they can use two Talents equally well. They are known as 'Dual Talents', and represent significantly less than 1% of the magically capable.

Only one full 'Triple Talent' – Ellie Hart – has been confirmed in the UK in the last fifty years, and she died from exhaustion and a brain haemorrhage at the age of twenty. Full Quad Talents have been known, but you are more likely to meet a Dodo walking down Kensington High Street than one of them.

Amongst the rarest multi-Talent is a *euste*, a person who can employ any Talent that another mage nearby possesses without having to have that Talent themselves. There have only been eight full-power *euste* confirmed in the last 200 years. Beyond that are the *kea*, who are hugely powerful but so lacking in control that they can't safely – or reliably – do almost anything. Finally there are the *mamua*, who possess all of the Talents at full strength and are consequently so powerful that they can do everything. Their existence, however, is entirely theoretical.

It is possible to join components of spells together to make bigger and more complicated ones, but you should only do this if you are highly trained, properly supervised or if you want your brain turned into the brassica of your choice.

The energy to cast a spell is drawn directly from the person casting it, and although objects can carry spells, no external source for more than slight amounts of energy has been created yet – and it's not for the want of trying. Almost nobody works – can work – fully in two Talents until they reach *Jaun* rank. There are common features between the Talents of course – pushing something is the same spell if it's clouds, blood, ice, boulders or pizza – which is one of the things that makes magic so dangerous for the undertrained.

There are physical effect spells – push, pull, lift and so forth, which are based on manipulating forces like gravity, momentum and so on. How they actually work is immensely complex, but they do, and a mage doesn't have to understand the nuts and bolts to use them. This is what *kemen* specialists study.

Control comes with age, practice, experience and whether you are suicidally impatient. Your Talent normally surfaces at or just after puberty, and which Talent you have becomes certain during the first term at college. Some people arrive knowing; Healers almost always seem to know before they arrive.

The neural mutations that allow this control are evenly spread across the sexes, but not across the world. Nobody has come up with a remotely convincing theory about why. It isn't to do with ethnic origin either; the figures are constant, whatever the person's ethnicity , religion, sexuality, genetic background or favourite beer.

In Europe, it's about one person in 20,000. In Africa and Australasia, it's about the same, but it's nearer one in 25,000 around the Indian Ocean and in South America. That goes out to one in 200,000 in the Far East, but those mages tend to be enormously powerful. Native Americans score about the same as Europeans, but non-native Americans seem to have the magical abilities of a hat stand – one in 750,000. I blame it on all the cheeseburgers.

Not all of these people end up as full-blown mages, of course – many have minor Talents that never develop beyond a basic level. These are what we, perhaps a bit snootily, call the Allied Trades. They are things like *gidari*, a person who can locate magical objects, spells and so forth, but can do nothing else. Their training is highly specialised but relatively brief, which is why the colleges enrol only about 100 potential mages every year.

The most extraordinary race are the Basques, a tiny population of around 2 million clinging to the hillsides between France and Spain. For them it's one in 300. Not 300,000 – 300, although they rarely achieve *Jaun* grades. Again, nobody knows why. As they are – or at least were – mostly sheep farmers or fishermen, I suppose that they had a lot of time to think about how things work.

That's also why all our spell words sound like a pissed Glaswegian ordering drinks in a Spanish bar. They often don't translate directly, having been subjected to lazy usage, linguistic drift and egregious mispronunciation for decades, but the roots are clear enough.

You can use any language you like, of course, but since Russian sounds like you're starting a fight and Latin makes everyone think we go to Hogwarts or work for the Folly, we stick to the old ways.

That's all the explanation you're likely to get. It works because it works. It is a truth unacknowledged that being able to describe something isn't the same as understanding it, even though most people think it is. I mean, consider electricity, or the popularity of the 'Birdy Song'.

*

The next few days passed in a blur of patchy snow and icy winds that did nothing for my temper or the RTC statistics. Sam vanished under layers of coats and jumpers, and Amy claimed she was going to fit snow chains to her wheelchair for the times when I wasn't pushing her. Clara started to turn blue, which is a good trick when your skin is the colour of dark chocolate. Sometimes all I could see were her eyelashes.

The only people who were smugly warm were my friend Jerry and the other fire Talents, who could heat up a small room just by thinking about it. Useful in Nottinghamshire in the winter, bugger all use in Sicily in August.

We have a professor for each of the Talents. Alex Tahy is the boss of the Healers and Catriona Gowan covers earth Talents, and so is in charge of me and Clara. Andrew Weaver deals with *kemen* and Maria Ngozi with fire. Andrius Denisov is the boss of the water Talents, which is where Amy hangs out. The almost unpronounceable Sigrún Magnúsdóttir is one of the most senior air Talents in Europe and, when she isn't working with Sam, spends a lot of time away. Professor Ngozi isn't here just now either – some sort of family issue back in Stroud, and Denisov only seems to come in about once a month anyway. They all have an assistant head of department, and there are plenty of others to do the day to day teaching when the boss isn't in.

As newly, not to say abruptly, promoted *Ikasberri*, Sam and I were treated with envy, congratulation, suspicion and downright disbelief by most people. Well, when I say Sam and I, I mean me. Nobody was even vaguely surprised about Sam – if there had been such a thing as a thaumato-meter she'd have broken the needle on her first day here. She didn't really come here to learn how to do magic, just how to control it.

After two days everyone had decided that my being promoted was either a mistake or reflected glory. Meanwhile we were discovering what our elevation really meant; access to higher-level spells of course, but also more responsibilities, a lot more work for the college itself and even some teaching of first years. But at least no more vanishing vehicles crashed into anything that week, so people started to relax a tiny bit.

In the meantime, Sam and I had to do a very rigorous conversion course. Without any time at *Iksale* 1, and the usual several months of preparation, the move from *Iksale* to *Ikasberri* was going to be… quite difficult. A lot of being an *Ikasberri* is about what you understand about magic, not how you use it. The more skilled you get, the more complex the spells, the more you have to know how it works at a fundamental level – because the more advanced the spell, the more it draws on that basic power.

Normally you get lots of time to get ready for this, sometimes years, time to learn how to control the magic so that it doesn't slip away if you push it too hard or hold it too tight. We had to pick this up in a few days. Plus, an apprentice doesn't only have to understand how magic works, but also how to work effectively with another mage that isn't their *erdikide*. It was going to be bloody hard, especially as we didn't know who we were going to be apprenticed to afterwards. Sometimes you don't find someone to work with at all.

It was a week away in York, some expenses paid. I was looking forward to it, but Sam wasn't. We would be at King's Manor, which was a part of the archaeology department of the University of York. Our colleges often get stuck in the archaeology department, but I don't know why. Maybe it's because both are about things that are very old which we don't fully understand.

"I not like city," Sam said as we were planning the trip.

"York? Why not?" I looked at the briefing pack we'd been given. We'd spread it over a big table in the common room and I couldn't see anything objectionable.

"Not just York, all big city. I not like too big city."

"Too big! You come from Hong Kong – isn't that like a bazillion times bigger than everywhere?"

"Hong Kong not just city. It a territory. I from Chuen Lung, right on edge of Ti Mo Shan."

"Ti Mo…?"

"Is country park. Lots hills, not many people." I've known Sam for ages, but for some reason this particular thing had never come up. I had always imagined her growing up amidst the thronged bodies and bright lights of a huge city with a population density twenty-five times that of the UK, not some dusty mountain village. There was a silence you could have rested a plate on.

"Anyway, York," I said after a moment. "Any thoughts on where you'd like to stay?"

She looked at the hotel list. "Gray's Court? Mount Royale?"

"I don't think we'd get away with that," I laughed. They were the most luxurious, and expensive.

"As long as it warm." Even in the common room she was wearing a scarf.

"I'll find somewhere nice. Shall we drive?"

"No drive. Train. Like to stretch legs and get food still moving. It only a couple of hours anyway." She stopped. "You OK with going on train? Can drive if you want." She rested her slim hand on my arm.

"It's fine. Back on the horse and all that." She smiled but I could see a frown hiding behind her eyes. "You sort the tickets and I'll deal with the accommodation."

*

We left the next Sunday, each carrying a modest bag of clothes and an immodest number of books, which we swore we'd read on the journey but never did. Instead I read the newspapers, because their reaction to the second crash had been very odd. The lack of attribution, or anything else, had made them so desperate for something to say that they had gone as far as door-stepping people who slept through the whole thing just to have something to put on the page.

But it was, nonetheless, serious. There was talk of terrorists and serial killers, of technological warfare; the word magic did come up, but only in the list of possible other causes, lower down than hackers (on a steam train?) but higher than aliens.

The police were all over it, but the entire thing somehow slid down the news order until it was litter-tray vintage within a couple of days. It had been urged there by several spectacular natural events – an isolated but previously dormant volcano erupting suddenly, for example – all of which seemed too well timed to be anything other than a diversion by The Powers That Be, which is a pretty scary thought.

When I finished reading Sam was asleep. With nobody to talk to I watched the cars on the quiet country roads, idly puzzling over who might be driving and where they were going. As we passed the rabbit-hutch dormitories on the outskirts of cities I wondered, not for the first time, how the residents managed to find their way home. It was mostly, I thought, by driving a rut between home and work, and living in a rut in both. It struck me again that the only difference between a rut and a grave is the depth.

I scratched my left shoulder as we started to slow, and Sam woke, blinking and frowning at me.

"You do think a lot of cock," she muttered as the train stopped with a hiss of brakes and the sound of desperate smokers scrambling for the exits.

She didn't seem disposed to talk and I had all the bags to carry, so I wasn't inclined to chat either. I know she can carry her own, but mum brought me up all proper like, and Sam always seemed content to let me, for some reason. I always say that I'm practising to be a gentleman, but I don't know if it's working yet. Sometimes people laugh.

The hotel was a decent little place just outside the city walls near Micklegate, clean, comfortable and modern without falling into the trap of drab, minimalist sterility. There were other *Ikasberri* there who were on the same course – Gilly and Blue from Falmouth, Seth and Tarik from Lincoln, Jojo and Paula from Newcastle, Matt and Gino from Marlborough and a couple of others. I gathered that there would be around a dozen pairs on the 'how to be an apprentice without cocking it up' course with us.

After checking in at a reception that was slightly too small but smelled deliciously of fresh coffee, we headed to our rooms to get ready for the first meeting and the inevitable, eye-wateringly embarrassing, ice breakers.

My room and Sam's were next to each other, with a connecting door that we didn't bother to lock. There is an odd intimacy with your *erdikide*; the word itself is a hybrid that roughly means 'partner', but it's only used for the magical type. There are few serious secrets between *erdikide,* but that doesn't mean that you are continually riding in each other's minds or reading each other's thoughts. Telepathy is not a known mage ability; you get impressions rather than words. I've never experienced what it's like when your *erdikide* has sex nearby, but they tell me it can be unsettling. I imagine sex between *erdikide* must be really interesting in an 'oh God I think I've melted my brain' sort of way.

It can also make you casual about going into their room, for example, because you know very clearly when they don't want you to, if not necessarily the exact reason. So I wasn't the least surprised when Sam wandered into my bedroom while I was getting changed.

"You like?" She twirled slowly and I admired her new outfit – a proper formal Chinese jacket thing in peacock blue and gold with fierce silky dragons, a high collar and slits up the thigh. Sam has short hair and is slim in the face as well as body, with modest curves and very nice legs, especially when she hasn't put her trousers on, like now. Red silk underwear, in case you're interested.

"You look great."

She peered at me and frowned. "What you done?"

"Sorry?"

"You shoulder. Blood." I twisted my neck but I couldn't see anything. "On shirt."

I didn't want to look. I'm very practical about medical stuff – years of helping to look after a wheelchair-bound grandma will do that – but just the thought of looking repelled me, revolted me, which was odd. My shoulder had been painful recently, and I'd assumed I'd hurt it at Paddington. But I still didn't want to look. There was a mirror on the dresser but I couldn't turn towards it.

She sighed. "Take off shirt."

"Now that's an offer I don't hear very often…" I said but then stopped when I saw the back of it. The patch of blood, mostly dried but some still red and wet, was larger than the palm of my hand. I flexed my shoulder, feeling the skin pulling and tightening as I did.

"What is it?" My voice suddenly had no power in it, and I slumped onto the rumpled blue bed cover as if I'd lost all the strength in my legs.

She stepped around, rested her hand on my shoulder and drew a sharp breath. "*Shuîniú de érzi*. It look like tattoo, but very small. When you get tattoo?"

"I haven't had a tattoo done, and certainly not recently enough that it would still be bleeding."

"Is tattoo," she insisted. "You see."

We cast a spell called *Mailegatu-Begi*, usually known as *Mail-Beg*, which roughly translates as 'borrowed eyes'. It allows one person to literally see through the eyes of another. It can only be done with the explicit consent and continual support of both parties, so it's no good for voyeurs, or for cheating in exams – the professors see to that.

It was very odd, seeing myself from behind. I'm fairly trim and muscular from all the karate I do, but my posture is quite poor. I focused on my shoulder; she was right, of course. There were two small tattoos, dark angular shapes, in the centre of my left shoulder blade.

"Can you get closer?"

As soon as she leaned in her vision started to dim and she quickly stepped back. I could feel her disquiet. "Is inhibition on it."

"Can you break it?"

"*Méiyôu.*"

I hadn't thought that she could – 'inhibition', properly called *Oztupato*, is a *Jaun*-level casting. It can make things very hard to see in the first place and, once seen, almost impossible to focus on for long enough to do anything with them. It's mainly used as a security tool, cast on locks, keypads and another access equipment. Sam had only seen the tattoos because the spell hadn't extended to cover the blood stain on my shirt.

"We show Professor Gowan later. I put dressing on." She broke the borrowed eyes, brought out a first aid kit, scrubbed the area with an alcohol wipe, which made me swear, and stuck a large dressing over it. "Amy tell you do this?"

"Amy? Why would I do anything she asked me to? If she had a needle anywhere near me she'd make sure it was full of strychnine, or something equally pleasant."

Sam chuckled and shook her head. "Amy you girlfriend."

"What? No, she isn't."

"OK, I think Amy want to be you girlfriend."

"The feeling is not mutual," I said, wondering if either of us was convinced by the denial.

"You say? Hard you be Amy girlfriend unless you very ugly ladyboy." I slipped on a clean shirt – going to the first meeting half-dressed would certainly break the ice, but in an 'oh look, there's the Titanic' sort of way. Laughing at her own wit, Sam went to finish getting changed, leaving me to puzzle how I'd managed to get two tattoos done without remembering it happening. I mean, I like the odd beer, but not that bloody much.

*

The first three days of the course were a blur of exhilaration, confusion and exhaustion. All of it was neatly and inconspicuously contained in the sixteenth-century buildings of King's Manor, and overseen by the gesturing luminary who guards the entrance.

Ikasberri have to do spells with much more control and precision, which makes it bloody hard work, especially on the *gogoan*, the magical part of the brain. When we trudged out of the King's Manor buildings, which are in splendid isolation from the rest of the university, we were all drawn and slack faced, stumbling into the Refectory – the old Great Dining Hall – at lunchtime and then back to the hotel after the sessions had finished.

Even the people who had been able to prepare for it weren't much better – Blue fell asleep one lunchtime and was only saved from going face down in a bowl of pasta when Paula prodded her with a spoon. I don't know what the hotel staff thought we were doing, but we got some very odd looks.

Old things and ancient places associated with magic have a power of their own, energy that they've soaked up over time. This place was built before Shakespeare put quill to parchment, so just being there should give us a serious boost. I didn't feel more powerful – I just felt exhausted.

On the fourth day Sam and I were so tired that even after we had shared what *Indar* we had, I could still barely walk, so we got a taxi back to the hotel. I could feel almost no thoughts in her mind, which worried me.

The traffic was awful, even over that short distance – not even a mile. The driver, a short tubby man with almost inflammable halitosis, was a combination of accusative, indignant and phlegmatic. We barely listened, but that didn't make any difference to him.

"It's another bleedin' crash, innit, this traffic," he said. He had that kind of stubbled aggression that made me wonder what he did when he went to football matches. "Council should do somethin' about this, I mean, the police put in these stupid detours and fings. An' this 'appens." He gestured to the grumpily immobile traffic. "Don't they know they're puttin' up the bleedin' Christmas lights? How's a 4-tonner supposed to get past a cherry-picker what's slingin' reindeer up the side of the town 'all?"

I hadn't the strength to answer, but he didn't notice. I didn't care – I was so tired I was almost frightened. I like York – we went to the Jorvik Centre when I was at school – but now it was buried in a grey haze of exhaustion. I think the driver might have said something else, but I don't remember any more until we got to the hotel.

Paula and Gino were in the lobby when we arrived, standing suspiciously close together, and they steered us upstairs. Paula helped Sam to bed and Gino watched from the doorway while I put myself to bed. Sleep was a black pit fourteen hours long, and climbing out of it the next morning was one of the hardest things I've ever done. I felt like I'd died but nobody had bothered to mention it to me. For the first time since Paddington I didn't dream, but my face was wet with tears when I woke up.

*

Over a very desultory breakfast we found out that what had delayed us had been another magical attack. A boat this time, a high-speed collision with the Ouse Bridge on the imaginatively named Bridge Street. It had clipped the bank just by the Kings Arms and then demolished the easternmost support, which had dropped the ancient stonework – and the people on it – into the freezing water. The pilotless boat vanished within two hours, leaving three dead and dozens injured, wet and annoyed.

The newspapers and media outlets predictably went bonkers, dragging out every even approximately expert they could find and plastering pictures of the 'reign of terror' (or 'rain of terror' as one tabloid news website put it) all over the place. Magic was raised again, but someone had been working hard on diversionary tactics and the talk was of small explosive vehicles with holographic images around them giving the appearance of being trains and so forth.

It was even suggested they were drones, because these days everything seems to be about drones. It used to be only clergy, school teachers and politicians who droned, but now it's everyone. The Internet experts loved it; the real experts were dubious, but still nobody claimed responsibility, so they were stuck. It was a time for mages to walk quietly.

Sam was troubled when we heard about the boat, but she wouldn't say specifically why until we saw Professor Gowan on the Monday morning after we got back. We passed the course, by the way, although not spectacularly, and we both slept all the way home, Sam curled up on my lap.

"And to what do I owe the pleasure of this festive visit?" It was only a couple of weeks before Christmas.

"These crash," said Sam, settling into one of the deep blue leather armchairs in Gowan's crowded and brightly lit office. The professor had a desk, but she treated it as a horizontal filing cabinet; I had been in her department for four years but I'd yet to see the top of it.

"I gather there was another while you were away." Her formal choice of words sounded odd in her soft Edinburgh accent. Possibly Edinburgh. Certainly Scottish.

"There was another *where* we were away," I said.

Gowan frowned. "And…?"

"Mike, take off shirt," said Sam.

"Hmm, let me see…" Gowan said a few words and made a brushing gesture. The pain that shot across my back was like being struck with a branding iron. I gritted my teeth and resisted the urge to shout.

"*Shuîniú de érzi*," I muttered.

"Well, daughter of one perhaps," said Gowan, but she looked grim. "That was a very powerful inhibition. Been there a while too. I don't recognise the *esku*. Now, let's have a look at whatever this is."

She and Sam peered at my shoulder. I was sweating and starting to shake, a quiver deep in the centre of me. It was most unpleasant. I felt like I was coming down with bird flu that I'd caught from an ostrich.

"I not see clear before," said Sam softly. In the polished wood and leather quiet of the room her voice was absorbed, muted, distant even. "But I think maybe it…"

"Yes," said Gowan shortly. "The… symbology of a train, a boat and a lorry, near enough."

"He no remember getting tattoo," said Sam. "Also, boat not there at start of week."

Gowan looked at me. "You were in London when the Paddington crash happened, weren't you?"

"In the station," I mumbled. I felt drunk, confused, as if talking was almost impossible. And frightened.

"Which do you prefer – lager or Real Ale?"

"Real Ale," I replied, suddenly free of whatever the hell was doing this to me. "Lager looks like piss and doesn't taste much better."

"Do you know where the Leicester crash was?"

"Yes."

"Did you have anything to do with it?"

"N." I tried again. "Nu."

"Do you want coffee?"

"Yes please." I looked at Sam and the professor. "What's happening to me?"

"Put your shirt on," said Gowan, leaning back.

"Someone has done something to you, and it's to do with these crashes."

"And the tattoos?" My shirt stuck to me as I pulled it on. Most unpleasant.

"They aren't. They're like… stigmata. There's something in your mind, or body, that's involved in these crashes, but your defences are strong enough that it's been contained in the marks on your back."

"How do I get rid of them?"

"You don't. I've taken the *esku* of the spell and I'm going to talk to some people I know. I'll get back to you after the break."

"What can I do about it now?"

"Well, try not to crash into anything," she replied drily.

I stood up. "I'm not going to sit still. I can't. I must find a way to drive this crap out of me. It's a corrosion in my soul. I'm going to set up some defensive screens and…" I may have been a little hysterical at this point.

"Seriously, Michael, you mustn't even try; it could be dangerous," said Gowan urgently. "You push too hard and you could do yourself a lot of damage."

With a great effort I calmed myself down, breathing slowly and carefully as the adrenaline faded, while Sam held my hand and offered mute reassurance.

"Good," said Gowan. "Now enjoy Christmas and forget about this."

I nodded, but I knew that however good Christmas was, there was no way I could forget about any of it.

5

After all the fuss, Christmas nearly didn't happen at all.

"Well, you won't be interested in anything religious now, will you?" Mum said one evening, totally out of the blue. Well, totally out of a sherry bottle, but that's another story.

"Why not? I love Christmas."

"But this thing you do now – it isn't really a Christian thing, is it?"

I refrained from observing that Christmas isn't for most other people either. I also didn't mention that I'd been doing 'this thing' for nearly seven years and that 'this thing' is thousands of years older than Christianity – all religions probably. And, unlike religion, we could prove that our way of looking at the universe is accurate. You cast *Argilabur* and a ball of light *will* appear – you don't have to plead for the intercession of some dead bloke and his intangible dad.

As a great man nearly said 'prayer is just a sophisticated way of pleading with thunderstorms'.

"Mum, doing… what I do is just another set of skills. Some people are born to be fast runners; some people are naturally good at languages; others have an innate talent for being useless." I meant Simon but I don't think she caught it. "I'm an environmental scientist and I love Christmas. Just because I haven't needed matches to light the candles for several years hasn't changed that." I was trying very hard to sound reasonable.

Mum was about to start again when dad lifted his face from his copy of *The Post*. "I believe that he has made his position clear." He turned to me. "You will always be welcome in this house, and especially so at Christmas." He smiled. "You should invite Sam over for a drink – it would be nice to meet him."

"Right. Thanks. I'll ask." I was about to explain that Sam is female but the newspaper was back in front of his face again and the moment passed. The matter was closed.

*

I did mention it to Sam next morning break in the college coffee shop. "Please present my apology," she said, after we'd both finished laughing. "Will be spending holiday with own family."

"I will deliver your apology," I replied, rising slightly and bowing. That ended abruptly when I was firmly – and accurately – jabbed in the backside. I looked around. "Oh it's you. What's up?"

Amy looked at me. "You being a prat again, Mike?"

"Oh, I like the 'again', Boudicca. You off to frighten some first years?"

"No. I was looking for you."

"Me?"

She looked at me quizzically. "Why would I want you, Mr oh-look-at-me-I'm-an-*Ikasberri*?" She paused. "Well done, by the way." She touched my hand briefly. "No. I was looking for Sam."

"You need?" Amy nodded. "We go now."

Amy is in a wheelchair because of her hips. I don't know

about anything else, but I do know that they will dislocate or something equally grim if she stands up for more than a few seconds, so she uses the chair. Sometimes Sam helps her with that and gives her some pain relief. I think there might be something female going on as well, so I didn't feel I could offer to help, or even enquire too closely.

*

You might get the impression that, bar a few overexcited headlines, the outside world wasn't paying much more than passing attention to all of this, but that wasn't the case. The news machine and social media rolled through gleeful shock and into the usual hunt for scapegoats and conspiracies every time something happened.

Mages and everybody else have always had an uneasy relationship. The wise woman and the cunning man have always existed, and little formal knots of learning began to form in the eighteenth century. This coincided with the beginnings of archaeology as an academic discipline, rather than the pastime of acquisitive gentlemen of leisure and curiosity. It may have been that researching magic could now be considered respectable, because it could be seen as investigating the rituals of the past. 'Ritual', by the way, is the catch-all explanation for anything archaeological that nobody can think of a plausible explanation for.

The study of magic just rumbled along, producing occasional high points and a list of spiritualists, like Conan Doyle, who never grasped that magic is a matter of physics not spectral intervention. Because of all the fuss caused by the Victorian Establishment, for whom everything they couldn't explain was either demonic or a threat to the Empire – or both – the use of magic went underground for decades.

Magic played almost no part in the First World War because it wasn't considered something that a gentleman would do, although it may have had a hand in the Angel of Mons incident.

It took an equally small part in the Second World War, simply because it was not well enough organised to be useful on the larger scale. Some individuals used their skills very effectively, especially on covert missions. It's estimated that between 15% and 20% of SOE operatives were Talents of some kind, often without knowing it. They fought as skilfully and bravely as anyone else, and died the same as everyone else.

But because there was no organised structure to be disrupted by the deaths, the development of magic continued almost without a break.

Nobody exposed magic to the world; mages, in the free and easy days of the 1960s, just did stuff, often under the influence of industrial-strength narcotics. Everyone fairly quickly accepted that some people could do things that nobody could explain, at least not now. After all, the world's like that – before Newton nobody knew why apples fell downwards; before the Curies nobody knew radiation would kill you; before Monty Python nobody knew that knocking someone into Teddington Lock with a really big fish was hysterically funny. Er… you get the idea.

But mages very quickly learned to keep things quiet, undramatic and out of the public eye, and so the habit of discretion was born. Magic isn't hidden so much as very much not talked about – largely because we all work extremely hard to make sure it stays that way. The smell of the smoke from burning witches never quite leaves the air.

*

The train thing had caused endless headlines, ranging

from 'Unexplained Crash at Paddington', or some slight variation of that in the more sensible newspapers, to *The Mail* which went with 'Train Crash Horror – Was the Driver an Immigrant?'. Papers with even more excitable editors offered things like 'Government Conceals Truth About Alien Train Mystery'. One even used 'Government Lies: Paddington Train Controlled by Aliens – Plans to Conceal Invasion from Space Revealed'. That one may have been in the *Church Times*, unless I'm remembering that wrongly.

The second crash produced an oddly muted response. No long-term hysteria, as if someone had decided that it was all just too weird, or that it really was terrorist related, so they weren't going to mislead people about it. Or possibly some woman with a large chest and the IQ of a sparrow had had a 'wardrobe malfunction' and they had pictures to splash. The third one barely made it to the front pages outside Yorkshire by the second day.

*

Mum had taken Simon Christmas shopping. She said it was because he wanted to get something for dad. I suspect it was more to do with dad saying, 'I know the boy's on holiday, but if he doesn't get off those bloody stupid computer games and out into the fresh air there's going to be trouble'. Dad is contemptuous of computer games – the violent ones especially. 'There is enough real misery in the world, why would you want to make up more?' is his mantra. Normally it would be me helping mum, but I'd been allowed a day off – provided I did the prep for dinner.

Dad had gone very quiet when he read the reports. "This is something to do with your lot, isn't it?"

"Well, the vanishing vehicles have to be, based on the reports, but I've no idea who's doing it or why. There aren't even rumours. There is an investigation going on, but..."

"Destruction for its own sake? Terrorism of some kind?"

"Terrorists usually claim responsibility, otherwise what's the point?"

"Er... rogue magician?"

"Seriously?" I would have peered over my glasses at him, if I'd been wearing any.

He shrugged. "Um." Dad's very bright but not too comfortable with the interpersonal stuff. "I er... gather that you don't have a girlfriend at the moment?" I nodded. "Boyfriend perhaps?" The parents are totally cool about Simon and Idris.

"Not boyfriend, no." I paused. "There is a girl... a girl who is a friend rather than a girlfriend, but..." I shrugged.

Even in the warm familiarity of the sitting room there was a silence that would have become painfully embarrassing without the distraction of coffee.

"I know there was," he thought for a moment, "Miranda, in the first year?" I nodded. "Then... whatever happened to... Paula, was it?"

"Patricia."

"Yes, her."

"Her family moved to Canada – her mum's a petroleum geologist – so Pat transferred to the college at Yellowknife. We e-mail occasionally."

"Pity. I liked her."

"Yeah, me too," I replied glumly. Pat leaving had put an unpleasant taint on the previous summer break.

"So who's this new girl then?"

"Amy." I explained about her and the whole wheelchair business.

"Well, if she decides to visit, please ensure we have a couple of days' notice so we can put the furniture back to where it was… before."

Grandma, dad's mum, who we called Nonna, had lived with us for several years. She had been in a wheelchair and suffering from increasing dementia for most of them. She'd died, not at all quickly, a couple of months before. I'd been the only person in the house at the time, and I hadn't enjoyed the experience at all.

"I was thinking of asking Amy if she wanted to come here for Christmas. Her parents live in the Far East." I paused. "I don't like the idea of her being alone."

"You should do that. Make sure you tell your mother as soon as she agrees."

"Of course. Idris is supposed to be here for Christmas too. Should make it an interesting day."

"Oh good," he replied, with the faintest hint of sarcasm. "Why is he coming here? Again."

"His dad's on duty all day and his mum's on lates." He nodded. Idris' dad is a fire fighter and his mum is a specialist nurse in ICU at the local hospital.

"Oh. Well, what do you want for Christmas then? A new wand?"

"We don't use wands, dad. Merlin and Harry Potter use wands – real mages don't."

"Takes some getting used to."

"I know," I replied, with feeling.

"Um… why is it that we know so little about what you do? I mean, you're the only person I am aware of that does that sort of thing." He paused and smiled slightly. "That came out really badly, didn't it?"

"Yes."

"Sorry. You know what I mean though."

"Yes, I do. We hear it all the bloody time." I sighed. "We stay in the background because if we come too far forward people will expect us to wave our hands and fix everything – poverty, disease, global warming, ridiculous politicians, lost lottery tickets, broken hearts and flatulence."

"And you can't."

"No. If we could, we would. We can do some stuff of course, but quietly, always quietly, often in support of the emergency services. One thing we can't do anything about is the human mind and all the venal idiocy and dangerous nonsense that flows from it. We can mitigate the fallout but we can't fix the cause of the problem. We do what we can."

"But why is so little said about it?" He was puzzled and insistent. "I thought the tabloids would be all over you like a rash the whole time."

"We can't do what they want, can't be what they want us to be." Or frequently won't be, truth be told. "It's like having a kid who is only just good enough to swim a length of the pool – what they do is great but you know they're never going to get to school team level, so you don't mention it too much." I shrugged. I bloody hate having to justify being a mage; it's like having to justify having brown hair. I didn't mention that we have an entire department whose sole purpose is to keep us out of the public eye, something they mostly achieve by being very dull and staging inventive distractions.

Dad looked at me for a long moment. "You hoped you could do more."

"I hoped I could do *something*. I still do, but every time I get deeper into it, the more I realise that what we can actually do is surprisingly little. We can heal to some extent – it's very good for emergency first aid and the advanced stuff is used to deal with things that can't be treated otherwise, like problems in the brain or inoperable tumours."

"I didn't know that."

"The Healers who do it are almost always doctors as well – a lot of people would be uncomfortable if they knew that someone who wasn't a doctor was treating them, especially using magic."

"Isn't it unethical, not telling them what you are doing?"

"Not really. Patients don't know what the anaesthetist does to them or even what the surgeon does, other than in a general sense. They say, 'we'll be performing a procedure that will fix the damage to your Achilles tendon'. They go to sleep, they wake up, it's fixed. The fact that it's a Healer stimulating regrowth rather than a surgeon with some glue or a needle… it doesn't matter." I felt myself flushing and forced myself to relax again.

"I see," said dad, affecting not to notice. "Are you a Healer? You were always good at first aid."

"No. I'm too squeamish." That wasn't why – your Talent isn't a matter of choice. You're a Healer or you aren't; you can't choose to be one any more than you can choose how big your nose is. "I'm an earth Talent, so I specialise in environmental control; making water clean, removing toxins from crops, making them immune to pests and diseases, that kind of thing. We can also change the structure of trees just enough to make it worthless to fell them. It's people like me that are bringing the rainforests back."

"Oh. I didn't realise."

"You wouldn't. We don't advertise that we're using magic to do it."

"I've never seen magic," he said abruptly. "I've heard stories of course, but the plural of 'anecdote' isn't 'data'." I suspect he'd been trying to get to that since we'd started talking, and had only just steeled himself to ask.

"*Argilabur.*" I put a very little energy into the spell and a soft sphere of light about the size of a tennis ball appeared, floating above the coffee table.

Dad stared, clearly fascinated. He reached out his hand, the light reflecting off his glasses making him look vaguely insectoid. He stopped just short of the surface. "It's cold."

"The light isn't caused by combustion," I said. "I'm altering the wavelength of the energy within the sphere so that it comes into the visible part of the spectrum."

He pushed his finger into the light. It doesn't feel any different, but it takes some courage to do that for the first time. "Where does the energy come from?"

"Me. The energy for a spell always comes from the caster."

He nodded. "So that's why you eat so much and never put on weight. I thought it was all the karate."

"Partly I suppose. You'll rarely see a fat mage, at least not one who's practising regularly."

"Haven't you got something like a battery, that you can use to store the power?"

I shook my head. "Nobody's been able to make one yet. It would be very useful if they had, because…" I stopped. Dad wasn't listening any more.

"How do you move it?"

"Like this." I made the sphere slide sideways down the length of the table and back. "Although strictly speaking I'm not actually moving it."

"Then how… oh, I see, you're creating a new globe in each position, so it just looks like it's moving." Like I said, dad is really bright. "What's the increment?"

"It can be at a quantum level."

"That small?"

"My tutor says that if you make the smallest possible shift it can be measured in Angstroms."

Dad nodded again, his eyes drawn back to the light as the front door opened with an icy whoosh and mum and Simon came in. I doused the light just as Simon stuck his head around the door.

"I hate shopping," he announced in a disgruntled tone.

"Put the kettle on," replied dad. Sighing like he'd been asked to clean the Eiffel Tower with a toothbrush, Simon wandered into the kitchen.

"Thank you," said dad softly.

"Any time."

*

We reached the end of term without anyone crashing into anything – well, no more than normal for the time of year anyway. Sam vanished – I mean she left, although I suspect she could actually vanish if she put her mind to it. Ambrose had gone too, and Jerry, and most of the ancillary staff and the various hangers-on that seem to infest the college. In the end, there was me, Amy, Professor Gowan and three first year girls, looking pretty much the same in whatever was passing for teenage fashion that week.

Nineteen years old, slim, conventionally pretty and with the world at their identically clad feet, they should have been shaking the foundations of civilisation. Instead they were discussing the civilising effects of a good foundation. I understand this is to do with make-up. I know, I sound like an old fart. My brother maintains that I had a tweed romper suit with leather elbow patches when I was a baby. I maintain that when mum and dad brought him home from the hospital they left his brain behind in the incubator.

I sipped my coffee as Amy wheeled her way over. Despite our combative relationship I was pleased that she had, and we decided to play 'Slide'. It's a simple enough game. You put an object on a cluttered table, then use a push spell like *Jaso* to knock it off on your opponent's side without touching anything else. It's good training for precision and an opportunity to pour salt, beer or anything else suitably messy into the other person's lap. We had fought to a stalemate when Professor Gowan arrived.

"I've a solution for that," she said. The salt cellar, which I had just bashed into, lifted a foot into the air and then jumped onto the table behind me.

Amy looked up. "We weren't sliding that."

"Oh," said Gowan, as I pushed the bowl of sugar sachets into Amy's lap.

"Cheat."

"So," said the professor, "off home for the break, are you?"

"Yes," I said. "Full parental Christmas dinner – mum's not a bad cook, but dad's excellent and it's his turn. You back up to Edinburgh, is it?"

She nodded. "How about you, Amy? You and Clara doing something?"

Amy shook her head. "Clara's gone to St Lucia to see her brother – new niece to go soppy over. They're at the ancestral pile, which is halfway up the volcano and about as wheelchair friendly as a climbing wall."

"So you've nowhere to go?"

"Just home." Amy's parents live in Laos. She doesn't see them much.

I couldn't bear the thought of her spending Christmas alone in her flat with no company but the river that flows at the end of her garden, and anyone she met in the pub, of course.

"You could come to mine," I said. "The house is all set up for wheelchairs because of Grandma, so…"

"And you aren't cooking?"

"No."

"Or choosing the wine?"

"No."

"Do you play board games after dinner?"

"No."

"Thank fuck for that. Okay, I'll come. Thanks."

*

Amy arrived early on Christmas Eve. Dad brought us both chocolate wands and Simon got me a Harry Potter dressing-up set – which mystified Idris and made Amy laugh like a drain after she insisted that I put it on. Mum gave me the washing-up to do.

Amy brought something innocuously domestic as a house present, and spent most of the time being charming and telling clean jokes – I hadn't known that she knew any. By the end of the day mum was calling her 'dear' and dad was eyeing me speculatively. Even Simon warmed to her, although Idris, who is otherwise a nice lad, was unimpressed, possibly because he was no longer being treated as the special guest for the day.

After we had finished eating they all repaired to the living room for coffee and burping. Amy and I made short work of clearing the table. "Your mum and dad are nice," she said, as the plates stacked themselves into the dishwasher.

"Yes, I suppose so."

"Mine sent me a four-line text," she replied bleakly. "That was unusually vociferous for them."

I perched on a kitchen chair and hugged her. "You'll always be welcome with me."

She kissed me – I had expected a peck on the cheek, but this was rather more enthusiastic than that. Then, slightly embarrassed, we went through to find the parents had taken their customary seats in the conservatory and were snoozing as the gentle snowfall on the roof darkened the room. Simon and Idris, both of whom had hit the wine a bit hard, were cuddled up on the couch. They sprang apart when we came in, and I guessed that things would have got out of hand (or into hand, if you get my drift) if we hadn't interrupted.

"You two really shouldn't be doing that down here," said Amy, hiding a smile.

"Why? Because you say so?" This was Idris being bullish. Simon didn't speak but, to his faint credit, he did look a bit embarrassed.

"Because if you carry on I'll pull your head off and fill it with snakes," Amy replied sweetly. Despite being a bit of an earth-mother type, she does good threat.

"What, from there?" None of us liked the sneer in his voice and, unsurprisingly, Amy took particular exception.

Amy can stand up for a bit, but it isn't easy, so it surprised the crap out of Idris when she stood up, grabbed him by the front of his tasteless Christmas jumper and lifted him clear off the ground. His squealing woke the parents.

"Yes. Problem?" Idris shook his head. "Good boy. Now piss off." She dropped him, and he and Simon scampered out of the room as she lowered herself carefully back into her chair.

Dad was chuckling quietly. "I always had my doubts about that boy's manners. I hope that will be a salutary lesson."

"It certainly surprised me," Mum added. "Michael told me that you weren't permanently in the chair, dear, but I didn't realise that you were that mobile."

Amy looked at me and grinned. I smiled back, feeling a genuine, and slightly unsettling, surge of affection for her based on something other than lust. Anyone who can silence Simon and his gobby boyfriend that quickly is all right in my book.

"I didn't do it," she replied. "Mike did."

"Michael did?" Mum frowned. "But he wasn't anywhere near him."

I raised one hand a little and an empty cup lifted off the

coffee table, traced a small circle and then settled back into place. She jumped slightly.

"Oh. And you…" She made a similar gesture but aimed vaguely at Amy.

"That's right," Amy replied. "Mike did the lifting and I did the swearing."

Dad looked at me. "I can see why you might want to." I nodded and he looked at Amy. "Brandy?"

"Yes, please," she replied, smiling. He rose to pour but Amy held up her hand. "Let me show you my party trick."

She concentrated hard and the brandy bottle gave off an odd bluish glow, one that was soon visible in Amy's glass. When it had faded, the liquid was in her balloon. Water Talent, yeah?

"Oh my," said Mum. "That must be very useful at times."

"Can be," I said as she drank. "One of the people I started training with tried to do something like it with his girlfriend's underwear."

"Tried?" Amy asked with a small grin.

"She tried to block it, but she was a first year as well." I shrugged. "His eyebrows had grown back by the summer."

They laughed and Christmas continued. I enjoyed it very much.

*

The day after, Boxing Day afternoon, was the time for Amy to go, and it was then I realised that I didn't want her to. Not in a fierce or soppy way, but because I enjoyed her company. I liked just being with her, which should have given me a hint about what was going on inside my head, but it didn't register.

It was blisteringly cold with a wind that bit, so she got into her adapted Audi quite quickly – lifting spells are useful for more things than just startling teenagers – while I put her bag in the boot. The cars that lined the street had a smooth half inch of snow over them and looked like they hadn't moved in a week.

"Thanks," she said. "I enjoyed that."

"Good. I'm… glad you came."

She sighed. "Maybe one day." She turned to me with a bright smile. "That Idris is a bit of a tosser, isn't he?"

"He's all right really, just a bit too convinced that he's more important than he actually is."

She nodded. "Anyway, I must go – people to do, things to see."

I smiled and touched her shoulder as she started the car. She quickly reached up and held my hand in place, then kissed it gently. "I would like to prove something to you soon," she said quietly.

"What?"

"That it's only the hip joints that don't work." She let go of my hand, flicked the door shut with a thought and drove off through the light snow that was falling again. I'm dreaming of a white Christmas and all that. I took my erection inside, glad that the icy wind could explain the almost radioactive glow on my cheeks.

6

The next day was typical of Twixmas, the flat time between the acquisitive hyperbole of Christmas and the celebration of our version of the New Year.

The morning was dragging its feet through weary minutes that felt like hours, so I decided to go for a walk. I like walking. It's peaceful and I can think – when Simon is at full roar at home it's like living in a spin dryer full of bricks. I had just got enough layers on when mum came into the hall.

"Sam," she said and handed me the phone.

"Sam?" I was puzzled – she almost never calls me on the landline, and it didn't feel like her anyway. "Hello?"

"It's Anthony."

"Oh. Hi." Anthony is Sam's elder brother, whose name is actually Zhang Wei. If they phoned me here it was normally him that called because we hadn't wanted the parents to think Sam was my girlfriend, or find out any more details about what we did. I can't give you a reasonable explanation for that now.

Sam shares a house with her brother and his girlfriend, Lian. He came to this country about five years before Sam did, and if pressed he will allow you to believe that he works in a takeaway. He's actually a forensic accountant who does so much work for the police that he tends to keep a low profile. Besides which, his sweet and sour sauce looks like wallpaper paste and doesn't taste much better.

"What you done now?" Sam said, after Zhang Wei had handed over the phone.

"I done… I've done nothing. What's happened?"

"Aeroplane crash. How you shoulder?"

"Fine. Why do you think it was me?"

"Lot of mess, lot of noise, achieve nothing."

"Thanks," I replied after a moment. Sam is not so much affectionate towards me as tolerant. Her boyfriend, Sho, who claims to have black belts in judo, kung fu and egg fried rice, really doesn't like me. He resents the fact that sometimes I know what Sam is thinking; half the time I don't believe he knows what he's thinking himself, let alone anyone else.

"Where?"

"Bristol, early this morning. Prof want see us."

"Where? When?"

"Like now, our café in Town Square."

"Okay, um, twenty minutes?"

"You not there in fifteen, I send search party." She hung up. It took me five minutes to get my car down the slippery drive, but there was some parking near the coffee shop – a minor miracle – so I walked in just on eighteen minutes to find nobody there. I guessed that they were downstairs, so I grabbed a huge coffee and headed down the narrow staircase.

I was expecting Sam, Professor Gowan and possibly Professor Wicks. I was wrong. There were about ten people in there, and the power radiating off them was like walking under a sun lamp.

"Morning," I said as casually as I could, sitting in the one empty seat.

"Morning," replied Gowan. "I take it Sam has told you there's been another one?"

"Yes, an aeroplane at Bristol Airport." The news broadcasts on the car radio had been full of 'Christmas terror outrage'. "I wasn't in Bristol over Christmas – I spent the whole time at home with my family." I wasn't sure if I felt aggrieved, but I certainly felt accused.

"We know. We've heard all about it."

"How?" Gowan didn't answer. "Amy? Did you send her to watch me?" I was shocked, partly that they might have thought to do that, but mostly that it might have been Amy's motive for coming.

"No," said Gowan. "We just asked her afterwards. Her being there was nothing to do with this, or with us. It must have been your wit and charming personality."

"I've got my doubts about that girl's common sense," muttered Professor Wicks. The man next to her smiled for an instant, but it never touched his eyes, and he never looked away from me.

"This is Mr Slater," said Gowan.

I kept my face still but felt that cold quiver in my gut that I used to get whenever I was sent to the head at school; this time it was fully justified – Richard Slater is one of the Triumvirate, the three mages that are notionally in charge of the Central College and, thus, all the active mages in the country. I swallowed and nodded politely. At least Anne Collister and Nadia Hussain, the other members of the Triumvirate, weren't here.

Gowan introduced the others, more of the Central College authorities whose names I barely heard and never remembered. I had no doubt that the strangers at the table were Richard Slater's hench–people, or whatever the politically correct term is this week; I paid them less attention than I probably should, apart from one red-haired woman who looked like she would bite me if I annoyed her.

"Michael," said Slater. His voice was soft but had a penetrative quality and a hint of an accent. He is also a big solid bloke in his forties; his lack of hair was made up for by having more chins than he was born with.

"Yes, sir?"

"We are aware that you were not involved in the incident at Bristol Airport," he said carefully. "The death tolls are getting higher with each event, and the media is finally starting to get some intelligent ideas. The relevant authorities – and one or two people who think they are the relevant authorities – are starting to ask difficult questions that we have no answers for. I regret to say that you are the only conduit that we can work with to resolve this."

"Conduit? Someone is working through... the only one... there was another?"

"Two. The first was in southern Scotland during the summer. We had no idea what it was about at the time, but it seems to have been a test."

"How much damage was done?"

"None. This is why we think it was a test; no one was injured except the conduit."

"Badly?"

"Burned out." I winced. Overusing magic can deplete a mage's energy reserves so badly that they can never cast again. It almost always results in some degree of brain damage as well.

"The other was the incident at Bristol. The mage who was the conduit – she was *Iksale* 2 – was located almost immediately afterwards, on the perimeter of the airfield."

"So what actually happened?"

"An incorporeal aeroplane ploughed into the flight line and wrecked most of the aircraft that were at the gates. At least ten dead, more than forty injured," he added glumly. "It could have been a lot worse – the airport carries more than eight million passengers a year, but it was relatively quiet when it happened."

"But still," I said.

"Quite," said Slater. "And currently we aren't really sure where all the power necessary is coming from. It's far too much for any *Iksale* to produce." There was a brooding silence that I filled by drinking my coffee, or at least starting to. It was a bit cool so I added some heat, a trick I had learned from Jerry the fire master ages ago. It was startling to think that I now outranked him.

My brain hurt because of the implications of what Slater had just said. Conduit – which meant someone or something was using junior mages to create mayhem and death. I mean, fucking hell. Why did they choose me? I saw Slater staring at me oddly and wondered what on earth I'd done *now*. Wicks looked at me expectantly, and I guessed they were waiting for me to work something out.

"Were all the others earth Talents?"

Gowan smiled. "I told you he was bright."

Slater nodded. "Yes." He made a gesture, and I could feel a power surge, but it didn't seem to do anything.

"What happened to the Bristol conduit?"

"She died," said Slater. The pain in my head faded.

"Oh shit." Another thought made me go cold. "Why didn't I die? Am I going to die?"

Gowan stirred. "No. Because you're too strong. The pair of you are too strong, I should say."

"What happened to the other *erdikide*?"

"The Scottish one is fine. The Bristol one, who we found lying next to her, is in a fugue."

"Shit."

"Quite." A fugue is a sort of mental blockage caused by

the effect of an *erdikide* dying traumatically or something similar. It doesn't always happen, thank god, but it's common if the partners are linked at the time. If the conduit was badly depleted they may have been sharing *Indar*, and that would be enough to create a fugue.

Just the idea of a fugue made me shudder. It's like locked-in syndrome. Mages who fall into a fugue never come out. Never. It's something you wouldn't wish on your worst enemy. "So what happens now?"

"You two need to come to Central," said Slater gravely. "The person who is doing this will have left some trace which we can work on."

"When?"

"Tomorrow morning. Expect to be away for at least a week, probably somewhat longer."

"You are excused classes," Wicks added drily.

"We'll come for you," he pointed to me, "at ten tomorrow morning. Be ready."

"Yes, sir."

He turned to Sam. "Can you be at his house then?"

She looked at me and shook her head. "Not possible. Maybe better he come to me."

"Very well. Miss Lee's house at ten."

"Yes sir," we chorused. The assembled hierarchy of mages rose to their collective feet and left the room. I looked at Sam.

"Oh bollocks."

"But it prove you right."

"What do you mean?"

"You always say you done nothing – this time it true."

*

The colleges were in turmoil, and many meetings happened,

most of them utterly fruitless. Meanwhile Sam and I went to Central, a car journey to London that gave us ample time to fret. We knew that the Central College was near Blackfriars, but neither of us had been there before and every person we asked had a different version of what it was like.

You might have expected it to be something like Hogwarts, or maybe the Folly, full of deep-instilled magic seeping from the ancient stones of a grand and imposing building. Sam suggested that they might have gone ultra-modern and be somewhere like the Shard, or that ugly car-melting thing that looks like a walkie-talkie, or some other prizewinning architectural eyesore. It isn't that the location is secret, but it's very heavily not advertised.

So where did we end up? Underneath St Paul's Cathedral. Seriously, St Paul's is one of the ancient 'places of power' – there are several dozen in this country – which are natural sources of really powerful magic. A lot of them have been inhabited since before anyone was able to work out why they were inhabiting them. A large proportion have been annexed by the church, on the theory that if people are going to worship there anyway you might as well stick a church on it and call it Christian; or by the National Trust, who do the same thing, but with tea rooms and gift shops.

St Paul's is a fine example of both. There is a huge crypt that the public can visit, where a load of famous dead people – or dead famous people – are stored. If you go into one of the side chapels – St Somebody I've Never Heard Of – there's a door that looks like it hasn't been opened since Chaucer was a lad. You know the type, hinges clogged with rust and spiders, a huge lock that Shakespeare probably lost the key for... yes, I know, this St Paul's wasn't built until after the Great Fire in 1666, and he'd been dead for ninety-odd years when it was finished, but you get the idea.

It looked like it didn't open because it actually didn't – when it was activated the whole frame dropped back and slid sideways. I don't know what happens if the wrong spell is cast but I didn't want to find out; sometimes spontaneous combustion isn't all that spontaneous, if you catch my drift.

"What the…?" was all I could manage before the door slid shut behind us. The stone corridor glowed, not from lights but from the stone itself. A simple enough spell, simple to apply, and impressive as hell – but I wondered why. I mean, this is the access to the Central College, and people who come here aren't going to be impressed by things like this. Sam appeared equally puzzled and our driver, the red-haired woman from the coffee shop meeting, recognised this.

"Back entrance," she said briefly. She had introduced herself as Katherine, and seemed to be permanently cross about something.

The tunnel was a quarter-mile of mediaeval unremarkableness, although you had to admire the neatness of the stonework. It ended at a steel door, streaked with rust and dusty spiderwebs, which wouldn't have looked out of place as the entrance to a Second World War bunker or as an obvious trap in a zombie film. Katherine waved her hand and the door opened with a theatrical creak.

The lighting inside really should have been eldritch or spooky or something like that, but it was a yellowing neon tube that flickered. I felt slightly cheated.

"Back door, yes?" Katherine didn't smile, but her tone was wry and vaguely amused. I suppose we both looked annoyed or confused or, in my case, in need of the toilet.

Then we hit the security screens and things went weird on us. First they froze us – as in kept still, not iceberg – and a green light tracked up and down our bodies. Then the room went black and they fired UV light at us; our teeth and eyeballs glowed but nothing else.

The door opened with an unimpressive whoosh – more Tube train than Starship Enterprise – and we were propelled into another room. This was equipped with two office chairs of the standard torture-chamber specification, one desk, one lamp and three people – a burly white man dressed in black and a thin, studious-looking Afro-Caribbean in a white lab coat. Behind them was a woman not much older than me, Asian heritage, in draggy jeans, a jumper that a Nordic detective would have killed for, and biker boots. She was looking at us sceptically.

"You have got to be kidding me. No way."

Lab Coat sniffed, while the man in black swallowed a smile.

"Thank you for that insight ma'am, but we still have to test them," said Lab Coat.

"If you must." She looked at us, sighed, then slowly lowered her feet from the desk and walked over. She wasn't much taller than Sam but you got the feeling that she was going to savage you at any moment.

She peered at Sam, rested one muscled hand on the top of her head and whistled. "Ye gods," she said, turning to look at Lab Coat. "You be careful with this one, Lionel. I know you're good, but she could pull your brains out through your ears as easy as sneezing."

She turned to me, shrugging with her eyebrows, but then stopped. "Ah, that would explain it," she muttered. "I don't think he's aware of it, but he's a Dual Talent." She frowned. "There's something odd going on too, like there's something… in the way." That comment worried me, even though I had no idea what she meant.

"A Dual Talent; just like Bristol," said Lionel.

"And that poor lass in Coldstream. Interesting." She paused, then turned to us. "Don't worry, Lionel here is a bit of an old woman but he knows his stuff. I'll see you later." She left.

"Please sit," said presumably-Lionel.

Neither of us moved.

"Why?" Sam asked, suddenly sounding like the member of the nobility that she was. 'Duchess' isn't quite the right title, but her status is close enough to give the average middle-class social climber palpitations. She rarely uses it, but when she does it's like being hit over the head with a big stick.

"I'm not going to explain until later," said Lionel. "Otherwise what I need to do won't work. I do not wish to compel you, but…"

"Try me," I said, and gathered a little power. Lionel waved one hand and I was pulled to the floor like gravity had trebled. Sam didn't move, but there was a vague bluish haze around her, and Lionel grunted. The man in black stepped forward and Sam raised her hand.

"You ask us nice, we do what you say. Going to be watching you."

"Please sit," said Lionel, "this won't take long."

We did and it did – the delightful Lionel had a bloody good rummage around inside my head until he was happy I wasn't 'infected' with anything they didn't approve of, but wouldn't say what that might be. I felt cold and sick and still needed the toilet when he'd finished. Then he tried to do the same to Sam. It was very hard not to laugh.

"He's clean," he told Katherine when she came to collect us, indicating me. "She's clean – as far as I can tell," was his verdict on Sam, which made Katherine smirk.

"Come with me," she said, removing us from Lionel and his taciturn friend. She led us down some very bland corridors – thankfully equipped with toilets – to a room that wouldn't have looked out of place in a tax office. If this was how they treated their friends I doubted they had any enemies left. Or friends, for that matter.

We were ushered into the room, and Katherine went

across to the other side and leant against the wall. The Asian lady was waiting for us, booted feet on the table again, doing something on her mobile phone. She looked up.

"Oh, you're finished." She chuckled. "You did give poor Lionel a hard time, Miss Lee, and as for you, Mr Frost, what a tiny surprise you turned out to be." She swung her feet down. "I'm Nadia Hussain, by the way." She saw the look on my face and laughed. "Don't worry, I don't bite. Well, not unless you want me to."

Oh for fuck's sake, I thought. *This is supposed to be serious. She's one of the highest rated mages in the country, about fourth highest in Europe or something, and she's making feeble jokes.* I looked at Sam, who seemed about as relaxed as a terracotta warrior.

"No idea," she muttered. "Go with flow. They on our side…"

"Sure?"

"*Meíyôu.*"

I wasn't either, but I followed her down the corridor anyway.

"Come on through." The room we went into looked like any hotel conference room you care to fall asleep in, and had an elevated view of the river, even though we hadn't got into a lift.

The Thames flowed past the heavily tinted window in a turbulent stretch of shit-coloured water sprinkled with boats, barges, litter and dead seagulls. We were halfway between the Millennium and Blackfriars bridges, and opposite the uninspiring frontage of the Tate Modern and all the other detritus of the arty-farty Bankside development. I guessed we were on White Lion Hill. In case you were wondering how I know that, Dad's from London and I have uncles, cousins and other familial hangers-on infesting most of the area from Kensington to Canary Wharf.

"How…?" I pointed to the view.

73

"That's just us showing off, Mike, don't worry about it," said Nadia.

Sam sniffed. "What you want with us?"

Nadia's smile faded just a notch, and I realised that her eyes had always been slightly distant. I sent out a small probe and met a shield so solid that my aura almost got bruises on it.

"And it's not even mine," Nadia replied. I asked a question with my eyes. It was Katherine who raised her finger.

"Oh."

"Right," said Nadia, "let's get on with this. You know that there have been several attacks using hard-light entities to wreak death and destruction on the population. No explanation or attribution has been forthcoming. The only connection is that in each case a Dual Talent has been used as a conduit for the power required."

"Not the source?"

"No. This is very advanced magic that needs lots of power, big serious stuff. You know about the probable practice run in Scotland and the thing at Bristol Airport?" I nodded. "The other three have used you, Mike, and it can only be because of Sam's extraordinary power that you survived what killed two other mages with a single exposure."

"Yay us," said Sam drily.

"Yeah," Nadia replied, equally drily.

"Do you think I'm in danger again?"

"No. As soon as we realised what was going on Catriona Gowan put a, well, it's a kind of shield on you, and then Richard made it secure. You're safe, unless you do something especially stupid."

"Splendid." I wasn't feeling too good, so I went to the side of the room where there was a coffee machine. "You don't know who's doing this, do you?" I said, as it burbled.

"No."

"You want to use me to find out."

"Yes." Now while I appreciate honesty, and direct speaking rarely offends or upsets me, this seemed a little too blunt.

"Will I survive?" I felt obscurely remote to the idea, like it didn't really matter.

Nadia seemed genuinely shocked. "That's the plan. It may not be very pleasant, and you're both going to have to learn some more advanced spells, but there's no suggestion that we're going to put you in danger."

And if you believe that, I thought, *I have some title deeds to the Eiffel Tower that you might be interested in.*

"So why we come through back door?" Sam asked. She never stops thinking. "Why all checking?"

"Because," said Katherine seriously, "we believe the person doing this may be trying to discredit magic users. Or it could be the build-up to a direct assault on us. If you were going to attack magery in general, where better than here?"

"Understand that. Why back door?"

"We don't want whoever is doing this to know you're here."

"So we sit by window?"

Nadia smiled gently. "It's one-way glass and the image it shows on the outside is of an office full of jaunty motivational posters that nobody reads, and staff that are dying of terminal ennui. This is Baynard House, which is notionally a BT office, and we're careful to do nothing to suggest anything different."

*

Central, as it is inevitably known, has moved several times since its creation in around 1815. The records are fragmentary and one day I may write a brief history – maybe if I've broken both legs or something. Anyway, it used to be housed in a number of locations around Westminster, many quite grand, although one was a floating coffee house near Borough Market that doubled as a knocking shop for discerning ladies and gentlemen. This was back in the days when not *all* the elected occupants of the Palace of Westminster were either powerless idealists or self-serving wankers.

The trouble came when the number of people wanting to be involved in the control of magic in this country (in the Empire, in fact), quickly overwhelmed the available space. So, after a brief and occasionally amusing interlude in a converted warehouse in Poplar, and another in a building on Canary Wharf that used to house the East India Company, Central arrived at its current location in the early 1970s. Ostensibly an eye-wateringly unattractive BT office about 200 metres from Blackfriars Station, the fact that it looks about as interesting as mud on a broken fence has proved a very effective form of camouflage.

I had a suspicion that settling in this location was not necessarily fortuitous – the fact that there is a tunnel from St Paul's to the building troubled me until Mr Hildebrand, the Nottingham college librarian-cum-archivist, pointed out that it had originally led to the banks of the Thames and was constructed as an escape route – although when, and who was escaping from whom, he wasn't sure.

Sandwiching the hub of magic between somewhere as powerful as St Paul's and a huge river like the Thames seems wise to me, because all rivers inherently have a lot of water Talent power in them. I suspect that it's because they are the junction between water Talent territory and earth Talent territory that such liminal spaces – where one thing becomes another – have always fascinated me.

*

I sipped my coffee. It was delicious. "Is this coffee real or have you been tinkering with the flavonoids?" I needed to ask something that I was fairly sure didn't have a scary answer. I'd had enough of being scared.

"It's real," replied Nadia, picking up her mobile, which had been buzzing like a demented bee for the last two minutes. "Okay, we'll start tomorrow morning. Kat will show you to your rooms. We don't want you to leave this building, and we have everything you could possibly need right here, so don't try. Bye."

She was already tapping the screen when Katherine ushered us out. "Your rooms are 412 and 414, and the doors are keyed to your *esku*. Just cast a light spell or something and they'll open."

"You have our *esku* registered here?"

"Of course." She sounded surprised. "You two successfully jumped from *Iksale 2* to *Ikasberri* in one go, which is almost unheard of; Sam here has enough power to melt a housing estate and you are a powerful, oddly previously undetected, and rather ambiguous, Dual Talent. You have," she added with a portentous voice and a grin, "been noticed."

That made me pause. A Dual Talent is someone who operates two Talents with equal power at the same time. "Earth and…?"

"Fire. Probably the rarest combination. It's strong, but they aren't a clean pairing."

Sam is an air Talent, in case you were wondering. "Oh, I didn't realise." That was mild, considering how shocked I was. Even in that bland corridor and surrounded by all the skills there are, I still felt the world slipping away from me.

"Hmm. Anyway, your rooms."

They could have been rooms in any mid-range business travellers' hotel; fairly comfortable, fairly spacious and utterly characterless. Our bags, which we had left in the car, were already in them. It took maybe ten minutes to unpack and put everything away, and Sam was already waiting outside when I came out. By now it was mid-afternoon, so we headed for somewhere where more interesting stuff was going on.

7

While this was happening, life at the Nottingham college was getting rather more interesting than anyone really wanted.

Our college buildings are loosely attached to the archaeology department, but from the outside you wouldn't know it wasn't the Department of Media Studies And Reflexive Cynicism, or something like that. It has lecture rooms, study areas, workshops, a library – all the usual stuff, plus our own coffee shop. This was, with pathetic inevitability, known as The Leaky Cauldron. I believe it was originally called 'The Coffee Shop' by the dullards who are in charge of these things.

In the first week after Christmas staff and students tend to be unenthusiastic bordering on sluggish, as if two weeks away from buggering about with the fundamental forces of the universe is somehow tiring.

Each term brings a new set of lectures, and each requires particular equipment and specific materials. Some of these have to be brought from locations that are secure, or shielded, or at the bottom of a coal mine, so there tends to be quite a lot of stuff coming and going at the start of term.

That's why nobody noticed yet another case being dropped off by an ordinary post office van, one of several that day. We don't have broomsticks or magic carpets, by the way; I drive a battered blue VW (and no, I didn't get it from Harry Dresden, and anyway, it's not a Beetle); Amy has a converted Audi something; Clara has her poxy little Fiat 500 and Sam drives a Trumpchi which she brought with her from Hong Kong. It's a terrible car, but she's irrationally fond of it.

It was the job of one of the staff *Ikasberri* to take the deliveries to the appropriate departments and remove them from their protective cases. This one, I am meanly relieved to note, was someone who I didn't really know.

The object didn't explode in the conventional sense – no blast, smoke, fire, bits flying everywhere or anything like that. This was a magical explosion; well, not explosion. Oh crap, this is hard to explain. It's the equivalent of a neutron bomb – no damage but a lot of dead people. Or in this case, unconscious.

Unfortunately the *Ikasberri* who triggered it was standing very close, and he was brain-dead in a heartbeat, the rest of his body failing before anyone found him.

Everyone in the building below *Iksale* 1 was rendered unconscious within seconds. Nobody was spared, and several people were injured when they blacked out halfway through walking or, in one notable case, standing on a chair to get something off a shelf.

Only the most senior grades didn't succumb instantly because of the protective shields they habitually wrap around themselves. Students are advised to do that as well, but they listen with the same set of ears that they listen to advice about not drinking too much with, so…

Of course, we do have non-magical people in the college, mostly of a domestic nature – coffee shop staff, technicians, cleaners and so forth; they suffered no injury unless they fell over, but they were put into a dream-like state. To put it simply, everyone fell asleep, then woke up when the device discharged itself about ten minutes later. All that remained was a metallic cube about a hand span across with some designs incised into one face. This is what is known as a *magia garraiolari*, a 'spell carrier' – or 'thaumatological effect transport system', if you want that translated into jargon – which are about as common and unremarkable as a data stick, which is the thing they most closely resemble.

Nobody could work out where it had come from; it had been sent from a large post office branch in Leeds by somebody who didn't show up on the CCTV and the staff couldn't recall clearly. Nothing was missing from the college, nothing was broken for any reason other than the obvious, and nothing untoward had been brought into the building.

The department responsible for ensuring the safety of the colleges had a lot of explaining to do. This mostly consisted of shrugging, looking embarrassed and saying 'beats the shit out on me, mate'. This was notionally Professor Weaver's bailiwick, and he said he was bringing in a new man to oversee the staff and building security. The next day the colleges in Newcastle and Bristol were attacked in the same way. Guess which colleges the other two conduits went to?

*

We were constrained in the illusionary London office block while all this was going on. Nadia had introduced us to a Healer named Beverley Hinch, and reacquainted us with Katherine Duncan, our driver and, we now discovered, Nadia's right-hand person.

I spent the first two days in the medical facility on the top floor at Central, just lying down. This wasn't nearly as much fun as it might have been, because I was face down on a table with two technical types and Bev trying to work out what had happened to my shoulder. Or how. Or why. Or possibly which way the wind was blowing on Jupiter. I don't bloody know. All I know is that it hurt and they said they couldn't give me any pain relief because they needed to know what it felt like. Bloody sadists. The medical section looked and smelled like a small but well-equipped hospital, clean enough to make the average mysophobic nod appreciatively.

The room we were in – and I was heartily sick of – was like any reasonably equipped doctor's surgery, so designed to be effective, efficient and about as comforting as the edge of an axe. The ranked medical equipment reminded me of the inside of the line of ambulances at Paddington. It made me uncomfortable, but thankfully nothing more. I tried not to think about it too much.

I was surprised to find that Sam wasn't there to give me hugs and *Indar*. In fact, when I saw her at dinner on the first night she looked worse than me, and her thoughts were troubled and cloudy. God knows what mine were like.

The eatery was called The Popina, because somebody did Latin at school, and was halfway between a restaurant and a canteen. And because enhanced taste buds are not part of a mage's mutation, the food was massively disappointing after dad's cooking. Fortunately I barely tasted a thing. I think the first night it was roof insulation *en croute* with mashed polystyrene and boiled musket balls. I have no idea what the pudding was, but I ate it with my eyes closed.

Bev saw me to my room. "You need to sleep now."

"I know," I mumbled. I sat down to take off my shoes but flopped back onto the bed, as boneless as a jellyfish.

"Get into bed," said Bev. On another day that might have seemed like an invitation, but tonight I wouldn't have been able to raise a smile, let alone anything else. Bev is my height, Afro-Caribbean and slim, with the same sort of smoky sexiness that Clara has. I mean, you don't look a gift… in the… er… I think I'll shut up now.

She pulled off my shoes. "Come on," she said briskly.

I wanted to move, I really did, but I couldn't. I wanted Sam to give me some *Indar*, or coffee, or even a back rub, but she wasn't there. In fact, I could tell she was already asleep, so far down that I couldn't possibly reach her.

I felt tears wet my eyes, and Bev's breath on my lips, hot and close, and power flowed into me like I'd got new batteries. This wasn't *Indar*, this was something quite different, something I didn't recognise, something that I'd never felt before.

Then I realised it was pure Healing energy. Using it on a whole person, rather than to deal with some specific problem, is technically impossible because there is no target for it. But that didn't seem to bother Bev, even if it confused the hell out of me. I had no idea why she decided to deliver it by kissing me either. I started to feel fizzing hot and made to sit up, but she kept me pressed to the bed for another few seconds, then leant back, sitting next to me.

"Wow," I said. "I mean, fucking wow. What was that?" I felt properly alert for the first time since Paddington.

She smiled, looking like a smug genie. "Fire. We've started to release a lot of things, but mainly your fire Talent. You've been operating at half strength for ages, only using your earth Talent. It's like running a marathon on only one leg – and yet you still reached *Ikasberri* three years quicker than average." She shook her head. "There's something very odd about you."

"Oh." I won't say I felt clear-headed and bouncy, but I could feel a liberating warmth flowing through me; my muscles felt loose and powerful. I couldn't have run ten miles – ten metres is normally enough for me – but I did feel like I could a lift a bus with a thought. Well, a minibus anyway.

"Now go to sleep. I'll get you up in the morning." I opened my mouth but she slid off the bed and pointed a stern finger at me. "No jokes. Go to sleep. You'll dream of fire, but it won't trouble you. Goodnight."

She left, and I was asleep within five minutes. I did dream, but I woke at 5am with my 'tattooed' shoulder hurting so badly it was an effort to withhold a scream.

A Healer arrived almost immediately – I hadn't even managed to call for help – and he gave me some honest-to-god morphine. I crashed back into unconsciousness within seconds, too distracted to wonder why a Healer had been monitoring me so closely that the morphine was on its way down the corridor before I'd even woken up.

*

Day two was basically a repeat of day one, including most of the unpleasant bits, but by the end of it the not-actually-tattoos had been removed from my back. You can't tell that they were ever there, apart from a small round patch that doesn't look quite like the rest – Sam called it my reset button. By the end of the day I was feeling better, but 'better' isn't a synonym for 'well'.

We met at dinner, with Bev and Katherine keeping a weather eye on us, and I have to say that Sam had improved. Mind you, I've seen dead people who looked better than she had the day before. Once we'd finished eating – Vermicelli made with real worms and a sauce that owed more to cornflour than cheese – she wanted to talk.

"So, they sort you out?"

"Er…"

She looked at Bev. "You not tell him? Why not? You think he not big enough boy to cope?"

Katherine stirred, setting her spoon down with a slow,

deliberate motion; if she had held up a sign that said 'I Am Now Going To Say Something Important' it couldn't have been more obvious. "Mike was a two-part... er, problem. Not a problem really. Situation. Thing."

I made a hurry-up gesture. "I know – emergent duality and being a conduit."

"Er... no. Nearly, but no. Your duality was..." she broke off.

"A bloody nuisance," said Nadia, putting her cup on the table and looking at me expectantly. Unsure what Mrs Uber-Witch wanted, I sipped my coffee, then nearly spat it across the table. It was disgusting.

Nadia looked at Bev. "That's a fiver you owe me." Katherine laughed and so, I was irritated to note, did Sam.

With a glare that had absolutely no impact on any of them, I stomped over to the servery, discarded my coffee with a feeling of revulsion, and got myself some tea. I sipped it carefully before I headed back towards the table. I normally find tea insipid going on flavourless, but this was delicious.

All the women were laughing together, and didn't seem to have noticed that I'd left, so I found a different table over by the window, sat back, sipped my drink and closed my eyes. I could have done with a lot more sleep or Bev's magic snogging. Instead, I had tea and a head full of smoke.

I heard a noise at the table and opened my eyes. There was a man sitting opposite me, looking at me very carefully. His gaze was disconcerting, and I wasn't sure if he was trying to read me or he wanted to see if I could do magic snogging too. I thought of asking what he wanted but I couldn't be bothered. After two days of this shit I'd just about had enough.

"Michael," he said, then held out his hand. "Patrick Fintan. Please, call me Pat." He had a soft rolling voice, Irish probably, and looked to be in his fifties.

I shook his hand briefly. It was cold and rough and one

nail was chipped. *If this man wanted some wood cut he would use an axe not a spell*, I thought.

"Yes?" Mum had tried to inculcate nice manners, which is why 'what the fuck do you want?' didn't get past my teeth.

"I'm here to help." I just looked at him. "I know you've had some troubles lately..." I didn't answer. I wasn't looking for talking therapy. "What with the crash and the whole conduit business." I still didn't speak. I just didn't want to. I scanned my own mind, but this muteness wasn't something that was being done to me. I didn't know who this Fintan bloke was, so I didn't trust him – in fact all I wanted was for him to just go away and leave me alone. I *needed* some peace.

He looked at me for a long second. "You aren't really here, are you? Or, at least, not as far as I'm concerned." He left a pause long enough for me to not answer in. "Maybe you should go to bed."

"I don't want to."

"Oh, it does speak. Progress at last. Do you know who I am?"

"The bloke who's getting in my face when all I want to do is sit quietly with a cup of tea?"

"Am I annoying you?" I didn't answer. "So you don't trust me?"

"I wouldn't trust you if you gave me a personal reference from the Queen written in Richard Slater's blood and countersigned by Mother Teresa and the Dalai Lama."

"They're both dead," he replied, "or they are at the moment, in the Dalai Lama's case." I carried on looking at him, feeling increasingly hostile. He grunted. "Drink your tea."

I pushed it away from me.

"OK, don't drink your tea."

"Why don't you just piss off?" I said coldly, balling my fist. Fintan was probably a higher grade mage than me, but he was several inches shorter, older, and not so heavily built. I wanted to hit something. Or someone. I had no idea what was wrong, but I just wanted whatever it was to stop.

"OK." He stood up, so abruptly it made me jump, looked across at the women and then stalked out of the room. He was replaced a few seconds later by Sam and Bev. Katherine had vanished but Nadia was still watching, amazingly not doing something on her phone. Her dark-eyed stare was disconcerting, and I couldn't meet her gaze. For all that she's quite attractive, in an idiosyncratic sort of way, I will admit that, at that moment, something about her scared me.

"You not okay," said Sam. It wasn't a question, and she felt agitated.

"Was Pat being intrusive?" Bev asked.

"No, he was being a pain in the arse," I replied. The headache was coming back, and with it the eyes of the man who had been crushed at Paddington. Bev took my hand. The gentle flow from her drove the pain away, or back at least, but the core of it remained. My eyes closed, without me being involved in the movement in any way, and when I opened them Nadia, and an older woman who I didn't recognise, were there as well. There were more tears, and a terrible sense that I had failed, or done something wrong. I felt fucking awful.

"Do you need to...?" Nadia asked.

Bev nodded. "Now. Both of them." I felt myself falling and grabbed for the table, but somehow failed to connect. My vision went grey and wavery and the room swung around me. It took me several seconds to realise that I'd actually been lowered to the floor.

I had a vague impression of being wafted out of the room and wondering why so many people were even interested in the fact that I wasn't very well. I saw lights and a lift, then a corridor that smelt of antiseptic, alcohol hand rub and fear that just had to be on the medical floor. At some point in that part of the journey, I passed out.

*

I don't remember the next day, not really. I remember a room, and I remember being in bed, but other than that it's all a bit vague. I know Sam was there for at least part of the time, and Bev seemed to be a permanent fixture. I'm sure there were other people but they were mostly drifting, insubstantial shapes. Nadia was there for a bit, and I think that Richard Slater turned up at one point, but it could equally well have been the Queen of Sheba and the Jeddak of Barsoom.

I do remember the pain, the terrible sapping confusion and the pictures in my mind that I didn't want to see but couldn't look away from. I was also very hot, burning up, my mind doing pinwheels in the roaring darkness. In the centre of it was my *gogoan*. That's the word for the special magical part of the brain, which sounds a lot more metaphysical than it really is. Brains have sight centres and hearing centres – this is just the magical centre. It gives you the extra set of mental dimensions that only mages have, a part of the mutation. It's an interesting place to visit, but you really wouldn't want to live there.

Mine is a landscape of jagged stone and disturbed black sand. In the middle of it were three stable points, like pimples on the arse of the universe. There was a burning swirl, like a fire tornado, that didn't interact with them; they were just places of stillness that it caught on and dragged at as it went past.

I knew one of the points was me, my core magical self. You get shown this early in your training so you know what you have to protect. If somebody or something gets hold of that, it's over. Previously mine had been a non-specific dark colour, which is normal for an earth Talent, but now it was tinged with an unstable red. Fire. I was gaining control over fire.

Another was Sam, the pure white of an air Talent. *Erdikide* are always present in each other's minds. Water Talents show blue, *kemen* is yellow and Healing is silver. Like mine, hers was also tinged with red, although less strongly, and both were ragged around the edges, like stars being sucked into a black hole.

The third was an alien thing. It was trying to steal power from both of us, and didn't care about how much damage it did in the process. No possibility of symbiosis here – this was a parasite, pure and simple.

The power of the thing had an odd... flavour, but it wasn't overwhelming. Nevertheless, I knew that while I might be able to resist it, I couldn't defeat it, and I certainly couldn't remove it. So I built walls and shields around us, including Sam behind every layer. Although she couldn't build any defences in here herself, she certainly could feed power into mine.

My attention wavered as a grinding pain arrived, smothering the clear stars of my personal universe. I'm sure I cried out, and I may have wept. I know I moved, thrashed even, and I felt hands gentle me to a stillness. Then a Healer took the pain away and the space was filled with something I had never experienced, even when I was deep in contact with Professor Gowan or Professor Weaver back in Nottingham.

It was clouds gathering over the starscape, and soon it was raining golden dust. Where it touched, it stuck. Soon the intruder, the parasite, was coated in a fine layer of the dust and its light was dimming, or being smothered, by this auric coating. Sam and I had a sprinkling too, and some of the gold had got through where the skin was ragged from the turbulence. The parasite started to shrink, to diminish from my mind, as if the weight of it all was simply too much for it to bear.

Then – which could have been seconds or days later, I had no idea – the rain changed colour to a lustrous metallic green, not unlike our *Ikasberri* bracelets. The parasite was further coated, and more of the rain entered me, but Sam seemed immune to this beneficent precipitation.

Beneficent precipitation? That's how far out of it I was. I'll start going on about the Ur-Spirit, the Paradigm of Relevance and the Immutable Power of the fucking Universe in a minute. Shoot me now.

The green rain became purple and unfamiliar – I hadn't realised that the gold and the green *were* familiar – and the parasite stopped moving, stopped fighting. It started to fold in on itself. It didn't diminish in power, but it shrank until it was tiny. There's no point in giving you a size comparison, because all of this was taking place in a part of my brain about the size of a walnut.

Sam was also immune to the purple shimmer, but I was filled with them all until I looked like a glitter ball. I heard voices, out in the real world, and a hum which seemed familiar, even though I couldn't quite place it.

"Are you sure he can take another? Won't it be too much for him?" I think that was Nadia.

"He'll be fine. There's far more going on than we originally thought. He's got plenty of capacity and having that one there should steady him." Even though it sounded like someone shouting under water, I'm fairly certain that was Bev – she has a quite distinctive way of talking, like she's about to start chuckling at any moment.

Then a fourth existence appeared in my mind. It didn't give me power, sprinkle us with fairy dust or attack the parasite on a white charger; blue for water, it just being there connected me to me in a way I hadn't realised was missing. I felt grounded and, because I was drawing power from the earth, stronger – but strong like a mountain, not like a lightning bolt. Does that make sense? It does to me. I heard a voice impose itself on my mind.

"Now".

I have no idea what I did. That's not actually true – I know *what* I did, I just haven't the vaguest idea of *how* I did it. I gathered up a stream of energy – the people who do the special effects for movies like *Stargate* would have loved it – and sent it spiralling away from my shield and straight at the parasite. There was a lot of anger and the need to hurt in there too. The fourth power watched, supportive but otherwise uninvolved. I briefly wondered how it could be so immune, then noticed it was contained within a faint but shiny silver sphere.

My energy beam – my phaser if you like – hit the parasite and splashed, like a hose aimed at a wall. The outer shell of resistance didn't last long, and it started to erode, layers ablating like onion skins peeling off. Remembering my sprites, I made little darts from the gold and the green and fired them at the parasite, which by now was a pale and sickly lemon–grey, wrinkled like fingers that have been in water too long.

Each impact caused a crack in the shell, a flaw, a weakness. I used my anger to drill a hole into the heart of it and filled it with fire. It started to scream. The noise was a keening, high-pitched and windblown, and then the parasite exploded. Its shield fragmented and vanished, and the tiny core, corroded by the fire and the falling dust and the fury, quickly vanished.

I heard a voice in the outside world say, "I think he's done it", the warmth of a hand in mine, and then everything went black.

*

It was just after dawn when I woke. I didn't ask, 'where am I?' because I knew I was still on the medical floor at Central. I knew perfectly well who I was, especially all the stupid and embarrassing bits that stick in your memory even when the good stuff doesn't. The questions pressing on my mind at that point were 'when am I?' and 'can I get a cup of coffee?'.

I wasn't surprised when a Healer came into the room a few moments later.

"I bet you could do with a drink." She held up a small cup of water with a straw in it. I took a shivery mouthful and swallowed gratefully. It was like drinking sandpaper and razor blades, and as I didn't have a cold I guessed I'd been doing quite a lot of shouting. I think she started to ask me how I was feeling, but a great weight landed on my chest and the darkness took me.

*

When I surfaced again the room was empty and so was I. I felt like a sere reed with the pith out. Still, at peace, with all the ground-in turbulence of the Paddington crash finally gone, my mind was almost blank. Sam would say that was its normal state and I smiled at the thought, at the recollection of her and her kindness; of Amy, and Ambrose and Jerry and even that twit Brian. I was still grinning inanely when the door opened.

"Hello, Mike." It was Beverley of the Amazing Kisses.

"Hello. How am I today?"

"You are well, for the most part." That meant there must be another part which wasn't, but I didn't care. "You need to rest and gather your strength," she went on. "The last little while has taken more out of you than you can possibly imagine. If you do this right, and are sensible about it, you'll be absolutely fine. You should be able to get up in a couple of days."

"Why?"

"Don't you want to get up?"

I blinked – this was such an alien concept that I was having trouble processing it. I was in bed, so that was what I did. Someone else would have to do the 'getting up' thing. "Um..."

"Not to worry," said Bev gently. "You can get up when you want to. Is there anything you need?"

"Tea, Earl Grey, hot." She smiled. "And I would like to kiss you."

"Why? The kissing I mean."

"You did it before and it made me feel great." My thinking was bizarrely linear at this point, so that made perfect sense to me.

"Would you like to feel like that again?"

The muscles in my face moved, and it took me a moment to realise that they were trying to form a smile. "Yes."

"Then you'll have to come here." She was standing by the window.

I looked at the floor. I didn't want to stand on it. It looked indefinably dangerous. I wanted to stay here, where I was safe.

"Later then," said Bev. She walked back to the bedside, touched my head gently and I fell into a dream–wracked sleep that lasted for longer than I could guess.

*

I was much more myself when I woke again – confused, grumpy, bogging for a drink and severely in need of a piss. I was walking back to my bed when I realised I had walked on *that* floor, without a thought.

The door opened. This time it was Sam, and I was surprised to see that she was in pyjamas too, even though it was just after ten o'clock in the morning.

"Hello, you," she said and sat on the bed.

"Hello, you. How's things?"

"Thing are good. You did very good. Not surprised you sleep so long."

"Long?"

"You been asleep two days."

"Two days? Fuck."

"OK." She started to unbutton her top but stopped just when I'd got a glimpse of her underwear – red silk again – and grinned impishly. "I think you too tired for that." Sometimes she's more like the older sister that I never wanted.

"Oh, I don't know," I replied, making a playful grab for her. It's something we do occasionally, but we're not even vaguely serious about it. It would be like wanting to have sex with your maiden aunt.

She held up a magisterial hand. "You rest now. You fight big fight, lots to integrate. Lots to… forget."

Then she did the most extraordinary thing. She reached out one soft hand and laid it on my stubbly cheek. She ran a thumb over the bristles, making a tiny rasping noise. Her eyes were big and bright with tears. "I thought I lose you," she said softly.

I put my hand over hers, for a moment utterly lost in the surge of concern and affection that I was feeling from her. The idea that I might not survive had never occurred to me. "Was it that bad? You thought I'd die?"

"You did," said a voice from the doorway. "Twice. Nearly gave me a bloody heart attack, you selfish git."

It was, to my astonishment, Amy. Disappointingly, she wasn't wearing pyjamas. Sam lifted her hand away, offered a wan smile and settled on the end of the bed.

"Died?"

"Yup," said Amy, wheeling up beside me. "I know they tinkered with your brain – after they finally located it – and that sent your taste buds screwy, but one cup of coffee just about did it for you. They told me you collapsed in the canteen and the Healers had to put you in stasis to stop you spilling bodily fluids all over the floor. I don't blame them – I mean, the amount of paperwork is appalling and it takes ages to get rid of the smell."

I laughed. I laughed until it hurt, until Sam had to get Bev to calm me down. I took both of them by the hand. "I don't know which one of you I love the most," I said.

"He's delirious," said Amy, shaking her head sadly. "He's a lovely bloke, usually, but I think it's time you put him back to sleep."

Bev chuckled. "I think it's time for you to leave before he says something else he later regrets."

Sam looked at her oddly. "I don't think he regret saying that."

"Go on, push off," said Bev.

They did, Sam giggling moistly while Amy swooped around the corridor outside making noises like a Tie Fighter defending the Death Star.

Bev handed me a cup. "Tea, Earl Grey, hot." I drank. It was horrible. She gave me another one. Coffee, cheap but delicious. "That's good," she said. "It shows that we've managed to untangle and release those neural circuits. There are some others that need a bit more work."

"There are others? How badly did you mangle my synapses? I feel fine."

"Mike, you died." She perched on the edge of my bed, suddenly very serious. "In fact you died twice. The first time, in the canteen, you were clinically dead for over a minute before we could get a stasis spell onto you. It's only thanks to Sam pumping you full of *Indar* that you made it at all." She paused, as if looking for a way to express something that I might not be able to grasp.

"She spent more than twelve hours in recovery, profoundly unconscious, because she gave you so much. If we hadn't stopped her, she would probably have given you so much that she would have died herself." There was a tableau moment while I absorbed that.

"She's too kind to me." That, of course, was not what I was thinking. We aren't talking about intimations of mortality here, just being really, really frightened. Stasis spells like *Oraindik* don't always work, and the best of them only last a couple of minutes anyway. I was more than a little concerned that, despite being in the Central College and within the purlieu of some of the most powerful Healers in the country, it was only Sam and her supercharged *Indar* that had saved me. There needs to be a word other than gratitude, or indebtedness, to describe what had happened there. The only one I could think of was 'love'.

"She cares for you as much as you care for her," said Bev.

"Hardly."

She clicked her tongue. "After the locator spell with Professor Weaver back in Nottingham, she was so weak that she almost passed out before she'd even left the workroom. If you hadn't been there, I suspect she would have needed to be hospitalised; what the bloody hell Weaver thought he was doing draining her like that I have no idea. Bo Hinxman was very angry and rightly so." Bo is one of the senior Healers at the college.

"You brought her back to full strength in less than five minutes, with surprisingly little ill effect to yourself." She shook her head. "I have no idea how you managed that – there's a huge amount of power in you somewhere. How did you feel when you did that?"

"Hot mostly, and very concerned for her. It's rare that any form of spell work takes that much out of her."

"My point exactly – you two are very strongly connected, unusually strongly in fact. I suspect that you'll spend the rest of your lives saving each other, in one way or another. Then you died again, about twenty-four hours later, but you were here, so we were able to bring you back quite easily. We don't know why you died that time, and the neural traces we got back when you recovered were very… odd."

"Odd?"

"Atypical for a Dual Talent," she said after a moment.

"So what were they typical of?"

"Nothing I've ever seen before." I had the feeling she wasn't being completely truthful. "I don't know what it was, but something caused a big change in your brain Mike, and I'm still trying to work out what it did. Now go to sleep."

"But I'm not tired," I protested unconvincingly.

Bev smiled. "You sound like my son at bedtime. He's six and is never sleepy until the moment he starts snoring." She touched my head. "*Loaren.*"

The sleep spell landed like a bus that's been dropped from orbit. My eyelids drooped and my feet started to feel warm. Bev shut the curtains with a gesture, and I drifted off, wondering why it had never occurred to me for one second that she might be married with children.

*

By Monday – day eight in the Big House – I was able to go back to my room. Sam was in hers, to the left of mine and, I was surprised to find, Amy was on the other side. Every time I heard the whirr of her wheelchair I would go to the door, hoping she'd knock. Sometimes she did, and then Sam would be there too and I would be happy.

Sam is a part of me, just as I am a part of her, but I was beginning to think that it was happening with Amy too. Which is supposed to be impossible, at least in a magical sense. I strongly suspect I wouldn't have been so torn, so confused, if Sam had been a bloke. Being so close to Sam may have helped me to understand my feminine side, but I have to tell you that phantom period pains are no fun. God knows what real ones are like. During that time I also developed a recipe for waterproof custard creams. No idea where that came from.

Over lunch Amy told me that Bev and the Healers thought that they might be able to do something about her dodgy hips, but the tests which left her in pain. This hurt me as well, and I couldn't work out why. Sam suggested it was because I wasn't able to help her. Paddington thinking again, and it made me teary until Amy told me to stop being such a softy and concentrate on getting myself well before worrying about anyone else, even her.

*

The mood had changed the next morning, and not for the better. It was Katherine who told us. "There's been another one. Southampton. A small naval vessel, like a World War II MTB, rammed the gangway of one of the Isle of Wight ferries while people were disembarking." The desultory way people were nibbling toast and the bleakness of their faces suggested this was not a secret.

"*Lâ shî*," said Sam. Even Amy looked pale, which is difficult for somebody who is already very fair with green eyes and hair that would be reddish-blonde if she'd stop using spells to make it weird colours. It was purple that day.

"How many dead?"

"Not sure yet, but there's around two dozen lost or injured. Drowned, crushed, gone in the water."

"That's horrible," said Amy. "Celebrate Christmas, get drowned on the way home. You got to be some kind of shit – or a proper psycho – to want to do that."

"And you got no idea who doing it or why?" Sam asked.

"None."

"Who was the conduit this time?" I asked, thankful that it wasn't me.

"We don't know yet – nobody's been reported missing and we haven't found a body, so we'll just have to see."

An image flashed into my mind, paused for the tiniest of moments and then fled. "There's an old jetty, a sort of pier thing, next to the Red Funnel terminal in Southampton. He's in there somewhere, and still alive, just." I felt shaky, slightly sick and disorientated for a moment.

They stared at me. "How the hell do you know that?" Katherine asked, sounding seriously concerned.

"I have no idea."

They found him an hour later, left for dead, half in the water, his *erdikide* dead beside him. He was a second year at the Southampton college and a recognised dual-fuel – earth and water, the most common pairing, but still rare in the scheme of things.

They moved him to the local hospital until his condition stabilised, and he was airlifted to the medical floor at Central the next day. That was when I discovered that there is a helipad on the roof.

"So how near to the attack site does the conduit have to be?" I asked Nadia as they were bringing him in.

She shrugged. "It seems to be about half a mile."

"How far does the caster have to be from the conduit?"

"Not sure. Close enough to use the victim to channel the power, so I would guess not more than a mile, but that is very much a guess."

"How did the parasite get planted in the other conduits?"

She gave me a dead-eyed look. "Really no idea." She shook her head. "If we could work that out, we'd be a lot closer to finding out who's doing this."

"So if this bastard gets within about a mile of me I could be used again."

"Hmm. Well, we've put in some protection, but you seeing where this conduit was suggests that some more might be in order."

The boy from Southampton never regained consciousness, and died two days later. His death felt like a cold ghost passing through the building. Something left as he died and it was horribly, sickeningly, familiar. There had been a parasite inside him too, and I felt it die with him. But I hadn't felt that before, which meant mine was still active inside me.

8

Predictably the press went nuts, and all non-emergency magical activity was suspended. Questions were asked in Parliament, none of which got answered, of course. They finally gave me some proper protection spells, both from the parasite and from the outside world. I'd hoped for fireballs like bullets and shooting electricity from your hands like the baddies in *Star Wars*. I didn't get either – disappointingly, the spells were all defensive and were mostly beefed-up versions of things I already knew.

Nadia taught me '*Armarria*' which is a *Jaun* 1 shield spell. It can block almost all magical effects and any physical object travelling faster than about two miles an hour – otherwise if you cast it around yourself you'd suffocate. She also taught me *Isila* – which makes whatever it's cast on completely silent, although I doubt even that would work on Simon when he goes off on one.

Katherine taught me *Ezaxolatu*; it means 'ignore'. It doesn't make you invisible, just persistently unnoticed. She also told me how to make parts of my body hot, a variation of the spell *Ukitu Beroa*. No, not those parts. It's useful for being able to touch really hot objects without taking damage, burning off ropes if you get tied up, or melting plastic car seats if you get carried away at the wrong moment, I discovered.

I learned *Kuxin,* a variation of 'thicken', which places a cushion of air between you and the floor. It isn't like an airbag; it's part of the *Oreka* group of spells – the word means 'balance' – because it pushes up with the same force that you are pushing down with. It's how mages appear to float. I also picked up *Kax*, which is a stun. I even learned *Iheki*, which I wasn't supposed to. With that you can create several identical copies of anything. They are only projections, like images on a Holodeck, but they're very convincing. I found that I could make the copies very, very small and then suddenly huge, so they looked like they'd arrived in an instant. It was all go in the Blackfriars Spell Factory.

Nadia and 'her people' were puzzled about how quickly I picked it all up, and the ease with which I learned to combine them. I wasn't, and as a Dual Talent I thought I was supposed to be able to do things like that. I was just glad I had something new to defend us with.

The only vaguely offensive thing I learnt, apart from some belting new Mandarin swear words from Sam, was *Biziagotu*, which lets you enhance the volume of things like distant conversations. When I asked if you could use it to make nearby things very loud, Nadia sighed and conceded that although it was possible it was unwise, as the caster would need ear defenders to avoid damaging their own hearing.

My motor spells – push, pull, lift, et cetera – improved markedly. I found them easy to remember and easy to cast, so by the end of the week I was screaming with boredom. Amy and Sam weren't doing much better, which tinged my pleasure at them being there with a certain amount of guilt.

Just before the Escape Committee convened, Nadia asked to see us. Her office could have been any middle manager's workspace and it looked about as magical as a filing cabinet.

"Right, I just want to clear up a couple of things," she said, "so you don't go home confused, worried and frightened."

"Confused is my ground state," I replied shortly. I should have been more respectful, probably, but after a week of being disassembled I didn't really feel like it. I thought that when they put me back together they'd still had a handful of screws and springs left over. We are IKEA people, built without spares.

"Before you collapsed Katherine told you that there were two things that made your life difficult, but they weren't emergent duality and being used as a conduit."

"Did she?" I shook my head. "I remember someone called Patrick something being a pain, and then feeling like I'd been dropped into a puddle of hot oil."

"Interesting description," Nadia replied. Today she was in trainers, leggings and a saggy sweatshirt with something impolite on the front.

"You tell me," said Sam suddenly, "why you dress like this? Nobody else does."

Nadia laughed. "You're the only person who's ever had the guts to ask me that. I dress like this because it pisses Richard off no end. Given free choice he would insist that I look like a geography teacher."

"What about Mrs Collister? What she think?"

"Anne doesn't care. Anyway, this is about the inside of your head, Mike, not the outside of my body." I carefully didn't say anything. "One of the two things that influenced your situation was that, unusually, your second Talent was completely hidden."

"I'm lost."

"Most people present with their two Talents from the start and they develop in tandem. Late presenters usually have a major Talent and a minor, and the minor one rarely achieves more than 25% power even when at full strength." I nodded impatiently – this was common knowledge. "In your case, unusually, the fire Talent is as strong as the earth. When Bev started to release it, the whole thing went nuts and we had to virtually rewrite your neurology, which is why you were in such a mess. Fifty years ago you would have either died or spent the rest of your life in an asylum."

"Charming," I replied faintly.

"The other conduits were known Dual Talents, one of which was always earth. As far as we can tell, the attacker burned out both Talents equally when using them to mount the attack. But with you he used only the earth Talent – because the fire was still hidden – which is why you survived. Having Sam as your *erdikide* made a big difference too. We suspect that's why he – or she, or them, or it – chose you, despite there being no prior evidence of you being a Dual Talent. We can't think of another reason."

"How truly fucking splendid." Nadia nodded, then waited expectantly. "So it had to be someone close enough to me to realise the strength of the link between me and Sam." She nodded.

"They must be *Jaun* 3, at least," added Sam.

"At least," Nadia confirmed.

I watched a questing gull investigating a discarded chip wrapper outside the building while I thought. "So it has to be someone who has taught me somewhere."

"Probably but not certainly," she replied carefully. There was something intense and unnerving about her gaze. "You know that senior mages move around a lot, research placements, lecture tours, consultations and stuff."

I nodded. "I don't think Andrius Denisov has set foot in Nottingham for about two months, so it could be someone who was at the college but isn't there any more." There was quite a long silence as we contemplated the number of people who would fit that description. Then a thought occurred to me.

"How did Mr Slater spot the second Talent? Couldn't someone else have done the same thing without me realising it?"

"You demonstrated it, without knowing what you were doing, when you were in the coffee shop," said Nadia. "To say it was a surprise is like saying that the surface of the sun is a little warm."

I had no idea what she was talking about – it doesn't require a fire Talent to drink coffee or look confused, which is all I remember doing that day. "Go on then, astonish me."

"You warmed up your coffee."

"It's just a trick." I shrugged. "Jerry showed it to a lot of us."

"As he should – it's a useful thing to be able to do for people. Richard said that you had a bucketful of coffee and you heated it from tepid to drinkable in about a second."

"So?"

"That's at least twenty times faster than someone with the trick but not the Talent would be able to do it. He identified it and sealed it until we could release it safely, which is what we're doing now. Other things are… unclear, so it wouldn't be a good idea to rush it."

"Okay, fine, so if I sneeze hard I'll set fire to my nose. What was the other thing?"

"The entity you call 'the parasite'."

"I thought that was just a residual thing, left over from whatever the hell that bastard did to me," I said, with more hope than certainty.

"No, it isn't. The last set of tests we did showed that not only did we not manage to get rid of it completely, but it's also still a live connection."

"Oh *gross*," I said, not actually surprised. "He can't use me again, can he?"

"We aren't sure. It might be that he thought he might try to use you again but we've got in the way. Or, more likely, it just got trapped when Richard sealed that part of your *gogoan* to protect you from your fire Talent."

I stopped. I had shown no sign of a second Talent before, but I remembered a moment of despair in Paddington when I couldn't stop the teenage girl bleeding, and then the blood had almost stopped and the wound was partially cauterised. I realised I was sweating.

"Whatever. I'm just bloody glad that he can't do anything with it any more." I thought about what we had done over the last week or so. "I'm just curious; why did you involve Amy in all this?"

She smiled. "I think that's a conversation that you're going to have to have with her." Sam was looking at me pityingly, an expression she reserves for times when I've said something particularly stupid because I've no idea what's going on. It's rather familiar.

*

Sam and I were allowed to leave a couple of days later, but Amy and her hips had become a pet project with Bev and the other Healers, so she stayed a little longer.

They gave us a car and driver, but not Katherine this time. I wasn't completely recovered and I just wanted to sleep anyway, and the M1 provided a splendid opportunity for torpor. We sat in the back of the nondescript car and drowsed, cuddled together despite the seat belts. It had all been rather intense and I was still more tired, detached and unsettled than I felt I should be. I won't go into the details of what we did in the last few days at Central because it's very technical, very specialised and consequentially very dull for people outside the job. You know, the sort of thing that makes people say *'really, how interesting, anyway, did you see that film…'* when you talk about it.

We were not far from the RAF museum at Hendon when we were both jerked from our comfortable stupor by a huge and powerful spell being cast very close by. Even the driver felt it, and swerved the car out of sheer reflex. This garnered him a forest of waving fingers and many suggestions about his parentage and habits. He continued to slow as Sam and I felt around, looking for whatever the hell had happened – it could be nothing to do with us, but we had to be sure. Someone trying to kill you can have that effect.

Nothing seemed to have changed as we rolled down the hill past a motorway sign that was telling us everything was fine. The train running on the line parallel to the road was clearly unaffected. I think Sam spotted the shimmer across the road a second before the first car ploughed into it and crunched to a burning halt in the middle of the carriageway. "Across road," she shouted. "Colour it."

I did, and our driver braked to an abrupt halt as a deep blue cast appeared on the barrier. It stood across the whole of the northbound carriageway like a wall about eight feet high and, from the damage done to the two cars that had already struck it, completely solid.

"*Là shǐ,*" said Sam, which isn't very polite. I grabbed her hand and drew in as much power as I could. I threw *Loditu* (thicken) as far across it as I could, and the air in front of the barrier became denser, like a heavy industrial grease. To a drumroll of airbags going off, all the cars in range slowed abruptly. I increased the spell density incrementally as it neared the barrier, until the last six feet were effectively impenetrable. Thankfully nobody else hit it, and the M1 slowed to a gluey halt barely yards from it. We looked at the cars that we hadn't been able to stop, but the drivers were beyond any help that wasn't based on theology.

"What...?"

I shook my head – I didn't know what the hell it was either. The Great British Driving Public – that amorphous mass of confusion, impulse, anger and impatience – were either blowing their horns, like that would help in any way, or leaning out of their vehicles and peering ahead. Our driver was already on the phone, first alerting the emergency services and then calling Central.

Order came over the scene once the blue lights had started streaming in, although that made me twitch. For the drivers at the back at least, it became just another day on the overstuffed motorway system. At least it was a nice day – doing this in heavy rain would have been horrible.

When we'd reached the aimlessly milling around stage, about fifteen minutes later, I strolled quietly forward to examine the barrier. There were no casualties beyond the exploded cars, but I still felt a flutter of panic. It wasn't, as I had expected, a smooth wall. Close up, you could see that the surface was uneven, but the colour I had put into it was starting to fade and I couldn't quite make out the surface detail. I reinforced the wavelength shift and stepped sharply backwards; the whole face was covered in spikes about five feet long, which made them long enough to penetrate the drivers' compartments of most of the vehicles that travelled on the M1 every day.

The tip of each spike had quite a different composition, energetically speaking. This was very inventive and particularly nasty – once they came close to something alive, like a person, they would release a burst of multiphasic energy across the full spectrum width. This would cause agitation in the shell energies and a lot of molecular bonds would be catastrophically released.

Or, in plain English, each spike was tipped with a high-powered explosive that would blow everything in a ten-foot radius into flaming splinters, whatever it happened to be – a horse box, an HGV full of toilet rolls, Ivy and her old mum on their way back from a day at the seaside or a bus full of school children on a sanctioned skive.

I knew it had been intended for us, but the callousness behind such an indiscriminate weapon made me go cold. Magic can be used for many things, some of which can be unpleasant, but this was the sort of thing a terrorist would use, randomly destructive and calculatedly nasty. It also explained why the cars that had hit the barrier were so badly damaged.

I turned away to find myself being scrutinised by a young-ish looking policeman in an expensive but rumpled dark grey suit. Other police officers were being deferential at him, which meant he was either toxically flatulent or a Very Senior Officer.

"This yours, is it?" He didn't ask if it was magic – such a twitchy word at the moment – and I guessed that he'd seen me change the colour.

I shook my head. "Not personally, no. My field if you like, but not my work."

"Whose then?"

"I don't know. There are some very clever people from our... HQ... trying to work out exactly that."

"You not one of them?"

I laughed. "Good God no. I'm the equivalent of a junior PC – I go where I get sent, do what I'm told when I'm there and then, if I'm really lucky, someone might tell me what the hell has been going on, but only once it's all finished."

He brooded on that for a moment. "We've got some dash-cam footage that suggests that this... thing... was invisible when it first arrived but then turned blue and forced everyone to stop."

"Not quite. I think it was supposed to be invisible the whole time, but as soon as I realised something was there I put some colour into it…"

"How?"

"I altered the wavelength of the energy coming off it so it was visible. That's why it's blue – it's the first visible part of the spectrum you come to from where it was." He grunted.

"And the slowing down?"

"That was me too. I did something to slow all the vehicles, then made another barrier in front of that one so nobody could reach it. Only my one is soft and doesn't explode when you touch it."

He grunted again. "I wish some of my PCs were as switched on as you. Thank you," he went on. "We're going to have to talk to you again."

"Of course. I'll have to let my bosses know." He nodded, unsurprised. "I dare say they'll send someone who can answer the technical questions."

"You can't?"

"Junior PC, remember? This stuff is like a smart phone – I can use one but I've no idea how it works."

He chuckled. "When my computer at home breaks down I don't contact an engineer, I get my daughter to fix it. She's fourteen."

"That's it." I pulled out a notebook and wrote down all my contact details. He gave me a card – Chief Inspector Tony Addison, Special Investigations. "You aren't traffic then?"

"And you aren't a bewildered driver wondering what the hell is going on." He smiled. "Thanks for stopping the other cars hitting it, Mr Frost."

I nodded. I couldn't have done anything else – the spell had been casting itself almost before I reached for Sam's hand. Without her, I wouldn't have had enough power to stop half of them.

He looked at me for a moment. "Any idea how to get rid of it?"

"Well, it should vanish all by itself in about an hour and a half." As soon as I said that I paused. All the other attacks had been hard-light vehicles crashing into things. This was something entirely different, so I actually had no idea what would happen, but I didn't mention that.

"Any chance you can, er, speed it up?"

"I'll try." I nudged Sam and she joined us a few moments later.

"Another one?" Addison asked, glancing at her.

"Yes. This is Miss Lee." He nodded but Sam ignored him as she stood in front of me – it's the best position for a tightly controlled directional casting and the optimum for reflective enhancement. We both extended our hands towards the barrier and colour rippled out, red and orange, like tie-dyed cloth in a high wind. People began to chatter and a forest of camera phones started to record what was going on. None of them would capture anything, of course. Funny how that always happens.

"It a weave," said Sam. Addison frowned. "Weave has bounce, can throw cars back into oncoming traffic."

"Can you, er, unweave it?"

"*Dāngrán, wǒ kěyǐ,*" she replied, frowning. Addison looked confused.

"That means yes, with added irritation," I said quietly, trying not to disturb Sam's concentration. Cars rolled past on the other carriageway, every one of them slowing to have a good look. The brisk wind and smell of petrol fumes made me shiver.

"Oh. Right then."

I could feel a huge power surge and gave it everything I

could. On this scale, the spell Sam was using, *Etent* (disrupt), needs far more energy than even she could muster by herself.

Redness spread out in waves from where her spell hit the barrier, like ripples across a pond. Soon it started to show patches where it had become thinner. Then, in a moment, it crumbled into nothing, dropping glowing ash and burning a line more than a foot deep through the surface of the road. The Scene Commander was organising the immediate repair of at least one lane before Sam and I relaxed.

"That was... interesting," said Addison. "Is it all gone?"

"All gone," confirmed Sam.

"Thank you."

"I go," she replied. She can do inscrutable very well when she doesn't want to talk to someone. She left.

"Traffic can sort this out now," said Addison as we walked back up the lines of cars. "Thank you for your help, Mr Frost. We'll be in touch."

As we shook hands I felt a thread of power coming from him. He could have been a mage; he still might be. I wondered if that was why he got jobs like this. Still gripping his hand I said, "Hold your other hand out flat." He looked at me for a moment, then did it. "Now say *Argilabur*."

As he did I loosened a little of his power and a softly glowing ball appeared above his palm. "That's you doing that," I said. "I'm just... steering."

He said *Argilabur* again, mangling the pronunciation, and it got brighter. I let go of his hand and it didn't go out. "Fucking hell." He actually looked startled.

"Quite." I folded his open fingers and the glow died. "When my people contact you to sort out the interview you *must* tell them that this has happened. It's important for your own safety that you do." He stared at me, eyes wide with wonder and even a little fear. "I think your life is about to get very interesting."

We made it home without further incident. Everyone wanted to know if we'd had a nice holiday – I just wanted to know how the hell Sam had cast a *Jaun* 2 spell pretty much by herself.

*

Then, all on a sudden, nothing happened, and it carried on happening. It was bloody unnerving but it gave me a chance to get back on balance, and the nightmares finally started to fade.

Amy returned nearly a week after us. I met Tony Addison again, and we spent more time talking about magic than what happened on the M1 – Central didn't know who did it, so what chance had the police got? There were six fatalities, but no more than a few minor injuries beside. 'Lucky escape' the newspapers said, while signally failing to have the slightest clue what everyone had luckily escaped from.

After about two days the press finally connected it to the hard-light vehicles, without realising that it was completely different. The consensus was that it was the work of a group of particularly clever terrorists and, if it wasn't magic, then there had to be some sort of advanced technology involved. China was hinted at; so was Russia and, for some inexplicable reason, Sweden.

A couple of the more excitable and less reliable newspapers persisted with the idea of magic being involved. But the publicity department at Central – actually the 'make sure there isn't any' publicity department at Central – carried on its customary role of downplaying the power of magic.

They always maintained that it was just odd, dull, and only very occasionally useful loopholes in the classical laws of physics. It might occasionally get out of hand but less often than, say, Millwall fans or 'disgusted of Tunbridge Wells' when confronted with an egregious breach of etiquette at Lords. Dullness and distraction shoved us back towards the sports section within two days.

*

The attacks on the colleges were more of a problem, because while they had clearly been designed to cause disruption and distraction, nobody was stupid enough to think that was *all* they were intended to do. Or that they were the work of a lunatic; someone with delusions perhaps, but that didn't help identify them.

Mages have had a hard time for as long as anyone remembers, mostly from people who don't understand how we do things, and why they can't – although I've yet to find a record of an Olympic gymnast being burned at the stake or a concert pianist being subjected to the ducking stool.

Magic, not being subject to 'common sense', makes a splendid scapegoat for all sorts of troubles that defy 'rational' explanation. The habit of discretion is hard-wired into most mages, and even those who openly use their Talents in public often feel obliged to incorporate other things that observers can decipher to convince them it's legerdemain, not the manipulation of the electro-magnetic spectrum.

It was only the nature of the attack that convinced us that this wasn't a civilian getting cross because we wouldn't guarantee the weather for his village fete (which has happened) or because we can't locate the lottery ticket that they misplaced and are *certain* is a winner. The number of times we get asked for the winning numbers for next week's Lottery are beyond counting – most people think that we know them and are keeping them to ourselves. The truth is we don't, and the lottery equipment is shielded against magical interference anyway.

This was a mage attacking mages, but it was more than just an act of civil war because of its indiscriminate nature. Mages fall out with other mages just as often as ordinary people do. The result is more often embarrassment than violence, because spells that don't work properly can cause a lot of collateral damage, so fights rarely use the nasty ones, at least not where anyone else can see them.

9

When college reopened it was cleaner than I'd ever seen it before. The whole place had been emptied out and sterilised, both physically and magically. It had probably been exorcised, smudged and sprinkled with fairy dust as well.

Professor Wicks was scathing when she gathered everyone at the beginning of term. "Either he's bloody rubbish or incredibly good, 'cos we ain't got nothing. You all gotta be real careful over the next while in case anything happens that ain't supposed to. Apart from what you lot normally get up to." As usual, her American accent got stronger when she was grumbling.

When classes resumed Sam and I were in the *Ikasberri* group; the training is like having a toothache but in your whole head, and all the time. We did light spells that were very familiar, but I'd never understood the depth and subtlety that could be applied to them. We learned *Foku*, a very precise wavelength adjustment that can turn a sunbeam into a laser and *Bira*, which makes a tiny horizontal whirlwind that can make a zephyr into a drill. All of these extraordinary things and more were taught in tones of dusty and abstract academe in a classroom that looked like a thousand others across the country.

It was complicated, tiring, difficult and didn't always work. I slept like I'd been unplugged; ate like I was in danger of starvation and I still felt like crap. I was constantly confused, bemused and a lot of similar things, which made me tetchy at the very least. This was, I was reassured, often the consequence of such a rapid advancement. Sam seemed to be having no trouble at all, the cow. Wicks couldn't find anyone for us to be apprentices to either, which was a bit awkward.

"What's up with you, grumpy?" Amy asked, pulling up next to me in the coffee shop as I brooded over an ignored Danish pastry. Despite the heating I felt cold and vaguely defensive of my isolation.

"Nothing." Even in the large space of the common room the word was hard and slightly too loud. A few heads turned.

"Liar."

I bit my lip and breathed down my nose. "What do you want?"

"I want to know what's wrong with you, you clot." She reached out and took my hand, uncurled my fingers one by one, then sandwiched my hand between hers and gently rubbed it until the muscles started to relax. I felt no urge to pull away. "You are so hot."

"All evidence to the contrary," I grunted, but a tiny flicker of a smile still tugged at the corner of my mouth.

"God, you can be a pain when you're in this mood," said Amy, leaning forward in her wheelchair, one elbow on the table in front of me. "I mean your hand is really hot."

"Feels fine to me."

"It would." She put one finger on my chin and turned my face towards her. She looked at me for a long moment, and I noticed that her hair was much whiter now, but it didn't look like it had been bleached; it was properly white, and seemed to glow from the inside. She blew out a long breath. "You are worrying a lot of people right now."

117

"Why? Why would anyone give a damn about me? I'm just… oh shit, I don't know."

"I get that. Why?"

"What do you mean why? What difference does it make?"

She surprised me. She stood up out of her wheelchair and sat in the chair next to me. I couldn't have been more astonished if the table had started reciting Shakespeare. "How did you…?"

"Bev said she could help with the hips. This is as far as we've got."

"I'm… that's wonderful." It was my turn to grip her hand, genuinely delighted.

"Yes, it is." She touched her hair and sighed slightly. "So I'm doing well. Sam is getting much more controlled. The only people who aren't doing well are you and Professor Weaver."

"Weaver? What's up with him?"

"I don't know, but he looks like he hasn't slept since Christmas." She paused. "You've been in two of his classes a week for the last month, and you hadn't noticed, had you?"

I turned my head away, not wanting to reply. I felt like I was being told off, found fault with, being got at, and I didn't like it.

"Was there something you specifically wanted?" I tried to soften it with a smile, but my throat was too tight.

"Oh for fuck's sake, Mike, I'm worried about you." Her tone was pure exasperation. "You've been like a bear with a boil on its bum ever since London. You get plenty of sleep, you eat like a combine harvester but you're even skinnier than before, and you have the attention span of a concussed budgie." She leaned across and draped her arm around my shoulders. I couldn't help notice a wince chase across her face, but she didn't stop. Her hand was soft, and she smelled of citrus and salt.

"You may find this hard to believe, but there are people

around here who really care about you, although sometimes I wonder why," she said softly, touching my face again, an unsettling echo of Sam's gesture the month before. "For God's sake, even Simon's wondering what's wrong."

"I'm amazed he's noticed." I stopped, then frowned. "How do you know that?"

"Because I've been talking to your parents, you nit." She sighed. "I've met your mum for coffee a few times since Christmas. Your dad has put some different rails in the downstairs loo to make it easier for me. Not that you've noticed."

"You sound like you're moving in."

She leant back a little and smiled. "Finally, Captain Clueless gets it." Her lashes clumped with tears. "I want to be with you, you halfwit. I want to live with you. I even want to sleep with you, even though Sam says you snore really loudly sometimes."

If she had said that she was taking up Appalachian clog dancing I couldn't have been more surprised. My mouth opened and closed like a goldfish and eventually a noise came out – I think it was 'unk', which is perhaps not the best response to the suggestion that we should live together.

She eased herself back into her wheelchair. "You think about it." She made to leave, not looking at me, but I stretched my mind and turned her chair towards me.

"Yes. I will. I do. When can I come and collect your stuff? And all that." There was a certain amount of kissing, which Clara and Sam got the drift of quite quickly, despite being at the other end of the building. They arrived with Jerry, Ambrose and several others in tow, all smirking loudly. This created a general stir and a heightening of interest in the rest of the room.

"About bloody time," said Clara, rolling her eyes and hugging me. She smelled of something musty and spicy, like smoked chilli.

"Ugly ladyboy," Sam whispered, and I laughed. I would have kissed them both but I don't think Amy would have been very impressed.

Jerry shook my hand, caught my eye and made a circle with his finger that remained in the air like the best persistence of vision experiment you've ever seen.

"Go on," he said. "If you're gonna do it, do it right. We'll help."

I picked up Amy's unresisting right hand and made a cold fire loop around her third finger. Her eyes were bright and full of joy. This was big, serious and sudden, but I was utterly certain that it was the right thing to do. Casual relationships don't feel like this – no thunderbolt of certainty, for a start. She held up her hand, turning it slightly and looking at the circling light, and then nodded. "Red gold."

When mages get together properly they don't buy a ring, they make one. It isn't actually a spell; it's more like an intention solidified by willpower. You don't need to be taught how to do it, either.

I pulled in all my power, felt it reinforced by Sam and Jerry, and drew elements from who knows where. The circle of light dimmed and then started to change. The colour shifted and a slender metal band formed. I was sweating hard by now, but then I felt the most enormous rush of power and the ring got slightly wider and thicker. Then another surge, quite beyond anything I could manage myself, and the top shimmered into lustrous channel-cut emeralds that filled a full third of the diameter. Amy flexed her hand and nodded, so I let the power drain away.

Standing behind me was Professor Gowan, looking like a dishevelled schoolgirl who had just been given a pony. Or in her case, a new box of hand grenades. Next to her was Professor Wicks, who was smiling at me again, which is always unnerving. Amy's ring was beautiful and suited her perfectly, because although the power came from me, the design came from her.

*

I'm not going to get mushy, or too graphic, but that was the first night we spent together. Her flat was surprisingly large and nicely decorated, with nonslip floors, no rugs, handrails, a bathroom that would not have looked out of place in *Bladerunner* and a large, low bed.

It was odd – I'd never been there before, but I knew where everything would be. Amy and I worked around each other in harmony, preparing a meal we would barely eat and drinking enough to get over any embarrassment or hesitation, but not too much – the spirit is willing but the flesh… you get the idea.

We'll close the bedroom door at this point and no, you can't watch. What happened was sufficiently tectonic that we knew that we would be able to repeat the event – all right, events – to our continuing satisfaction. I know that sounds like a coy line from one of the more vapourish kinds of bodice-ripper, but that's all you're getting, you nosy bugger.

*

I was woken by light trickling in through the imperfectly closed curtains and the noises from the river outside the window. I was warm under the duvet and reluctant to move.

"I do not love my body clock," I said. "Why doesn't it have a setting marked 'Sunday'?"

"Because it's Wednesday," came a voice from the kitchen.

"Yeah, there is that." I tried to find enough energy to get

up, to go for a shower, to get dressed – although I guess opening my eyes would have been a better first move.

"You," said the same voice, only much closer now, "should be out of bed. Classes will not wait for you, and even though the first one is Weaver of the Ballistic Cough, you can't rely on him being late."

"Go away," I muttered, not in the least bit seriously.

"No. There is coffee…" I felt the side of the bed sag as Amy lent on it, "… in the kitchen."

I opened one eye. She looked tousled and wonderful but, sadly, dressed. "Do you now see it as part of your role in life to torment me?"

"No, just one of the perks." I heard the wheelchair moving away. "Oh, and put some clothes on – Clara and Sam are here."

"What, already?"

"It's twenty past nine."

"Right."

When I got to the kitchen all three of them stopped talking at once and looked at me. To their credit, none of them giggled for at least thirty seconds.

"Three times?" Clara asked with a sly smile.

"At least," replied Amy. "I'd lost most of the feeling in my toes by then."

That did it – they all started laughing. It's very hard to maintain your dignity in the face of such provocation, especially if you are barefoot, wearing cargoes straight off the bedroom floor and a shirt that hadn't been closely acquainted with an iron for some time.

"Haven't you lot got homes to go to?"

"Yes," said Amy. "And I'm in it."

"I know, I mean… oh forget it. Good morning, Sam, good morning, Clara."

"Good morning, Mike," said Clara. "You should do your shirt up before another one of us gets ideas." Clara's grin was mischievous, and in other circumstances I might have considered that an invitation of some kind. But I'm not a fan of pain, so I said nothing. I looked down at my shirt and fingered the loose threads where several of the buttons should have been. Things had got a bit… urgent… at one point last night.

"Um…?"

"Top shelf in the wardrobe," said Amy, smirking slightly as she dropped more bread into the toaster, "there are some oversized sweatshirts."

They were not oversize. Well, maybe for her, and you could have put two of Sam into one of them, but the word 'snug' really doesn't do it. Amy had said I should wear shirts that show off my shape, but these were tight enough to cut off the blood supply to my face.

I'm going to be honest here – I hid. I'm not proud of it, but I did. Amy is in my heart and Sam is in my head, with Clara as a Lycra-clad and dreadlocked Greek chorus to all that mental activity. But I didn't want to share Amy with anyone; I'd only just found her – or she'd found me and beat me over the head until I recognised what I was feeling. Whatever; I didn't want to share, not just yet.

My bit of showboating over the ring had made quite an impact on the common room. Several people asked Sam why I'd chosen to do it just then – a lot of students, particularly in other years, had assumed that Amy and I had been a couple for ages. It seemed that the only person who hadn't noticed that Amy was my girlfriend was me.

*

Getting together with Amy put things into perspective. I stopped being so grumpy because I was aware of the people who cared about me. Plus I had someone to care about for reasons other than genetics and fate. It's an oddity with mages that although casual relationships are just the same, serious is very serious. There may be an evolutionary element to this, the drive not to dilute the magical genes.

We went to London the next week and she came back able to walk a little better, and with even whiter hair. Then we went looking for somewhere to live – with Sam and Clara now both permanent fixtures we needed a house with at least two extra bedrooms. We wanted them to be able stay with us without having to hotbed on the couch.

Mum and dad were delighted, as were busloads of aunts, uncles, cousins at various levels of removal, and other familial hangers-on who suddenly appeared out of the woodwork. They even started to ask about wedding dates – which seemed to be less to do with inviting Amy into the family and more to do with finding an opportunity for a free booze-up. Amy's parents gave their unenthusiastic blessing by Skype. All Simon wanted to know was if he could have my room when I left.

The girls in college thought Amy could have done better. All the guys kept asking me how the hell I had managed to inveigle her into my bed. My stock reply was 'wit, charm and elegance', a list of qualities so unlike me as to raise an ironic smile and allow me to avoid the truth – that I had absolutely no idea.

We studied too, possibly even harder. Just because two mages get together doesn't mean they've finished their training. And we didn't wander around holding hands or anything like that. Well, not much.

College carried on as before. The only person who really changed for me was Clara – now that Amy and I were a couple she was around much more. I didn't know her well, but she knew a worrying amount about me. I knew that her family was from St Lucia but I found out that she had been brought up in Corby. She'd had a steady boyfriend through school who'd run away – literally – when she became a mage, and no amount of support or encouragement from her parents could repair the emotional damage that had done. She was a runner, and her figure showed that, but there was always a kind of distance, a loneliness, behind her eyes that nobody ever seemed able to touch.

*

After an amazingly short time we found an empty house in a nearby suburb, and with no chain we bought it in a couple of weeks. It was a bungalow, of course, one which was suitable for adaptation for the wheelchair and also capable of being made magic resistant. Well, not exactly resistant, more like leak-proof, so nothing that we did inside the house would be detectable outside. Mages rarely do more than trivial magic at home, but with two of us in the house – often four – it was going to be necessary.

So we had furniture delivered. We chose a duvet set. I cleaned the house, repainted the bedroom and put up some pictures. The bathroom and kitchen were adapted by two extremely competent Polish men who bickered constantly. I think they were a couple who brought their domestic issues to work with them. Or they could have been discussing twentieth-century Bulgarian cinema for all I know. It was utterly, routinely domestic but still felt like an adventure. We decided to spend our first night there at the end of January.

We were in the house, making the bed, but the bedding got twisted – I might have had something to do with that –

so she got up to straighten it and slipped. There was a lot of swearing, and our first night together in our new house turned out to be our first night together in the Queen's Medical Centre while they put her left hip back in place. She was exhausted and in pain. I was exhausted and worried. She slept in a hospital bed, fitful and horizontal. I slept in a hospital chair next to her, fitful and slumped.

And while we slept, someone burned our house down.

10

I hesitate to use the word fortunately, but fortunately we were moving in stages, so not all of our stuff was actually in the house when it went on fire. The police officer that came to see us in the hospital was professionally supportive, but the one who talked to us in Amy's flat a couple of days later was both grave and confused. The startling colour scheme and the layout of the furniture, which made no sense unless you knew magic was being routinely used, obviously unnerved him.

"Er... yes. The fire. I'm sorry to say, Miss Deerborn, Mr Frost, there's no doubt that it was deliberate," she said, her expression unreadable.

This wasn't really news, but it was unsettling to have it so baldly stated. "How was it done?" I asked. "Petrol through the letterbox, or had someone got into the house?"

"Neither, sir. There was no sign of forced entry, and the fire investigation people could find no trace of accelerants anywhere in the property. The seat of the fire appears to have been the bed. They said it's as if the whole mattress burst into flames at the same moment."

Amy gripped my hand. Even with the new improved hip joint she would never have made it out of the room. I can carry her, but it's not much more than a barely controlled stagger, let alone a lithe sprint. I'm not saying she's heavy – I'm not suicidal – but she isn't a collection of matchsticks like Sam.

"Any idea who did it? Any forensic evidence?"

"No, sir. Not much clue as to how, either."

"But you said…"

"The whole bed caught fire, yes, but without an accelerant that's pretty much impossible. Contrary to what you see on the TV, bedding doesn't instantaneously flash into flame, so how the entire mattress – which the law requires to be flame resistant – did…" She shrugged and fell silent for a moment, apparently listening to the sounds of the river. "The investigation team is confused, and wanted me to ask if anything you had in the room could account for this?"

We glanced at each other and I shook my head. "All the painting stuff was in the shed in the garden – for exactly that reason – and we hadn't been using anything inflammable inside the house, unless you count wine."

"You've had no similar fires?" Amy asked.

"Not without a reasonable explanation, no. There are house fires all the time of course, but mostly it's toasters full of crumbs, overloaded plugs, overfilled chip pans, overconfident DIY or ignored candles." She stopped. "I hesitate to ask, so soon, but… can you think of anyone who might have wanted to do this?"

"We've been wondering about that, of course," said Amy, shifting slightly in her chair. Her hip was still very sore. "But we can't think of anyone. We've no enemies that I am aware of. I mean, there are people who don't necessarily like us, but that's at the level of not being invited to parties, not attempted murder. Could they have been after the property, rather than us?"

"It's early days, ma'am, so I can't really comment on that. Did you have insurance?"

"Of course," I said wearily. "It was going to be our first home together. We finish our university courses this summer and we've both got postgraduate work to follow, so we were going to be there for at least three years, probably a great deal longer."

"I see." The detective was young, in a cheap and ill-fitting suit, and a bit nervous. Amy in her wheelchair, with striking white hair despite obviously being in her early twenties, can be an unsettling sight, especially when she wants it to be.

"We'll continue to investigate, of course, but I wouldn't delay or defer any plans on the assumption that we'll come up with anything." On that startling piece of honesty, she finished her tea, shook our hands and left us to it. Two minutes later Sam and Clara came in from the patio.

"Who burn you house?"

"They don't know."

"Why burn you house?"

"They don't know."

"How it happen?"

"They don't know," I repeated sourly.

"I think I do," said Clara. "It's a broad area fire spell, yes? A sheet of flame that burns very hot and can go without fuel for several minutes? I called Jerry when I heard that. He said it's called *Irazeri Orri*."

"Never heard of it."

"Fire sheet?" Sam is quite good at the language beyond just learning the magical terms.

Clara nodded. "*Jaun* 2." She tipped her head on one side, setting her hair moving in a way that I knew Ambrose, for one, found interesting.

"Still not sure why attack house," said Sam.

"I don't think it was aimed at the house," Clara replied softly.

"But we weren't there," I protested.

"When you went to the hospital, did you leave any lights on?"

"Only in the hall."

"You went in your car? Not an ambulance?"

I nodded. "I can't drive hers, and it was much quicker if I drove."

"But you often go to the house in just Amy's car, don't you?"

"Yes," said Amy, "but I went straight there while Mike was picking up some kitchen stuff so we travelled separately... oh shit."

"Is right," said Sam. "Nothing to show you not in house at midnight."

"So it was attempted murder by means of magic." This made me feel sick, even though it wasn't really a surprise. We had only survived through a fortunate misfortune. Fear settled into my mind like a plum into custard.

"*Jaun* 2 at least," Clara reiterated. She sounded grim.

"What you done now?" Sam asked. I almost managed a smile.

"It's got to be to do with the crashes," said Amy, gripping my hand. "I know you can be as annoying as fuck sometimes, but even my desire to strangle you is usually only fleeting." She gave me her best charming, girly smile, which made me chuckle.

Clara sniggered. "Ah, the happy couple."

Perhaps sensing that this would be a good time to change the subject, Sam looked at her. "What about you and Dominic, that touchy-feely postgrad from Material Science?"

"What about him?"

"How touchy-feely he getting now?"

She smiled. "He touches what I let him. He feels... nice."

"He lucky man."

"Speaking of that," I added, "what about Sho? He still hanging around you like a bad smell?"

"No. Sho find someone else. He say he like big girl." She

looked down at her slight chest and shrugged. "I do better than him." She grinned. "Could have been stuck with you." She nodded towards me. "He still snore?"

"Rattles the windows," Amy replied. "What about Dominic?"

"Oh, he's a teeth grinder," said Clara. "He also maintains he's a sleep groper – it's like a sleepwalker, but better targeted."

"Sho like that, not keep hand to self. Sometime is okay, but one time he tore nail on bra strap, made big scratch…" at which point I left. All right, ran away.

*

Insurance forms are bloody complicated at the best of times, and when you've no flaming idea what happened, it's hopeless. There wasn't a box for 'it just fucking caught fire, all right'. We claimed for the house, of course, because the fire had rendered it suitable only for demolition, or possibly as an entry for the Turner Prize. A local developer had almost bitten my hand off buying the site from us.

We claimed for the furniture, the bedding and pictures, plus the stuff that was still sitting in cardboard boxes in the kitchen, waiting for us to work out what on earth we were going to do with it all. We couldn't claim for anguish, disappointment or grief. I think that the loss of what the house symbolised hurt more than the bricks, fabric and saucepans.

Jerry had done his fire Talent stuff on the smoking rubble a couple of days after it happened, but apart from confirming which spell had caused it, he could find nothing of any help. Honestly, we hadn't expected that he would, but it was important to him that he do that for us.

An insurance assessor contacted us two days after that, citing enough caveats and exceptions to make paying the premiums pretty much a waste of time. However, when he met Amy, conspicuously in her wheelchair and playing helpless, he revised his opinion sharply, especially when she said that her friends, colleagues and disability campaigners were monitoring her progress on social media.

So, by the end of February we had enough money to buy another one of the houses we'd seen, but to be honest, we were reluctant. No, that's not true. We were frightened, because we might be at home next time and... the thought was horrible.

*

After all that, and with our finals just a few months away, we decided to go on holiday. A big part of where we could go depended on Amy of course – what with the wheelchair, even getting transfers from the airport to the accommodation can be tricky, and finding accommodation that was wheelchair-friendly in the first place was difficult. A lot of people did that teeth-sucking thing which means that however hard they try, they aren't going to be able to help, even if they could be bothered to try in the first place.

We ended up in Malta – Maltese Airlines was brilliant and suggested a really nice place for us to stay, right by the sea on the north of the main island near Golden Bay. Compared to Nottingham it was pleasantly warm, even at this time of the year, with plenty of chances to float in the sea if you were feeling brave or the large, alarmingly bright blue swimming pool. The Healers said they'd done all they could for Amy at the moment, and that it would be best if she left her hip joint unstressed as much as possible, so floating was ideal.

Sam stayed in Nottingham, promising to tinker with the climate of the island to make it warmer. I don't think she was serious. Clara and Dominic joined us in the villa; by this time Dominic knew some of what Clara could do and, by extension, the rest of us, so we were able to drop our guard a bit. What with all the relaxing, the wine and everything, we kind of forgot that, airy and attractive though this house was, it wasn't leak-proof.

The area was lovely, with long walks – or long rolls in Amy's case – amongst trees that smelled of dust and olives, and light that made you squint just a little bit, even this early in the year. The comparative warmth soaked into our bones and we felt better each day. Meals were light and lunch would meld into afternoon glasses of pink wine and a convivial supper that took longer to wash up than it did to prepare.

"Your neck has got longer," said Amy one day.

"What do you mean?"

"Your shoulders aren't up around your ears any more." She stroked my neck and if I didn't purr it was nothing to do with me. "It's good." She eased herself higher on the couch. "Why don't we go outside for a bit?" I shook my head. "Why not?"

"One of my ancestors came from the north of Scotland: I have to lie in the sun for an hour just to go blue."

She laughed. "But your mum told me that one of your other grandparents was from Italy, so some sort of sun-soaked Mediterranean type."

"Er… no. Nonna was from Campestrin, an occasionally snow-bound village high up in the Dolomites, and met my grandad when she was working in an Italian restaurant in Stockport. Love at first pizza." I paused. "And ended her life in a wheelchair in a Nottingham suburb, singing lullabies in broken Italian and forgetting who her grandsons were." The pain must have shown on my face because Amy took my hand.

Not putting Nonna into a nursing home had been a

really important thing for us, as had been converting the dining room into her bedsit. The house wasn't all that large, and meals could get a bit cramped with five of us around the kitchen table, especially once she was in her wheelchair.

Watching her fade from a bright, funny and energetic person into a mute and immobile drain on our emotional resources had been horrible for all of us, but especially for Simon, who had loved her to bits. She was the one who helped him to understand what being gay meant, and taught him to be neither belligerent nor defensive. It's hard to get any emotional distance from someone when they're sitting next to you, and I might have left home even sooner if I hadn't been part of her care team.

"Come on," said Amy, squeezing my hand gently, "let's get a drink."

Dom and I were the first up for breakfast the next day.

"Morning," I said. We weren't close friends – in fact we had only met three times before the airport – but he's a decent enough bloke.

"Indeed yes," he replied. Clara told us that he comes from Brighton, but he instantly corrected her – 'Hove, actually' he'd said, only he pronounced 'actually' with an 'e'. I thought he was a bit of a twit – I suspect that he found me uncouth. He's also three inches taller than me and has a splendid nose, so he appears to be looking down it at everybody all the time. Sometimes it's hard not to take it personally.

"So, you and Clara, serious, is it?" I asked, buttering some *Hobz-Malti*, a lovely local bread I'd got from the local bakery just minutes before.

"Well, it is at the moment. I'm not sure about the longitude." I wasn't sure if his mangling of the language was idiotic management speak or just ordinary bad English – it's often hard to tell them apart. "You and Amy seem quite settled."

"Yeah, very much so."

He nodded, then addressed himself to his breakfast cornflakes while I watched the white flowers just off the terrace – I've no idea what they are, but they look a bit like daffodils – shimmy in the warm breeze. I could feel him trying to formulate a question.

"Doesn't it bother you, that Clara... knows what you're doing all the time?" he said in a rush, then flushed. "When you're with Amy, I mean."

Oh, great, I thought, *he thinks we're listening in while he and Clara are shagging.*

"It isn't like that."

"Really?" He didn't sound convinced. "I have to say that I find it... intrusive."

"Seriously, we aren't reading each other's minds all the time. Unless we make a real effort to communicate it's not much more than a vague impression. You may know that someone is asleep, but you have little idea where they are, and no idea at all what they're wearing or if they are alone or cuddled up to a dead elephant."

"Oh."

"Does do one thing though," I added, standing up and going to the coffee machine, "at least you know when they wake up." I put a mug of coffee in Amy's space and an orange juice in Clara's, taking my hand away just as they were picked up.

All right, I cheated. I have no real contact with Clara, but I had seen both of them heading down the corridor from the rooms – Dominic was sitting with his back to the door, something I hate doing.

"This magic thing..." he said, staring into his cup rather than looking directly at me. "I mean, Clara has shown me making a light and so forth, but... is there much more to it than that?"

"Oh yes, a lot more," said Amy.

"Well, Clara said about the Talents and the like, but... well, common sense and all that. Some of the things she was saying, well, they hardly seem possible."

I can only assume that Dominic is a bloody good shag, because otherwise I have no idea what Clara sees in him.

"If you get to a certain standard, you can do some amazing stuff," said Amy, "although once you get beyond light spells and the like, it often isn't obvious what you're doing."

Dominic the Rationalist lifted his long nose into the air and looked down at me. "Show me." He covered Clara's hand with his. She started to shake her head, but, probably typically, he ignored her.

Oh dear, I thought, *he's afraid I'll turn him into a frog, even though I can't*. It's a matter of mass, and I don't know how to anyway. Clara would have shown him simple, useful stuff to get him used to the idea – light, heating drinks, simple barriers against wind and rain – but he wasn't buying it. So unless we were going to fall out spectacularly, I was going to have to do something extremely convincing. I hate having to do things like this, but sometimes there is no option. This was supposed to be a holiday, a time for Amy – for all of us – to heal.

"Sure, I'll show you something." Earth Talents like me can, with some effort, make changes to gravity over larger areas than ordinary lifting spells like *Jaso*. I chose the swimming pool, defined the space and halved the mass pull of the Earth. I used the pool because accidently dropping a load of water does less damage than doing the same thing with, say, a car or half a house, especially if it's the bottom half.

It was quite difficult and I had to draw a lot of power from the surroundings. The water rose upwards until it was clear of the tiled edges of the pool. Then it started to drift towards us, because, despite pulling in all the power I could, I hadn't been able to fully compensate for the rotation of the Earth below the water mass. To be fair, it is about 750mph here.

Dominic sat, open-mouthed, as the ragged block of water slowly moved towards us. I suspect he thought I was showing off, whereas I was actually losing control. It was touching the flowers when Amy, expert water Talent that she is, grabbed the whole lot and deposited it back into the pool with barely a splash.

"Yes, I see, indeed, yes," Dominic mumbled and fled.

"You plonker," said Amy, "you nearly pulled up half the plants in the garden doing that."

"I know. I'll go and apologise to them later." I looked at Clara. "Sorry. He just wasn't taking it seriously."

"No," she said, standing up. "He wasn't taking you seriously." She was clearly annoyed. "That was too much," she added.

"Sorry," I said in a small voice.

Clara snorted and essayed a grin. "Maybe he'll be a little less dismissive from now on. I just hope you didn't piss off the locals too much."

*

The first hint that I'd been a little careless, if you could call a breach of magical etiquette the equivalent of smacking the Queen on the bum and calling her Lizzie careless, came the next afternoon.

Dominic, who had been avoiding me all day, was asleep and Amy was floating in the pool. Clara and I were doing desultory things in the small kitchen. We used times like this to get to know each other better. Clara also likes to stay alert when Amy is floating, because the regeneration she's undergoing is quite draining and we don't want her to drown or anything like that.

Friendships are built on mutual interest, but we knew that it couldn't be just Amy. The trouble was finding something else that we *did* have in common; I do karate, she runs; I like detective stories, she reads science fiction; we both have extended and sprawling families, but mine is in London and hers in St Lucia; she can draw pictures really well; I can just about draw a bath. Despite this a warmth grew between us, and while I doubted we'd ever skip off into the sunset holding hands, we quickly came to enjoy each other's company, even if not each other's taste in music. I like everything from Mozart to Motörhead, and I'm not averse to a bit of New Romantics or Bluebeat, but Boy Bands? Sheesh.

The knock on the front door was polite but firm, like a postman with a really heavy parcel he'd like you to take as soon as possible. There were three people on the doorstep, clearly locals, and not best pleased about something.

"*Tajjeb jum. Ahna kellu thaddet ta' magija,*" said the tall, swarthy man at the front, or something like that, sounding like he was trying to dislodge a particularly troublesome toast crumb.

Being English I felt the need to apologise for his assumption that I could understand him. "I'm sorry?"

"English?"

"Indeed yes." I have no idea why I said it like that. Defensive hyperliteration, probably, unless I just made that up.

He grunted. "We must speak." He started to step inside but I moved to block his way.

"Carry on."

"Not out in the world to hear." I didn't move and tried hard to send a loud nudge to Clara and Amy. I didn't like the way this was going. "It concern *magija.*"

By now Clara had heard the conversation and had come into the hallway behind me. I could feel her mustering the energy for a focused strike – she's an earth Talent too but she's been mates with Jerry since forever, and he's really good at fire spells and doesn't take shit from anybody.

"Not necessary," the man said to her. "*Dawl*." I felt the flow of power and a spiky red ball of light popped into existence between us. "*Magija*, yes?"

I stepped back and gestured them inside. Clara showed them into the airy main room, then went off to help Amy out of the pool.

"Sit."

"Not now. We have thing to say." He stopped and said something to his companions; one was a tall, generic Mediterranean man, the other a much darker woman with a copper's stare – eyes always moving, noticing everything without seeming to. It was obvious that she was the most magically powerful of them, but perhaps didn't speak very much English.

Amy and Clara arrived together. Man No. 2 looked at The Woman, raising an eyebrow. "*It-tnejn?*" he muttered, glancing between us.

"*Ghajjen*," she replied, and Man No. 2 laughed. Man No. 1 looked annoyed, but then broke into a smile. *It-tnejn* means 'both' and *ghajjen* means 'tired'. I don't mind people making assumptions about my prowess, but… well, anyway, it broke the ice.

"Please, we will sit. I am Vittor. This is Girgor and Melita. She is boss."

We all sat. "Okay, how can we help?" I asked.

"You using *magija*, yes?"

"Yes, small *magija* only." He nodded. That wasn't strictly true, but I wasn't about to split hairs in a language that he could barely speak. That's the problem with phrase books, they tell you what questions to ask, but give you no clue what the answers mean.

139

"Small *magija* it is okay. Lots of small *magija* all of place. But maybe bigger than small *magija*, yes?"

I shrugged. "Maybe."

He nodded again. "Is okay, it er… doctor *magija* we know." I'm sure he was being tactful.

"Know?" Amy frowned. "You detected it?" Melita was clearly *kemen*, at least *Jaun* 3.

"Yes, detect. Melita feel in Valetta. Is long kilometre away. So we know you here, but it cause small problem for spells in town. It not control. It okay as Healer *magija*, but you should need tell before using."

"Understand. Sorry." I looked at Amy. It seemed that Bev had left some major residual energy in her to consolidate the alterations to her pelvis, and my attempts to help had probably been a bit heavy-handed.

"It's to repair an injury," Amy said, touching her hip. "Is problem?"

"Not healing, no. Very big doctor power for not Healer." Amy nodded, then glanced at me. "Problem… person search for you. Searching power cause big problem."

"Searching for me?" Amy sounded surprised.

"No. For you." Vittor indicated all three of us. "Search *magija*…" he made a sweeping gesture, "across all island, moving, cause problems many things."

This was worrying but also slightly reassuring – unless there is more than one of you, and you can use triangulation on a motionless target, a single person has to get very close to their subject to be really accurate. This kind of search is like scanning with a searchlight; it's not the passive 'track and trace' stuff, which is like just listening really hard. The fact that the source of the search spell was moving suggested that whoever was doing this was working alone, at least in a magical sense; they could otherwise have an entire troop of jugglers and their own mariachi band with them for all I knew.

"This is not good," said Clara. "You know about the attacks in England?" They nodded – the hard-light vehicles had been really big news in the magical community across Europe, if not the world, and you could read speculation about them in any of two dozen languages. The only common conclusion was that the person doing it wasn't very nice.

I'll just say this here – there is no such thing as Black Magic, unless you're referring to the chocolates. Magic is a tool, one that can be turned to any use, like a knife – you can use it to make dinner or to stab someone; the knife itself has no moral position of its own.

"Was you?"

"We were part of it."

"You *Ikasberri*?"

"I am, they are *Iksale* 1." I didn't have to say that Amy and Clara were *erdikide* – what they imagined about our sleeping arrangements was up to them.

"Search is… hard, is not nice," said Vittor. "Not stop for any *Maltin*. We not feel any other not local *Ikasberri* on island. Think it be searching you."

"Shit." They seemed to have no trouble translating that. "Can you help us find the searcher?"

"No. Only six *Jaun* on island now; protecting, so not free to help. We think you this problem; you leave here."

I nodded, unable to disagree with their conclusion. "Thank you. We will talk and let you know what we will do."

"*Tajjeb hafna.*" Melita gave me a card with her email address on it. "For message."

They left, and the door closing behind them woke Dominic. He offered nothing to the discussion, just sitting and blinking in the sunshine. It took five minutes.

"Dom, we have to leave," said Clara. "Go and pack."

"Pack? Why?"

"Because the person who burnt their house down is on

the island and is hunting for us. We need to get home, back to where we can be properly protected."

"Oh."

We reached the airport forty-five minutes later, managed to get seats on two different flights, just to be on the safe side, and left the ground less than three hours after Vittor and his chums had come to the house.

*

All this caused a bit of a storm. Not a real one, although that can happen if you really piss off an air Talent. No, this one was in the hierarchy of European magic users, or rather, The Hierarchy of European Magic Users, which is how they would prefer it to be pronounced.

Malta, like all independent nations, has autonomy in its magic. Because of its location, it's part of the Southern Italian Regional Group, which is based in Palermo. Northern Italy and the southern Alps are overseen from Venice, and Central Italy and Sardinia from Naples. It should have been Rome, but some Pope got snotty about having mages littering up the place and taking the piss, so they had to set up shop further south.

Melita woke up Palermo just before we left the island, got bollocked for letting us leave, and then stood aside when a group of spotters were flown over, intent on finding us as well as the person looking for us. And no, they were not bloody Aurors.

Of course, by the time the bureaucracy had been sorted out we'd been gone for about twenty hours and all trace of the searcher had vanished as well. Hardly their finest hour, although I don't suppose our people would have done any better.

Magic is organised across the world, of course it is,

but it isn't to do with power levels or the number of *Jaun* mages in each country. It's to do with being able to create the most purblind, inept and top heavy bureaucratic sludge-fest imaginable.

Every country is directly accountable to all the countries they abut, and every country is also part of a larger regional group that doesn't necessarily respect ethnic boundaries, or logic, or common sense. Denmark, for example, is part of the South Scandinavian Group, even though it is physically connected to Germany, which is in the North East European Group.

These are the formal organisational structures but there is another, entirely informal arrangement which is to do with magical talent, experience and influence.

You won't be surprised to know that while the three people who run Central are noteworthy members of the formal organisation, Nadia is also in the informal one. It's called the *Jakintzaren Gizarteko*, which roughly means 'The Society of Knowledge'. If you ask her she affects to know nothing about it, in a *Fight Club* sort of way. It is, however, widely known that while the bureaucratic organisation moves things along in its own leaden way, it's the *Jakin* that is the real driving force behind European magic.

*

I'd contacted Nadia before we even got to the airport in Malta, and we were met at Heathrow by several people with grim expressions and nervous fireball fingers – most security staff are fire Talents – and taken straight to Central under guard. Not quite the relaxing break we'd had in mind.

Dominic went home; well, more like he bolted. Clara, grim faced, stayed with us. We told the parents that Amy needed some more hospital treatment but otherwise we were fine, that we'd had a smashing holiday and I had decided that I would stay in London with Amy. In Malta it was warm, sunny and calm. London was dank, rainy and dull, but despite that I was glad to have seen the last of Melita and her band of pirates.

11

I expected we would be in Nadia's care again, but after we settled in our rooms we were met by the most forbidding-looking woman I have ever seen in my life, and that includes my mum when, as a teenager, I forgot to delete my Internet history.

"I," she said austerely, "am Mrs Collister." Anne Collister is over six feet tall, mid forties, and built like a javelin. She looked like a greyhound with toothache and had a lamentable taste in clothes, almost as bad as Professor Gowan. Gossip had told me that she was a widow, but didn't know why her husband had died. The smart money was that she'd eaten him.

"Good morning," I said. Bev had already started on Amy's other hip, even though we had only arrived yesterday, so she was in her chair, and I was holding her hand. Bev had taught me a new spell before we went away – *Sorgortu*. This translates as 'numb', but it's really a kind of magical morphine and I was there to keep Amy topped up. She didn't speak – she was feeling quite sick a lot of the time; our hasty departure from Malta had been rough on her.

Mrs Collister sniffed. "As we are doing our best to render

you inconspicuous, we need you to observe some additional rules." She laid them out in terse sentences; in essence, we weren't to leave the building or do any magic beyond *Iksale* 4 without express permission. In other words, we had to stay out of the way while making ourselves available at a moment's notice. We might as well have been in Pentonville or Wormwood Scrubs, except that the food was better here and Amy and I were together.

"Miss Deerborn will, of course, be spending most of her time with the Healers." She held up a file with 'N. A. M. Deerborn' on the cover. "I think that Mrs Duncan will be keeping Mr Frost and Miss Downing busy in the meanwhile."

I nodded. "Can we contact our families?" I held up a hand. "Obviously giving no indication of where we are or why."

"Of course. We have an IP-invisible server so your emails can't be tracked."

"Thank you."

"I need to sleep," said Amy. Her face was still and slack, puffy beneath the eyes and worryingly pale. I was concerned, even though I trusted Bev and the Healers completely.

Mrs Collister dropped gracelessly onto the chair next to her. "Oh my dear," she said, laying her hand on Amy's arm. "Poor girl. To have such happiness and such suffering at the same time. And to lose your house – your home – too." She sighed. "Your courage is remarkable." She turned to me. "As is your dedication to each other."

She smiled. No, I'm not joking – she smiled. Or possibly bared her teeth for some other reason – an imperfectly suppressed belch perhaps – but I took it as a smile.

"You two need to look after each other," she went on. "This has all been terribly stressful. I'll ask one of our specialists to have a word." I nodded. "Now, take your wife back to your room and let her sleep."

"I will. Er… just to clarify, we aren't actually married."

She nearly smiled again. "And what would be different if you had that extra piece of paper?"

I looked at Amy. I didn't see the wheelchair or the adaptations we would need to make to our home; I didn't see spells or degrees or bust measurements or IQ or anything superficial like that. I saw her, and realised that I had fallen for her ages before, but had been too dense or self-absorbed to realise it. "Nothing. There are no pieces of paper that will change how much I love her. Not even a death certificate."

Yes, I know, bloody soppy, but true. Clara started to cry as I took Amy's hand. She smiled sleepily and I stretched my mind to turn her wheelchair. I could almost drive it with my thoughts by now. Anne Collister, Triumvirate member and Certified Scary Person, rubbed my back for a moment then turned around to give Clara an enveloping hug.

Having another man run away because of her magic had clearly upset her a lot, and I was sure that Anne could feel the jangling in her. I thought Clara needed a *Jaun*-level boyfriend to avoid it happening again.

I took Amy back to our room and lifted her into the bed. Bev arrived, pronounced her knackered but otherwise fine and told me to stop being such a soft sod and go away and let her sleep. I went to the coffee shop and tried to sort out what was going on, but I found it hard to concentrate. My head felt like it was full of cotton wool and concrete.

It wasn't long before Anne's specialist turned up. Unfortunately, I recognised him – the last time he had spoken to me had been immediately before I died. Pat the Nosy Bugger, who was actually Dr Patrick Fintan, psychologist – in other words, a Professional Nosy Bugger.

"Good to see you again," was his opening line. I sighed. What with being a conduit, psychic parasites, falling in love and the ongoing threat of being killed, my head was a bit of a mess and I really didn't want to say anything to him.

"Oh yes, you're the one who doesn't like to talk." My mother would not have recognised this description.

"Mrs Collister has detected a lot of confusion in you, and no small amount of fear."

"You know about Paddington, and what happened to my house?" He nodded. "And you wonder why I'm afraid?"

"No, I don't wonder why you are afraid," he said. "I know about Natasha too."

"Who?"

"Natasha. Your girlfriend?"

"Her name isn't Natasha, it's Amy."

He stopped. "Oh. Well, actually her name is Natasha Amy Marie Deerborn, born in Vientiane, Laos, to English parents..."

"I know this. Her mother is half French." But, unfortunately, not the half with the cooking skills, according to Amy. Pat Fintan just irritated me. He had a voice like a fire alarm and the bedside manner of an Ebola doctor with grim news. He swept his greying hair back from his forehead with a self-conscious gesture.

"Let's start again."

"Had we started? All you've managed to do so far is annoy me."

"Why?" I shrugged and sipped my coffee. "I am aware," he said carefully, "that you have suffered the trauma of being helplessly used to kill people. I am aware that your magical capabilities have been severely disrupted. I am aware you have been pursued. I am aware that your house was burned down and you only survived by happenstance. I am also aware that the only part of any of this that actually bothers you is that you aren't sure you can keep Amy safe." His voice held a tiny thread of wondering disapproval.

I couldn't meet his eye. It was all true, but there was a

kind of numbness about it, a feeling of dissociation. Fintan was watching me carefully, so I kept my face closed.

"Why don't you want to talk about this?"

I recognised an imposed reluctance to speak, which made my skin crawl. "I feel that I am being prevented," I said, without moving my mind. For no reason I could explain it felt easier if I used more formal language, almost as if it wasn't really me that was talking.

"Is this the same restriction you experienced previously?"

"I believe that may indeed be the case."

Fintan smiled. His teeth weren't very good but the expression seemed to be genuine. "Clever," he said distantly.

"In what manner could my actions be described in such terms of approval?"

"You don't know what you're doing?"

"I have not the least idea." By now the accent was kicking in, and I sounded like a BBC newsreader from the Lord Reith era being disapproving at Neville Chamberlain about something. One or two people were looking at us, but nobody intervened. Slightly weird is normal in places like this.

"I think it's part of the inhibition, Michael," said Fintan. "It doesn't allow you to discuss what's going on with the parasite, and other aspects of the matter, but because you're using a voice that makes the Queen sound like a chav, whatever it is doesn't seem to realise that it's you speaking. Which is actually rather odd."

I pondered this for a moment. "I find myself conversing with the mindset of a specialist in combustion." I was starting to sweat a little, and my hands were unsteady.

"Oh, I see. The inhibition is only on the earth Talent, because whoever did this to you didn't know about the fire Talent." He chuckled. "I'm afraid you're probably stuck with it now."

"What might it be that I will not be able to dissociate myself from?"

"The Duke of Conflagration voice. I suspect that, until you integrate it, every time you access fire alone you will end up talking like this, unless you concentrate really hard."

"I believe that I could be content with that, under the circumstances," I said.

He nodded. "Splendid. So, what can't your earth Talent talk about?"

"In simple, the parasite remains – or rather, a fragment remains. It is not active, but there is a latency, a residue of control that still grants access to that... particular thing to whosoever set it there."

"I see." He made some quick notes. "How does the idea of having it removed seem to you?"

My vison went grey and my ears began to buzz. I swayed slightly.

"Okay, we won't do that," said Fintan quickly, and the feeling of imminent death subsided. "How does his Dukeness regard the prospect?"

"I am in accord with the other, in that the prospect does not appeal, although in this pseudo-psychotic state physical symptoms are not manifesting themselves."

"Good. I will continue to speak to his Lordship, if I may?"

"You may call him Arthur, to avoid ambiguity and confusion."

"As in 'I am the God of...'?"

"Indeed."

"Very good," he said with a small smile. "How does Arthur feel about neutralising it?"

"A similar... disinclination."

"Access?"

"As the term is undefined in terms of process, it evinces little or no significant response." This was becoming a very peculiar experience, and an uncomfortable one too. I could feel a huge muscular tension gripping my body, as if I was putting actual physical force into controlling myself.

"That's good, that's good. Very well. I think we'll leave it there for now. Thank you, Arthur. I recommend a large drink."

"It's three in the afternoon."

"Your point being?"

"It was an observation, not an objection," I said, sounding much more like myself. My body relaxed. It felt like my muscles had been replaced with boiled string and marshmallow, and I was sticky with sweat.

Fintan nodded. "I admire the distinction. I shall report this to Mr Slater and he can decide what to do with the two of you."

"Fine."

He stood up. "So, do you trust me now?"

"No."

"Thought not." I was glad when he left. I'm sure it's not personal, but every time that bastard turns up something bad happens. First time I died, and now he's lured me into having a split personality. Lovely.

*

Amy was awake when I got back to our room, propped up on some pillows and reading a magazine with torpid inattention. Her face was drawn and grey, and her hair seemed whiter than ever.

"Hello."

"Hello, love," she replied, voice barely above a pallid whisper.

"How are you feeling?"

"Crap. You?"

"Certainly somewhere down that end of the digestive tract." She nodded, so I sat down on the bed. "Pain?"

"Bev gave me something."

"It doesn't seem to be working."

She looked at me a little dopily. "Should've seen me before."

I smiled, but it hurt that I couldn't help. All I could do was sit and hold her hand and watch her sleep until the healing was complete. I hate feeling helpless, which I suppose is why I ran towards the crash at Paddington and not away from it like any sensible person would have done.

A little bit more explanation might be appropriate here. The problem with Amy's hips is not the result of trauma but of dysplasia, which affects the cup of the hip joint on the pelvis. It's a congenital condition where they are too shallow, so the femoral head slips out very easily. To avoid the wheelchair being permanent, the early onset of arthritis or the need for a full hip replacement, Bev and the Healers weren't repairing damage but virtually rewriting Amy's DNA so that the sockets formed properly.

The pelvic bones are some of the largest, most structural and weight-bearing in the body; and of course, any distortion could be disastrous for bearing children, so they had to work slowly and carefully. I was just grateful that they could do anything at all. All I wanted was for Amy to be comfortable and pain free – in or out of the wheelchair, I didn't care, and I don't think that she really did either. She had slipped back into sleep again, even though the pain was still clear on her face, so I very quietly had a shower and put on some clothes that didn't look like I'd been swimming in them.

*

I was in the canteen resisting the urge to gloomily eat more cake when a member of staff came looking for me.

"Mr Frost?" I nodded. "Please come to the IT suite – there's a call for you from Nottingham."

It was Ambrose Kiru, *kemen* Talent and good friend, with what looked like most of the rest of the college clustered around the Webcam.

"Yo, bruv," he said, doing the mockney-cockney thing he does when he's worried or upset. "What's happening, dude? Where's Amy?"

"She's having some more work done on her hips, so she won't need the chair any more. I'm with her."

"So, where was ya? You, like, vanished."

"Sorry, mate, we were on holiday in Malta. I'd tell everyone, but you obviously weren't paying attention, as usual. Where's Jerry?" Jerry Denton is Ambrose's *erdikide*, and we've spent a lot of time in the pub over the years. I was surprised that he wasn't there.

"He's got himself a new girlfriend, Ariadne something or other. We ain't seein' him a whole lot just now."

"Not surprised, knowing him and his trouser snake. So, what's all this about you lot falling asleep then?"

We chatted for several minutes while a question pushed its way to the front of my mind, like a stroppy toddler nagging for sweets.

"How did you get through to me today?"

"Professor Wicks set it up. Everyone's been asking about you two, even Professor Weaver, believe it or not, so she said she'd sort it out. And, like usual, when the professor says she'll sort summat out, it gets sorted out."

"Oh, I see. Fair enough. Anyway, go and do some work and get promoted, you idle sod."

"Piss off," he laughed and I cut the connection. I could feel that Amy had woken up, and I was eager to go to her, but I only got as far as the lifts before being intercepted by Katherine Duncan and a nondescript man in ironed jeans and an old man's coat. She introduced him simply as James.

"Sorry, but Amy's awake…"

She cut me off. "She's with the Healers and will be for a while. The rebuilding is getting complicated. They don't need you there."

"Amy does."

"She's asleep."

I frowned. "Doesn't feel like it." I don't even know why I could feel Amy at all – we weren't *erdikide*, after all.

"*Loaren*," said Katherine. I nodded. *Loaren* is a Healer's spell, much more powerful than *Lo*, which just puts you to sleep; *Loaren* is no pain, no fear, no concerns and scant awareness. It's not anaesthesia but it's bloody close.

"Okay. I suppose you have something for me to do then? How about Clara?"

"She's busy; she's got a pile of work to get through because she's about to be promoted to *Ikasberri*." I wasn't surprised but it still pleased me, and not just because that meant Amy would be too.

"That's good. Sam?"

"She's helping Clara and fending off the advances of one of the Healers who is taking a persistent and, shall we say, non-professional interest in her."

"Really? Has he been hit on the head?"

She laughed. "No, although if he carries on I'm sure she'll be happy to oblige." I chuckled, although I felt suddenly lonely, unneeded, irrelevant even. "So we have a job for you. Well, you and James. There has been an incident not far from here and we need you two to go snouting around, see if you can find out what happened."

"What sort of incident?"

"Possibly another barrier. Something of that type, anyway."

"Where?"

"Piccadilly Line southbound at Russell Square Tube Station. A Tube carriage ran into something nobody could see."

"Injuries?"

"Just bumps and scrapes – it was rolling to a halt at the time, so only the people who'd stopped hanging on got knocked over."

"When did this happen?"

"Couple of hours ago."

"Why me?"

"You were close to the one on the M1 and involved with that other stuff – so we want you to tell us if it's the same thing, or related to it or whatever."

"Isn't there anyone…?"

"Mike, just bloody go." Thunderclouds gathered on her brow, cresting the storm front of her irritation. I felt like shuffling nervously backwards. "If you ask any more questions I might as well brief an *Iksale* 10 and wait for them to reach the same level as you. James, take him away."

We left through the front doors, which immediately struck me as odd because that let us straight out onto the extremely crowded Queen Victoria Street. The difference from inside Central was stark – the fresh-ish air, the swirl of tourists, the rolling energy from the river and the stink of petrol fumes. I turned and stuck out my hand. "Michael Frost, confused *Ikasberri*."

My companion shook it. "James Greylock, currently appointed as assistant to a confused *Ikasberri*." He sounded vaguely Welsh. "Straight there, or do you fancy a coffee?"

"Coffee, definitely coffee," I said. I didn't really want coffee, but if James Greylock was there to assist me then my middle name is Matilda.

We stopped at one of those pseudo-Italian chain coffee shops just up from Blackfriars Tube Station, and I allowed James to seat me where he could see all the sightlines and close to an exit.

Assistant my arse.

"So what can you tell me about this thing at Russell Square?" I drank my small coffee and thought big probing thoughts.

"Nothing much. Something happened, someone thought to report it to us and the boss wants you to look at it." He shrugged. "I'm just here to help."

OK, I thought, *if Katherine thinks I need a bodyguard, that means she has reason to believe I may be in danger. Yet she sends me out of the front door onto the streets of London in broad daylight. Great. I'm bait. The clever ones are back at Central developing strategies and looking for clues, while my job is to go out and be a target. Great. Shaggy and Scooby Doo, too dumb to be of any other use.*

"Okay, let's get to it." He gulped his drink down as I peered at the counter. "I wonder if they sell Scooby snacks?" James looked at me blankly, so we headed out of the door, back across the road and into the depths of the London Tube system.

The station at Russell Square was operating normally when we got there, trains passing the oddly dated green, black and white tiled walls in a gust of hot, oily air every two or three minutes. Fortunately we arrived at platform level – I didn't fancy the 171-step spiral staircase, even though I had raced my cousin Juliet up it once. James walked me to the far end of the platform, just short of the transponder that tells the car where to stop.

"There. It should have been moving at walking pace here but it stopped, very abruptly."

"Inattentive driver?"

"Automatic system."

I scanned the area, leaning over the bright metal of the track tops, to the increasing consternation of nearby commuters. They didn't care about me personally, but if I decided to kill myself – to be a 'one under' as it's known – then it would delay their journey, and that's just beyond the pale.

I tried to remember the *esku* of the M1 barrier; it had been a woven ripple that moved across the road rather than appearing in place all in one go – one lorry had been clipped by it and had ended up pirouetting down the carriageway like a drunken ballerina. I wasn't getting anything like that.

You can feel the 'vibrations' hanging around for hours after a spell of that magnitude. The Tube train may not have been travelling very fast, but each one of the carriages weighs more than twenty-five tons, even when they're empty. Even at walking pace, that's a hell of a lot of momentum for each one, about the same as the average car travelling at thirty mph, and there had been six of them and they were full. That needs a lot of power.

I touched the floors, I touched the walls and people started to edge away from me. Fortunately a member of the transport police arrived and, after a brief consultation with James the Assistant, stood next to us while I poked around.

There was something here, something I didn't recognise. Well, I sort of did, but not in any specific... look, I can recognise a pistol, right, but I don't know if it's a Colt, a Browning or a Glock. This is the same. It was a magical device with a weak inhibition on it – not the great beast of a thing I'd got stuck with, but something to make it unnoticeable, like all the empty glasses on the table when it's your round.

"James, come and look at this." He crouched next to me, careful not to get his hands dirty, and looked at the grubby box that was attached under the lip of the platform.

"Oh." He seemed genuinely taken aback. "I had no idea there was..."

You weren't expecting me to find anything, were you, I thought. *Which makes my just being out in public the purpose of this exercise. Hey bait, get out there and wriggle like the fucking idiot you are.*

I reached inward, looking for the fire Talent in me. I found it easily, a hot, dark red place full of anger and frustration and the desire to lash out. I cautiously extended my hand and touched the box. Nothing catastrophic happened, but the concrete that had been holding it in place for God alone knows how long started to smoke and crumble. I kept going until I was able to lift the metal box, which was bloody heavy for its size, off the platform face. I passed it to him.

"Thank you," I said to the policeman, who I could see was looking concerned, even through the thicket of his beard. "Come on, Scooby," I said and James, still in the dark, trailed along behind me clutching the box.

We waited in the red tiled entrance of the Tube station until help arrived. A man with an alarmed expression and a stout container, like a ballistic box on steroids, kindly allowed James to gently lower the device into it, climbed smartly back into the car and sped off down Bernard Street without us.

"Oh," I said. "So, no car for us then?"

"Guess not," said James, not looking the least bit surprised. Well, not about that anyway. "Walk?"

"Bugger that." My dad was brought up near Bonnington Square, and my cousin Juliet still lives two streets away, so when the parents were doing the bi-monthly family visiting thing, she and I would go out and misbehave terribly. We'd have to get a night bus home because we'd drunk all our taxi money, spending most of the journey either snogging or giggling. I walked to the nearest bus stop, and checked the numbers on the pole. "Number 45 bus, takes us straight to Blackfriars."

"Oh." He seemed nonplussed. "I mean, bus, Russell Square, er, suspect device…"

I waited for him to run down, then leant back on the scratched plastic partition and squinted at the contrails homing in on Heathrow like a cheesy graphic of a missile attack. The wind was chilly and dark, classic weather for late February.

"So where do you expect him to try?"

"Er…"

"James, don't piss about. You aren't an assistant, you're a bodyguard, and if someone is going to go for me I'd rather be on the bus." I held up my hand. "I know the sides of the bus won't stop a bullet, but he might have more trouble spotting me at least. Moving target and all that. Plus it's cold, and the quicker I can get back to Amy the better."

He breathed slowly down his nose. "Bollocks," he said softly, his voice almost lost in the excited noises of children playing in the fountain.

"Seriously? You thought I wouldn't catch on?" He shrugged, looking very fed up. "So, what now?"

"Not my call. Come on, we'll take a taxi. She said it wouldn't work, but I thought… what gave it away?"

Apart from being extremely bleeding obvious? I thought. "If I need to tell you that, mate, you ain't nearly as good as you think you are."

He flagged down a taxi, which ignored him, so we waited for another. "She's going to kill me."

"Who?" I already knew it was Katherine.

"Nadia." Okay, I didn't already know.

"Why?"

"She's my boss. Nadia oversees the security of mages and the Allied Trades; Anne does all the higher-level interfaces with the non-magical world; Richard does pretty much everything else. They have teams under them of course, but they make the decisions."

"It sounds like the Ministry of Magic to me."

He snorted, scanning the street again. "If it was then the minister would have to be called Cornelius Fuck-Up."

London taxis doing what they do best – never being there when you need one – we ended up taking the bus anyway. For some reason James seemed reluctant to talk, especially once he understood I'd rumbled him just after we left Central.

I pondered about the thing I'd found – I couldn't think what the hell it could be and I was certain it had been there for a long time, long enough for anyone who saw it to assume it was part of much earlier building work on the platform. The station was opened in 1906, and it could have been there since then – or not. Clever concealment or genuinely old?

London passed in a blur of vaguely familiar images, but nothing of note happened. There were hints of small magics, because there is magic everywhere and a lot of people do it without knowing what they are doing, or why, or how. The apparently supernatural ability to find a parking space is normally done by placing a repulsion field – a bit like an inhibition – on an empty space so nobody takes it before you get there. People who are brilliant at finding things place 'tags' on the objects they are looking for, without needing to be able to see them – then 'miraculously' locate them. Such low-level, unintentional magic is very common, but it's irrelevant to the real practice of magic.

The real practice of magic: We were outside the Albion on New Bridge Street when something went click inside my head. *Ikasberri* had been a dream, like an undergraduate aspiring to a Master's degree, and I'd done it. Now I outranked nearly everyone in the Nottingham college that wasn't a teacher. *Iksale* are the background noise in colleges, the source of work, frustration and occasional, momentary, inspiration. But once you get to *Ikasberri* what you do and what you think starts to matter to other people.

My God, I'd turned into a grown-up.

And what do most grown-ups do when they have some serious thinking to do? They go to the pub. "I'm going for a drink," I said, over the noise of the diesel engine struggling with the fractious traffic.

"Why?"

"Because I want one."

"We should get back."

"No, you *think* we should get back; you *know* you should get back. I, on the other hand, am going to go and do what I want to do."

"I'm sorry, Mr Frost, but I really must insist."

"I'm sorry, Mr Greylock, but I really must ignore you." I started to rise and felt the distinct but distant tug of a spell as he tried to prevent me from moving.

In the quiet hours sitting with Amy in the medical wing, I had been doing a lot of thinking about the spell that had caused so much fuss when I disrupted Professor Gowan's sprites. It seemed like another lifetime, where things were fairly simple and nobody was trying to kill me.

The spell I had used wasn't specifically designed to stop the sprites – it was a generic counter spell, one that can neutralise almost any casting below a given level. It doesn't really cancel them either; instead it disconnects the active part of the energy, rendering it unable to function however much power is put in. The spell is still there, but it doesn't work, and usually the caster will stop once the counter has been applied. It's called *Hutsak*, which means 'hollow', as in to hollow out, to take the heart out.

I applied it to what James did and you'd have thought I'd tried to kiss him. "How the fuck are you doing that?" I just smiled, while the older people on the bus tutted at his language. "Who taught you that?"

I sketched out the circumstances as the bus slowed to a stop about a quarter of a mile from Blackfriars Station. He scrambled after me when I dismounted, and we started to walk downhill towards the river. He grabbed my arm and swung me around. He was really cross.

"My job is to keep you safe from all sorts of attacks, including ones mounted by practitioners. To do that I've been taught that… technique as well." He glanced around. We'd reached Apothecary Street by now, and the people queueing to use the cash machine on the corner had been listening in default of doing anything else. Some had even stopped looking at their mobile phones, which shows how interesting our conversation was.

"Jolly good."

"Mine will neutralise anything up to *Jaun* 3." I looked at him. "I tried to apply it to your… and it just… bounced off."

You use a lot of weak metaphors when discussing these things in public, because there isn't any other way of referring to this stuff without getting confused, needlessly metaphysical or talking crap. "That means that your… thing… must be at least level 4, although I suspect it's nearer five."

I blew out a long, and I have to confess slightly shaky, breath and started to walk again. "I see."

"And if you can do that then, in theory at least, you can do everything at that level," said James, his tone oddly subdued.

"Fucking hell. Now I really *do* need a drink." By this time we had reached the traffic lights by the turning to Watergate. Off on our left was what I needed – a pub. Specifically, the magnificently triangular and wonderfully art deco Black Friar, all green tiles and gold lettering, with the number 174 in huge figures over the door. This is the local for Central, barely 300 metres from the front door, and they're well used to magical types in there.

"Pint?"

Greylock shook his head. "What's the point?" His voice was sour, but there was an edge to it. "I'm supposed to be dealing with you, but you could probably reduce any attackers to cinders before I even noticed the threat."

"So maybe an orange juice then?"

"No. I'm going to see Nadia. This is way over my pay grade." He left, which was unfortunate, because the moment I finished my pint and stepped out of the pub, someone tried to kill me.

12

I could say that the attack came out of nowhere but it didn't; it came from the steps leading down to the Tube station about twenty metres away from the pub door. A figure, one of the many wrapped up against the cold, stopped with just its head visible above the steps, raised one hand and loosed a fireball about the size of a fist.

It was the fact that they stopped that caught my attention. I saw the fireball coming and cast *Armarria* (shield). The fireball bounced off and shot up into the sky, then vanished as the caster broke the spell.

Almost nobody noticed what was happening until someone bumped into my shield. She looked around, glared at a man standing innocently a few feet away and stalked off, muttering.

By then the next attack was on the way. It was a tightly focused disintegration spell called *Ebaki,* which destroys organic matter and leaves the rest untouched. I'd heard about it – Patricia told me that in Canada they use it for felling trees – but I hadn't seen it in action before.

It went through the *Armarria* like it wasn't there, and headed straight for a group of tourists that had meandered to a stop behind me.

I pushed them aside with a gust of wind, something I had no idea I could command, and then stepped smartly away from the impact. The spell splashed on the outer wall of the pub, stripping the Jolly Friar over the doorway of a layer of grime and pigeon shit. I didn't wait for the next spell, but drew a multi-layered globe of hardened *Armarria* around myself and charged straight at the attacker.

Unfortunately, my wind-powered tourists righted themselves just in time to get exactly in my way. My language skills are rudimentary, and I have no idea how to say 'please excuse me, I need to get past' in Japanese. Just 'move' would have done, but I didn't even have that, so by the time I'd got around them the fireball flinger had vanished – whether into the Tube, over the bridge or up the road I had no idea. There was no physical trace and little lingering magic, so after a minute of snouting around, I gave up.

Magic sometimes leaves a really big trace, usually if it has involved a building or the ground or large objects like a car. Sometimes the magic can alter the surroundings in unusual ways, anything from tiny changes that only a perceptive mage can spot to big things like gaping holes in walls. Sometimes magical fallout can have odd effects too – it can change the colour of fabrics, the way something smells, the accuracy of a clock and even the order of the tracks on a CD.

What I had been looking for outside the pub hadn't been what the spells had done – that was pretty obvious – but who had cast them and how.

How? Yes, how. There are different ways to create the same effect; it doesn't apply to all spells, of course, but it does to a significant number of more basic ones. It can arise from a mage using their own Talent, from a mage using a spell from another Talent, like the coffee-warming trick that Jerry taught me, or from using an object with a spell imbued into it. Very occasionally a spell can even be forced out of somebody who isn't a mage when they are *in extremis*.

This wasn't any of those; this was a mage using his own fire Talent to try to kill me. All of which I knew after the first attack, but I had to be sure.

Katherine was unimpressed when I got back, and told me that I needed to see Nadia as soon as she stopped bollocking James. I ignored her and went to see Amy instead.

*

"Hello, love," she said as soon as I walked into our room. She was pink and alert and sitting up in bed. She laid aside what I had assumed was an improving text. It wasn't; it was a battered copy of *Fifty Shades of Grey*, with marginal notes for the terminally unimaginative.

"Hi." I kissed her gently, as befits an invalid, but she grabbed me and did the whole enthusiastic snogging bit. "Oh. Good. Feeling better are we?"

"Fuck aye," she replied. "My left hip is pretty much fixed now, as well as will ever be possible, probably. I'll have to be careful while it muscles up, and they suggest I avoid trampolining, parachuting or horse riding for a while. As I have no desire to do any of them, ever, no problem."

"Brilliant. What about the other one?"

"Another time. We should be able to go home in a couple of days." She smiled. "So what have you been up to?"

"Studying the hard-light vehicles, learning some new control spells and other fascinating stuff like that."

"Interesting?"

"Not really, but I have to know it, apparently." I paused. "So how come you didn't tell me your first name is actually Natasha?"

"Oh, that." She shrugged. "I've never used it because I

don't like it. It's soppy – they got it from one of my aunts, apparently. And everyone shortens it to 'Tash', which makes me sound like facial hair."

"Do you think Amy is better?"

"I was born in Laos and none of the locals – not even my *ayah* – could pronounce 'Amelia'. So they called me '*Ame*', which is a pretty common local name. The parents gave up on Amelia, thank God, and when they finally got around to registering me as a UK citizen, Amy had stuck." She held me out at arm's length, frowning slightly. "What's happened to you?"

I told her the non-scary version, with the revelations about *Jaun*-level casting emphasised and the nearly getting killed bit barely mentioned.

"Of course you're *Jaun*-level now, you twit – anyone with two fully developed Talents is automatically *Jaun* 1, and you've gained so much power recently that I wouldn't be the least surprised if you're *Jaun* 2."

I was stunned. "Really? I didn't realise." *Iksale* 2 to *Jaun* 2 in less than six months. It should take years, if ever. Amy watched me while it sank in, but wisely refrained from saying anything.

"So who attacked you?"

"Fire Talent, at least *Jaun* 1, probably higher."

"Why?"

I shrugged and scratched my arm. My skin felt tender and sort of gritty. *I must have a shower*, I thought. "It has to be something to do with the hard-light attacks. If it isn't, I haven't the faintest idea."

"Does anyone else?"

"No. Well, not that they're telling me anyway." I scratched again. "I'm going to have a shower."

"Can I watch?"

"Scrub my back if you like."

She winced as she shifted on the bed. "No, I think I'll just watch for now, thanks. Feeling a bit sore at the moment."

I dropped my clothes in a heap, as was my usual practice, and was about to get wet when Amy gasped.

"What?"

"Look in the mirror."

The skin of my torso was coated in a fine, sticky grey dust, denser where the seams on my heavy cotton shirt had been. I picked it up – the fabric felt flimsy and stiff, like thin cardboard. My jacket, all artificial fibres, didn't seem to have been affected.

"Do not shower," said Amy urgently. "You better put some pants on though." A few seconds later Clara came in, looking concerned.

"Oh. Right. I'll get Bev and Katherine. Do you feel okay?"

"Itchy."

"Stay there."

She returned about three minutes later and the whole interrogation started. I had to describe the attacks in detail, and Amy was looking thunderous by the time I'd finished.

Bev nodded. "It's your shirt. The cotton fibres have been stripped of their outer layer by the *Ebaki*. It seems to have stopped when it reached your skin." She looked at Katherine. Her eyes were hidden behind her shoulder-length red hair for a moment as she drummed her fingers on the table. I noticed that the tip of her left little finger was missing and that she was wearing what looked like a jade wedding ring.

"No idea. If it hit you hard enough to do that to your shirt you should look like a chicken nugget." She turned to Amy. "He's fine. Once he's washed he needs to come to conference room six – both of you, if you're up to it. Something very odd is going on here."

They left. We looked at each other. "What have you done now?"

"I don't know." I searched for Sam, but she was in college and focused on something very complicated and meteorological. She acknowledged my existence, then gave me the mental equivalent of 'go away and leave me alone'.

So, just me then.

*

I thought it was just going to be another bloody circular chat, another pointless conversation about something that none of us understood, and at the end of it I might be allowed to go home – or to go and find a home anyway.

It wasn't. An official title would have been something like 'a multiagency meeting with expanded parameters to investigate the cause of the incident' or some such bloody waffle. It was a lot of people sitting around a big table either interrogating me or ignoring me. I would have liked to have Amy with me for moral support, but Bev had said she was too tired and thwarted her protestations by putting her to sleep.

The chair – why are people in authority named after furniture? The chair of a meeting, a board of directors, a bench of magistrates, a barstool of journalists… anyway, Richard Slater was steering things but Nadia did most of the talking, which seemed to be the normal arrangement. The only person I didn't at least vaguely recognise was a young dark-skinned chap in a medium-expensive suit who was simply introduced as Peter. I was told he represented 'external agencies', but nobody deigned to be more specific, which didn't surprise me either.

"This situation is complicated," said Slater. That's like saying that building a space rocket is a bit tricky. "We have two contiguous sets of magical events, and young Mr Frost here is the only connection. Nadia, could you bring us up to date?"

She looked up from the mobile phone she seemed to have permanently welded to her left hand. "What? Oh, right. Event one, the hard-light vehicle attacks."

"Motive?" This was Peter. His accent was pure Kentish Town.

"Unknown. The mechanism is the perpetrator using an earth-based dual Talent to create a vehicle by channelling very high-powered magic through them. This usually kills them."

"But not Mike," said Bev.

"But not Mike. This is where it gets properly odd. We know that he is powerful, but not extraordinarily so. We can only assume the perpetrator chose him not for his own power, but the power he has access to."

"Sam?" I asked. Peter glanced at his notes and nodded to himself.

"Yes Mike," said Slater. I swear he nearly smiled. "You and she share an unusually strong link and you unknowingly pull down power from her when you do very high-powered spells."

"Oh. And there I was thinking I was getting good at it all by myself." I hoped I sounded wryly amused, but it appears to have come out as grumpy.

Nadia chuckled. "Ah, the fragile male ego. She draws on you for control and fine adjustments – like most mages of her power levels, she has trouble controlling what she does." Nadia looked at Peter. "We spend an awful long time teaching them not to pull down a wall when they just want to open a door. Sam gets control from Mike, as Mike gets power from Sam, but without either being aware it's happening. It's the relationship between *erdikide* in a nutshell." Peter nodded.

"So," said Slater, "his choosing you was not a lucky coincidence but a very clear and deliberate decision on his part."

"His?" This was Peter again.

"His, hers, theirs, its," Slater replied, irritated. "We don't know." Peter nodded. I began to suspect that he was either police or a spook. "The other conduits died after a single event, so you surviving three of them troubled us."

I could see where this was going. "Even stealing power from Sam I shouldn't have survived, so you wondered if I was doing it myself."

"Yes," said Nadia. "Your tutors describe you as one of the quiet ones, good at the small-change interactions of everyday life, but not conspicuously making any particular friends. That could have been significant."

I just stared at them. I didn't think I was particularly quiet. Okay, I'm kind of private because who the hell would be interested in what I think about stuff? And I've got loads of friends.

"However, you and Amy getting together gave your professors a good excuse to investigate."

"Why didn't you just ask...?" I saw Peter raise one eyebrow. "Oh, yeah, sorry."

"And subsequent events have proved you were just a conduit, so that begs the question, how the hell did you survive?"

"I almost didn't. I may not next time."

Bev nodded. "I know. But not to worry, you're protected now."

"Thanks." I was trying for dry, but it may have ended up somewhere nearer fervent gratitude.

"So we did some more investigating and found out that not only did you have a fully developed but suppressed second Talent, but you also had a fragment of the control spell in your *gogoan*." Peter raised an eyebrow again, and made some hasty notes. This appeared to disturb him more than somewhat.

"I remember," I said. "I was there." Three days totally out of my tree with no clue what was happening or even if I was ever going to wake up. "You removed it."

"No."

"OK, I removed it with your help."

"No." This was Pat Fintan, who thankfully had been silent up until now. "When I was talking to you earlier, you said that part of it remains."

"An inert fragment I said."

"Yes, yes, but that doesn't matter." He was being annoying again, so I got up and went to the coffee machine. Yes, I drink a lot of coffee. In fact, I probably drink too much of it, but only when I'm away from Sam. Coffee is my *Indar* when she isn't around. Maybe having to support an unsuspected second Talent was why I needed so much caffeine to block my adenosine receptors.

"Mike," said Bev, bringing my attention back, "we think the inhibition is still there."

I looked at her and felt Arthur the Fire Talent stir. It was very odd, like thinking with someone else's brain. "I believe you may be correct in your assumption."

"So we have to ask why it's there," Slater said.

"Still," added Nadia from the other side of the table. "We need to investigate further." I twisted my head to look at each in turn. I felt like a tennis umpire.

"Enlighten me."

"We are now almost certain there is something in what remains of the parasite that will allow us to identify the perpetrator."

"Oh, how truly wonderful." I was sweating quite hard now and my coffee was starting to move in the mug like it was simmering on a stove. I put it down, felt myself swaying and almost fell.

Pat Fintan leaned forward and steadied me. "This line of discussion must cease immediately."

They held a long silence until my breathing calmed and I sat back in my chair. "Why was my fire Talent separate?"

"We don't know," said Richard.

"What could cause that?"

"It could be fear of the Talent; it could be resistance to having two active Talents; it could be the result of trauma, or just because shit happens."

"Trauma…"

"Yes, that occurred to us too," said Richard.

"Well, now it's been opened, why hasn't it been integrated?"

Nadia stirred. "We've blocked the integration until the parasite is gone. It's possible," she added with a caution that I did not like, "that if they were fully integrated the inhibition could kill you if we tried to remove it."

I pondered that for a bit, but nobody spoke. Fintan was making notes, and the scratching noise of his pen was just loud enough to compete with the hum of the air conditioning and the murmur of voices outside in the corridor. Unable to relax, I stood again, and went to the window. There was still just the reassurance of the Thames, an inert if not motionless lump of water, one that couldn't give the tiniest shit about what we did.

This was old power, deep power, something we could observe but never touch. This was blood and bone magic, the heart of the city. I could almost touch it, and it was amazing.

"Who could have done this to me? There can't be that many people who could, I mean, how long did it take to put the parasite in place? Why didn't I feel it? Why didn't Sam feel it? Why didn't the professors notice it was happening?"

Now it was Katherine's turn to bring Peter up to speed. "The person who did this to Mike must be someone who knows him well – he doesn't draw power from Sam all the time, so they must have been there when he did." Half looking over my shoulder, I nodded. Peter was writing again.

"They must be aware of what Mike can do. They must also have been able to magically interact with him in a way that he would consider normal and unthreatening, so he would effectively ignore what they were doing. But, they can't have been close enough to him, and of a sufficiently high level, to be able to spot that he had a suppressed second Talent."

"And the other conduits?" Peter asked. "What's the story with them?"

"We aren't sure, but it seems likely that the parasite was forcibly implanted very shortly before being used."

"So it's one of the tutors at college then," I said dully.

That generated a few mutters. "Well, they would fit the bill, certainly," Katherine conceded.

"So why do they want me dead now? My aftershave? My taste in jumpers? Because I don't like football?" I paused. "It's because I survived and so might be able to identify them, isn't it?"

"That's our working hypothesis," said Nadia softly.

"Fine. Just run up a list of all the people who meet the first criteria and then cross-reference them with their location."

Slater stirred. "No correlation."

"Oh." I was still looking out of the window. I could feel the cold falling off it and I touched the glass with my fingertips. I felt the hum of the power that fuelled the illusion as a skin over the surface, and I watched it ripple as I moved my hand. "You don't need to do this for me," I said, gesturing at the window.

"The illusion? Why not?"

"Because you sent me out there to get shot at." I was suddenly so weary of it all. "There's no point in hiding me any more. Whoever's doing this knows I'm here – he's probably sitting outside waiting for me to leave so he can have another go at killing me." I turned. "You couldn't find anyone hanging around, could you? So you invented that bloody stupid wild goose chase up to Russell Square to draw him out. Get out there, bait, and wiggle, so we can see who's trying to catch you. And you all think that's okay, do you?"

I must've been shouting, as all the noise outside the door stopped and everyone except Pat Fintan was looking shocked and serious. He just looked grim.

"I warned you," he grated, all signs of his previous jovial personality gone. "I told you he'd work it out, and that he wouldn't like it."

"Yes, Pat, you were right," said Nadia placatingly. She looked at me. "Don't worry, we'll get someone to repair the window." I looked back at it – where my fingertips had been touching it, the glass had melted clean through and the molten glass had trickled down the pane. It looked like tears, and I could feel the wind coming in through the holes, and with it the smell of river mud, petrol fumes and brick dust.

"We sent you a bodyguard," said Richard, sounding more defensive than I'd expected.

"James Greylock is not a bodyguard, unless he's an utterly fucking useless one. He's *kemen*. I know I'm not supposed to be able to work that out – so I'm wondering if having the parasite has given me some extra skills. Shades of bloody Voldemort." I lifted one hand a fraction and a gentle breeze stirred the papers that were scattered across the big table.

"An earth and fire Talent at my level shouldn't be able to do that either. So I suspect the person behind this may be an air Talent."

Slater nodded. "An interesting idea. How did you know about James?"

I sighed and sat down, slumped really, utterly drained. "I thought he was holding some power ready to use in case we were attacked – fireballs, that kind of stuff, but we've got a bloody genius fire Talent in Nottingham who I've known for ages, and it just felt wrong. I had a quick dig into James's *gogoan* – I know, I shouldn't be able to do that either, especially not when drinking coffee and talking about music venues, but it seems that I can, at least at the moment. I'm sure you'll be able to tell me why, or how, eventually."

"What did you find?" Peter asked, with soft emphasis. He did not look happy.

"That he wasn't a fire Talent holding a defensive spell ready for use – he's a *kemen* who was sending out a message like a fucking foghorn that just said, 'we are here'." I slammed my hand on the table. The plastic surface cracked, shooting spall marks to a radius of more than a metre. No, I don't know how – I didn't hurt my hand or anything.

"I won't be bait again. I want this bastard thing out of my head and then we are going to go home. And then you will leave us alone. You can sort out the attacks without me."

"I wish we could," said Nadia softly.

There was a really long silence, long enough to make me wonder if I had shown myself to be manly and determined or just petulant and scared. Peter looked at Nadia.

"I have some concerns about your methods, concerns I need to raise with you," he said. "In private."

"Amy's awake and is wondering about you," said Bev.

"How can she know what's happening to me? How can I *feel* what's happening to her?"

"I talked to Marika, one of our specialists, about that," said Bev calmly. "Even though normally you can't be *erdikide* to more than one person, she thinks your fire Talent was separate for so long it's becoming *erdikide* to Amy," said Bev. "Which is very odd in lots of ways, some of which you aren't aware of. Even without the hard-light attacks, I think you would have had some interesting times ahead."

A horrible thought struck me. "Will I lose Sam?"

"I have no idea," said Bev, taking me by the arm and helping me from the room. I was suddenly very weak. "Think of how much fun we'll have finding out."

13

After all that there wasn't very much else we could do in London. Richard Slater was certain that whoever was targeting me would decide not to have another go because we were alerted to their intentions. Yeah, right. I don't know what Peter said, but Nadia had a right face on the next time I saw her. Plus they couldn't fix the parasite just now and the Healers couldn't do any more for Amy for a while, so they sent us back to the tender care of the professors in Nottingham.

So we went home, because there wasn't much point in doing anything else. Whoever was doing this would find us – me – eventually. As I had no intention of spending my life hiding or running, I decided to let him come to me. 'Readiness is all' said Shakespeare or one of those guys, but that meant I had to get away from everyone I cared about so I didn't put them in danger, even though Nadia and Katherine had given me lots of protection, some of which I didn't really understand.

My control of my offensive capabilities was a concern. I knew that if I got into a fight and started chucking fire spells around, everyone within half a mile, even in aeroplanes flying overhead, could be in danger. I knew I was going to be bait, but I wanted to be bait that could bite back. I needed to learn to control my fire, and that meant talking to Jerry, in private and at length, without beer being involved. There's a first time for everything.

We met at a greasy spoon not far from his flat and I described my situation to him over coffee. He listened intently and he conceded that he was confused. Well, actually he said, "You're just a flaming weirdo, you are. I always said so." Which was true. "And you're going to be a pain in the arse."

"Well, thanks for that. Why?"

He took a long breath. "Because normally when we start to train a fire Talent they don't have a lot of power, so they can't do much damage when they inevitably cock something up. But you're a total monster when it comes to spell power, even without Sam, so if you screw it up we'll be picking up the pieces for a friggin' week."

"So what can I do?"

He thought for a moment. Jerry is Mediterranean dark and has the kind of face that looks vaguely grumpy even when he's asleep, but now it was troubled. After a couple of minutes, he sort of nodded.

"OK, let's try this. You know the amount of control layers you put on when you chuck a big spell around?" I nodded. You use things that are the equivalent of walls around the path of the spell so that it doesn't leak out of the sides. The usual analogy is a hosepipe that stops the water going anywhere other than the direction it's supposed to. For once, that's pretty accurate.

"You'll need that a lot when you start, but it won't be a problem – you can get Sam to control the path while you do the spell."

That led to a slightly awkward silence, and then, over the clatter of cutlery and the hiss of the coffee machine, I tried to explain my logic about not getting anyone else involved.

He snorted derisively, his dark eyebrows rising in surprise. "Good luck with that, you bloody maniac. Whoever did this to you is going to turn you into friggin' cat food if you try to do this by yourself."

Someone sat close enough to us that they would be able to overhear every word, so we left and walked around the local park. "The trouble is, I've no idea where or when it's going to happen," I said, "but I can't endanger the college, and I won't endanger my family or friends."

"Then I guess you're just going to have to lie to everybody," he said, looking like a mournful basset hound.

"I thought so," I replied. "I'm concerned that I'm going to have to leave here as well, because I won't know it's happening until it starts."

"If it starts." We sat on a bench and watched bored dog-walkers and muffled children wandering across the soggy grass. "Because from what you said I don't think that this dickhead is going to go anywhere near you."

"Why not? I've still got this thing in my head and that means I might be able to identify them." I hadn't meant to tell Jerry everything, but a lot of what I was asking made no sense if I didn't, so I'd filled him in.

"And you've spent a week at Central and they couldn't get it out. Now you're back here and however clever our professors are, if that lot at Central couldn't get it out then there's nobody here who can. While you're here, you're safe."

"Maybe." I would have liked to talk some more but his mobile rang and he answered in such warm and affectionate tones that I knew it had to be the new girlfriend, so I nodded to him, which he didn't notice, and left.

*

A dank last week in February turned into an identical first

179

week in March, and it was then that the last bit of fallout from the Paddington crash happened. I received a formal invitation to go to the town hall in Nottingham to be given a pat on the back for being stupidly brave, or possibly just stupid. I'd almost forgotten about it – well, not forgotten, because it isn't the kind of thing that you forget, but it wasn't always at the front of my mind any more, a demotion that had taken far too long. The embossed card suggested that I wear a suit or a uniform, and as I was fairly sure they didn't mean my old scout jumper, I squirmed into the grey three-piece, found some shoes that could take a vestige of polish, and presented myself as instructed.

I hadn't read the bit about there being a reception, so I was surprised when I, and several others, were ushered through some neo-baroque doors and were greeted by the Lord-Lieutenant of Nottinghamshire being formal and congratulatory.

After a while I gathered that, to my bemusement, I was being given the QGM, the Queen's Gallantry Medal, for failing to get squashed by a vanishing train. Apparently I had put myself in considerable danger and in the process saved at least four people from certain death. Which was nice.

At the first reasonable opportunity I headed to the toilet, which was a lot less posh than the rest of it, and phoned Amy. She called me 'my hero' a couple of times, while trying not to laugh.

Mum and Dad were impressed, unlike Simon, who thought I was making it up. They promised to look after my medal until we'd got another place to live. As far as I know they've still got it, somewhere.

*

It was not even a week later when we found our new home, a house that we had looked at before. The bungalow had been suburban, but looking at similar ones now made me feel hemmed in. This one – Whin Hill Farm – was a converted farm building north of Nottingham, not far from the village of Linby.

It's halfway up an irregular, sheep-scarred hillside topped with some substantial ruins, which Amy thinks were an old baronial hall or something like that. Most of the time the piles of stone are used by sheep as a place to keep out of the wind, which seems to blow most of the time in winter, and the rain which is horizontal, freezing and as insistent as a hungry cat.

The house was empty, so because we were buying it with insurance money and already had a mortgage, we were able to move in quickly. I felt utterly at home from the moment we arrived.

The place consisted of the triple-glazed house itself, a huge barn full of miscellaneous crap, a wood store, a Calor gas tank and two stone owls on the gatepost. There's also a huge picture window, which gives really big views over the countryside, and an awful lot of sky. Despite the apparent isolation it felt welcoming, and the almost unrestricted access to the countryside makes earth Talents who visit really calm and centred. Earth Talents need to be in contact with the earth to stay on balance. Suburban streets and tower blocks are fine to live in, but you have to get your feet on bare ground regularly.

The house is slightly out in the middle of nowhere, but that was deliberate – you can't see the bastards coming if you're surrounded by buildings. We covered the place with wards, shields and lots of other magical protection, plus more conventional defences, before we even moved in.

When we first looked at the house mum had said she liked the sense of space, and especially the long views from the picture window. Dad had noticed the large, dense copse down across the lane and declared the area 'satisfactorily bosky', i.e. having an adequate supply of bosk, whatever the hell that means.

We weren't really alone, of course; the village is less than a mile away, and the proper farmers – Jim Brennan and his wife Helena – lived about a quarter of a mile around the hill in a new build. There were other houses around and about too, and a whole shitload of things that go grunt, squeak, blart, moo and start singing far too bloody early in the morning. Despite the distance, and unless we had a bad case of tractors, the traffic was so light that it was sometimes quicker to get to the college from here than it had been from mum and dad's house.

The weather, we had been warned, could be an issue, especially on bad winter days; the snow falls like a bag of hammers and the fog can be thick enough to cut with a spoon. I didn't care, and neither did Amy or Sam. Clara did care, and complained endlessly about the drive. Mind you, if I had a poxy little car like hers, I probably would too. It's a lemon-yellow Fiat 500, with less power than mum's sewing machine and leaky windows.

Mum and dad came out to Whin Hill Farm one day to 'help us get settled', which is parent speak for 'have a nose around and see if the children are doing something you can disapprove of'. Dad hadn't wanted to disturb us but, as usual, mum had given in until she got her own way. They turned up about three days after we'd finished getting everything sorted out.

It would have been better if they'd warned us they were coming, or even mentioned that they might, because their arrival at around nine in the morning, on a Saturday yet, was something of a surprise. Fortunately we were up, showered, dressed and had finished breakfast when the doorbell went. Dad appeared at the top of the stable door

– no, I didn't fit the thing – when Amy opened it without crossing the room.

"Oh hello," she said, perking up and losing that soft, early morning look that I find so appealing.

"Good morning," he said with a grin, putting on his best smooth, slightly louche voice, the one he uses for winding up door-to-door salesmen and nuisance callers on the telephone. "May we?"

"Of course," said Amy, smiling and waving her hand to open the door all the way. Dad stepped confidently across the threshold, but mum was more hesitant. Dad's fine if he can understand the science behind something, but mum needs to be reassured that it's 'normal' before she's comfortable with it. In our house, she was going to have to learn a whole new version of normal.

I was upstairs when I heard the voices. I came down the wide staircase cautiously – I wasn't sure why they had turned up unannounced; it wasn't like them. I didn't read anything into the fact Simon wasn't there – I wouldn't expect him to come here unless he was orphaned, homeless, on the run, on the scrounge or had been evicted.

"Everything all right?"

"Everything's fine, dear," said mum, looking ostentatiously around the big main room. The last time she'd been here it had been stuffed with cardboard boxes and the other detritus of moving house. One end had a wood-burning stove and comfortable chairs; our huge wooden slab of a table was in the middle, with a big bookcase on the back wall, and a kitchen area at the other end. The smell of frying bacon and home-made bread lingered. "You've done this very nicely," she said.

"Thank you." I mouthed 'tea' and Amy scooted over to the side and chucked some teabags into our big brown ceramic teapot, which has a series of breaks painted onto the surface. It was a housewarming present from Professor Gowan, who said that Amy must be a crackpot to move in with me. Ho, ho, bleeding ho.

We have one of those built-in boiler units that delivers hot water like a tap – much better than using a kettle when you're in a wheelchair – but mum still bustled over, and no one bustles quite like mum, then took over, mostly as a bastion against the embarrassment of idleness.

Dad and I never saw that tea, because the women started gossiping and that was them for the next half an hour or so. I was glad that Amy had decided to be vaguely sensible about her hair colour that day – it had been an almost luminous green for most of the previous week.

I gave dad the guided tour, which didn't take long, and then we settled at the other end of the long room.

"Comfortable," was his considered verdict. "A little sparse of furniture…"

"Wheelchair."

"Of course. Shame you can't fly." I'm fairly sure he was joking.

"Can you imagine what air traffic control would say? They'd have conniptions if the skies were suddenly full of mages zooming around like hummingbirds on speed." He laughed. Dad has a generous sense of humour, but a well-developed sense of irony really is the only explanation for his choice of ties.

"Do you think you'll get many people coming to see you out here?"

"No, but that was part of the idea." Ambrose, Jerry and a few others from college had helped us move. Then we had the house-warming, when around thirty people turned up, drank all our booze and ate everything I'd set out, plus most of what was in the fridge too – it was like locusts, but without the sense of social responsibility.

That was also the first time we met Jerry's girlfriend,

Ariadne something-or-other. She's Greek, or from a Greek family, and she's smart and pretty and has a very silly sense of humour, so she fitted in just fine.

Even Brian had turned up, dressed like a normal member of the human race for once, and offering blessings for our new home; we had to stop him smudging the place and setting off the smoke detectors. It's inevitable that he would have been some kind of New-Age weirdo, even if he couldn't do magic. Other than that, our visitors so far had been postmen, delivery drivers, Jim the farmer and his wife and one rambler who was so lost that he thought I was lying when I pointed us out on the map.

"We have regular visitors like Sam and Clara of course." By now they knew that Sam was female, and understood the relationship between us. When Amy explained that it was the same between her and Clara, they accepted that it was just another weird thing about mages, although Simon made some suggestive comments that earned him a good glaring-at from mum.

We talked a little more, then went for a walk outside, despite the chill in the air. The cars were on the gravel drive, near the old barn that we'll put them in when I finally get around to clearing it out. A branching track joined the main farm road near the opening in the extremely substantial wall, with its carved sentinel owls, and then it was just the rolling and empty hills in the swirling wind.

"So, why did you actually come here today?"

"Impulse," he said after a long moment.

"You don't do anything on impulse, dad. It's not that we mind you coming of course, but…"

He shrugged uncomfortably, his sensible waterproof jacket rustling as he did. "Your mother's impulse then. We were out anyway – Simon is off on some school trip or other and we had to get him to school for stupid o'clock this morning, so we stopped in town for some breakfast and she thought we might drop in here on the way back."

I felt the wind moving my hair slightly. "Dad, his school is in the diametrically opposite direction to this house…" I didn't have to finish the sentence.

"Your mother is worried," he said, not looking at me. "She's cared for you for so long she's… oh dear, this is hard to phrase properly… concerned that Amy won't be able to keep up the same standard." He finished the sentence in a rush of breath.

"Because she's in a wheelchair."

Dad hesitated, but then did me the honour of being truthful. "That's certainly a part of it."

"I could be offended by that. I know Amy would be, because it's just bloody rude – she's been living independently, in her own flat, for the last four years, for God's sake – and about me, like I can't cope either. You know how much I did, and what I did, when Nonna was still with us."

"I know, and it hasn't been forgotten, but mum still thinks you can't manage without her." That was blunt, even for dad.

"Based on what evidence?"

"Mother's instinct," he said apologetically.

"Bollocks."

"I agree."

I walked around a bit, trying to separate maternal concern from irrational prejudice, then stopped when I noticed a grey car parked at the far end of the farm driveway. Sometimes people pull over to use the phone, or to turn around, but not very often because the little road doesn't go anywhere much.

"That was there when we arrived," said Dad. "One white man, dark hair, looking at the house."

"Did you get the number plate?"

"No." He looked at me sharply. "Why would I need to?"

"See if you can when you leave." I looked around as the front door opened. "Which seems to be about now."

I turned back to see the grey car pulling away. I made to speak but mum was there. "You certainly have done well with the house, despite everything."

"Thanks, mum."

"And I'm sure that you'll be fine together." I could hear Amy trying not to laugh, at least in my mind.

*

There was also a lot of sorting out to do at college. Mainly there was the question of our status, and that took bloody ages to resolve, unfortunately at the same time as we were moving into our new house. I won't bore you with all the testing we did – it bored the crap out of me and I was the one doing it. The result was that Sam and I were made probationary *Jaun* 2.

I'd never heard of probationary grades before, which I discovered was because they technically didn't exist – Professor Wicks made them up, because she couldn't think of a way to grade people with so much power but so little experience. Amy and Clara, very unusually, became *Jaun* 1, bypassing *Ikasberri* altogether. I thought that was incredibly impressive but also a bit of a swizz.

Because it was a large and abrupt promotion, the conversion course that Clara and Amy did wasn't a week away but a series of extra classes at Nottingham, overseen by Professor Ngozi. As the boss of the fire Talents, she wasn't involved with them directly and so could be impartial. It lasted more than two months and they passed without much trouble, although both the girls slept very poorly for most of the time.

I could feel the change in Amy, and her already impressive levels of precision and control improved dramatically. Clara didn't appear to change too much, but Amy told me that her casting had become more subtle and the amount of power she used to achieve the same result had been significantly reduced.

I know what the course in York did for Sam – hugely improved control – but I'm not at all clear what it did for me. They tell me that I have become a 'better' mage because of it. But from this side of the equals sign I can't detect any change, apart from rather more confusion than previously.

I was concerned when I saw the grey car again a few days later, this time parked near the pedestrian entrance to college. I took photos and was about to call Nadia or Richard when the person driving it – a young Muslim woman with a stunning royal blue and silver hijab and two small children – came back and loaded it with shopping. Then I realised it wasn't the same car.

From that moment onward I kept noticing small grey cars, until eventually I stopped registering them at all – it seems that non-clinical paranoia does wear off, eventually.

Then early one Thursday Nadia turned up at the college unexpectedly and vanished into a meeting with Wicks, Ngozi and Gowan that lasted all day. At lunchtime my kudos levels went through the roof when Nadia said 'Hi, Mike' when she walked past me, and I replied 'Hi, Nadia' without the sky falling on my head.

*

Sometimes, when some parts of your life are being quiet and normal – whatever the hell *that* means – the rest of it can suddenly get… tricky.

It happened just as we started to fill our house with books and videos for our MScs. Most of them should have been called *An Idiot's Guide to Sunken Ships and How to Excavate Them* or something. For mine I got lots of geology and geomorphology, plus quantum physics, electromagnetic theory and a whole raft of stuff about energy transfers for mage training. I'd known that I wouldn't be learning how to do card tricks, but getting my Talents into balance was proving to be a real pain. Jerry had been right about that, and on top of that we had loads of revision to do as we neared our finals. I don't talk about university stuff very much, but we do spend a lot of time doing it. Me sitting in a chair reading a learned discussion on upper air carbon residence time just isn't very interesting.

It was Professor Weaver, our *kemen* lecturer, who helped the most with balancing the Talents. We spent hours faffing about in some obscure corners of my *gogoan* trying to settle the Talents. I was always tired, and days when I didn't have a headache were a bonus. I actually fell asleep driving home once, and I only didn't crash because Sam felt me going and gave me the mental equivalent of a sharp poke in the ribs.

I pulled over at a shop near Southglade Park and bought industrial quantities of Red Bull and chocolate. It worried me because, leaving aside that business in York, however hard I'd worked before I had never been so weary. I wondered if I was coming down with something.

So the next day I drank lots of very strong coffee and drove home with the windows open while seriously in need of a piss. It was uncomfortable but it worked.

＊

Some days I just have to go and hit something. I suspect that was one of the reasons I took up karate; it's also a socially acceptable alternative to fratricide.

The club meets in a sports centre in the north of

Nottingham, the usual collection of empty rooms and gyms and squeaky floors. The whole place smells of sweat, swimming pool and a desperately reluctant adherence to New Year's resolutions.

I bowed to the teacher when I came in, and she nodded to show that she'd seen me. That's all I normally get from her – she's short and solid with cropped hair and a smile that would melt the heart of a statue.

Amin was already there, but Josh wasn't. As we did our warm-up I wondered out loud, "Where is he?"

"He said he wasn't coming."

"That sounds like it should have the word 'tonight' attached to it, but hasn't."

"I don't think that he was just talking about tonight."

"He's quit? Changed clubs?"

"I don't think that he finds it easy to be around you."

"Oh, for… sake. What's his problem?"

"He told me that it's like it says in your Bible – 'thou shalt not suffer the witch to live'."

"Eh?" We stopped doing press-ups and started stretching our hamstrings, which is always a bit of a trial. "Josh isn't a God-botherer. Why does he care what the Bible says?"

"I don't know. If I were a strict observer I would have to say the same. Such practices are condemned by God, although the Book also says you cannot harm anyone with them unless God wills it so."

"That's confusing."

He laughed. "It's religion, mate; it's supposed to be confusing for us mere mortals."

I nodded. This was something of a trope with us. "Yeah. And once the chief magician has put on his costume and cast his opening incantation, we are obliged to sit in awe of his majesty while he divulges the secrets hidden in his book of wonders…"

"And spouts a load of divisive bullshit," a voice behind us interjected. It was *sensei*, the teacher. "Time to stop your intellectual discussion and kick things."

"Happily," I replied. Amin and I are at the front of the class, so *sensei* uses us a lot to demonstrate techniques. It can hurt, but she's extremely good and I've learned a lot about placing kicks by tracking the pattern of bruises that she leaves on me.

We stopped for a drink after an hour or so. In between gasps Amin gulped water. "Josh is really uncomfortable about this," he said, after several goes.

"I get that. Why aren't you?"

"Mate, I've known you since you could only head-butt your dad in the knee. You may have developed some weird skills recently but you're still a prat, so who cares?"

"Yeah, and I love you too." Amin is the kind of friend you really need – doesn't give a shit about what you do, unless it's seriously dodgy. Gay? No problem. Like the bagpipes? Weird but fine. Mage? Who cares. Football supporter? Well, even he has standards – the crime rate drops sharply during a home match and domestic abuse increases when the home team loses; draw your own conclusions.

My musings took us back onto the mat, and *sensei* took the greatest delight in dumping me on my backside and nearly breaking my arm to remind me to pay attention. I'm sure some of the teachers at my school would have liked to do the same. Amy maintains I have the attention span of a mayfly either because I got dropped on my head as a baby, or possibly because I didn't.

This time it was Amin who threw me into the wall, so I dismissed Josh and his redundant opinions from my mind, and went back to bashing the crap out of anyone who came in range. I felt a lot better afterwards.

It seemed that the time of the hard-light vehicles was over. The next attack was on a college building in Sussex.

I knew the place slightly, so I was upset when the pictures came up on the news. It's an old house which is used to train Healers. There were thirty people in it at the time, and almost all of them died. The news media vacillated between 'terrorist outrage' and 'unexplained blast' to 'suspected gas explosion', depending.

Whatever they ascribed it to, the destruction went up through the middle of the building, tearing a ragged cylindrical hole from cellar to roof, which caused the rest of the building to fall in on itself. It went from a rather lovely neo-Georgian house on the Downs above Brighton to a pile of bloodstained rubble in ten alarming seconds.

The only people unharmed were, ironically, the four students who were stupid enough to still smoke, because they were outside at the time.

Mages use all sorts of different places to practise their craft. Sure, most of it is done in universities – all *kemen* work is, for example – but there are other places, ones you wouldn't necessarily think of. There are a couple of apparently disused army sites where some of the more ballistic skills of the fire Talents are honed, and water Talents are known to employ some of the larger RNLI bases. A lot of work is done at the end of the pier at Bembridge on the Isle of Wight, at Wells in Norfolk and at the Old Fort that overlooks the Port of Shoreham in Sussex. There is also talk of a small corner of the naval base at Faslane that is subject to mysterious lights and a lot of damp swearing.

Healers, naturally, infest almost every hospital in the country, whereas air Talents tend to go for big open spaces, and we're back to disused military bases again, although this time it's airfields, and they apparently have their own suite of offices in the Met Office complex in Exeter.

Earth Talents biggest training areas are the north end of the Welsh Marches near Oswestry, the North Downs around Box Hill – look for a field studies centre that never seems to host school parties – and a big chunk of Lincolnshire.

*

Professor Weaver was grave when I met him at college an hour or so after news from Sussex came through. "This is most unfortunate," he said, adding a suppressed cough. "So many dead." He looked upset, and I wondered if someone he knew had been in the building. "It was not a bomb, nor a 'gas explosion'," he added in a tone of acerbic disgust.

"Are you sure?" He looked at me sternly. "As in, what is it that makes you certain of that?"

He sniffed, which for Weaver means the grudging acceptance of an apology. "The first reports by the witnesses mentioned 'a column' rising through the structure, but nobody mentioned fire."

"Oh."

"I believe it is a variation, rather than an aspect of, the spell *Kendu*." I frowned. *Kendu* means 'remove'. It's normally part of other spells, like '*Kendu-Ura*', literally 'remove water', which water Talents use to extract water from somewhere or something. *Kendu-Suta* is the same for fire; it puts out fires by picking up all the flames and so forth and shifting them away from the source of fuel. It's actually much more complicated than that, as Jerry reminds me every time I cock something up while he's training me. I queried this. Several other people were listening now, and Weaver's tone became more didactic.

"At a sufficiently advanced level, *Kendu* is generic. With the low-level versions one has to specify what is to be… removed, but this one was applied to everything. I suspect that part of the speed of the collapse was because it removed the air too."

"It created a vacuum?"

"A partial one at least," he allowed, with a faint shrug. "However, it is a spell that requires considerable precision – not something that, for example, I would want you to use without a great deal more practice." He coughed again. "We must return to our work. The stabilisation of an emerging Talent is neither simply nor quickly achieved, although I must say that you are doing very well, thus far."

"Thank you."

He waved that away. "Oh, it's nothing that you are responsible for young man – that is the equivalent of being congratulated for having long fingers or small ears."

"Oh. Right." Charming.

That afternoon Weaver pulled his next trick for integrating my Talents, which was to pretty much reboot my brain. Unfortunately, part of the process didn't go very well. He had conceded that it was 'potentially a little dangerous', so Alex Tahy, the head of the Healers, sent *Jaun* 2 Healer Bo Hinxman along to make sure I didn't dissolve or turn into a seagull or something. Weaver was not pleased that he was there, and Bo was equally unhappy with the way Weaver was going about it.

I'd got to the stage of having the whirlies – like when you get drunk and you open your eyes and the light switch skids to a halt – when what amounted to a blazing row, conducted with venomous politeness and toxic courtesy, broke out.

"Professor, I ain't so sure that's the safest way to go along with this," said Bo, laying his hand on my shoulder. The sudden silence in the steel and wood workroom was startling.

"Young man," Weaver replied acerbically, "I have been dealing with this sort of thing for longer than you have been breathing. I know what I am doing."

"I ain't so certain you got it right this time."

"I am unconcerned about what you 'ain't'." Weaver flipped closed the folder that he'd had open on the desk.

Bo tried again. "I'm here as a Healer, to protect Mike from taking harm. There's something about the way you're doing this that don't sit right with me."

"I have had more than thirty years' experience of this kind of thing."

"You sure it ain't one year's experience thirty times?" Bo asked, *sotto voce*. "They ain't at all the same thing."

"That is insulting," said Weaver stiffly. Bo didn't reply. "I insist that you apologise."

"You going to carry on treating Mike the same way?"

"I don't believe that it's any of your business," replied Weaver, irritated and imperious.

"I got sent here by Professor Wicks and Professor Tahy. Seems they don't have so much faith in you, if'n they send me."

"You are being insulting again."

"Only if you think I am. I ain't the least bit happy about what you're doing, and I ain't gonna let Mike get hurt just because you've made a mistake but you're too stubborn to admit it," he said tightly.

Weaver was sputtering by this point and Professor Wicks felt it at the other end of the building and intervened. She put me into Sam's care and invited Weaver and Hinxman to continue the discussion in her office, preferably at a lower volume.

Sam gave me *Indar*, coffee and a huge bacon sandwich, then sat next to me on one of the couches in the common room, holding my hand, until the confusion and nausea abated. Then Alex Tahy arrived to sort out what had happened; he was extremely unimpressed – what Weaver had been doing could easily have been fatal in just a few hours because he had bypassed the safety protocols to speed things up – hence Bo stepping in to stop everything.

Alex, whose glower can be measured in P.S.I., discovered that Weaver had become so involved in his 'discussion' with Bo that he'd also failed to close off what he'd been doing, which left me psychologically vulnerable. I know that sounds a bit poncy, a bit touchy-feely, but it's like fixing a computer and then not putting the cover back on. It doesn't necessarily mean that anything undesirable is going to occur, just that it's an awful lot easier for something bad to happen than it would have been if you'd finished the job properly.

It took about an hour for Alex to sort it out, by which time he was bloody furious and I was absolutely knackered. At the end of it, all they could do was to get Amy to take me back home and put me to bed.

Magic is inherently very tiring because all the power behind the spells comes from the mage, so it requires a lot of mental and physical stamina. We all experience that special kind of exhaustion occasionally, but now I felt like a gutted fish on a slab. I tried to make a note to talk to Professor Gowan about it, but I fell asleep too quickly, and had forgotten about it when I woke up.

14

There was an unexpected phone call the next morning. "Mr Frost? Tony Addison. Do you have a moment?"

"Yes," I replied, then realised that I had used a questioning tone that made me sound very dubious – which was fair, because I was.

"Good." I could hear a suppressed chuckle. "We need your help."

"Yes," I said again, employing the same tone. By now Amy had finished getting out all the ingredients for making a cake and had come to sit next to me. Her eyebrows signalled an enquiry, so I put him on speaker phone.

"There has been an incident that we would like you to… look into."

"An incident." By now I was very suspicious. "The last time someone said that to me it was a surprise birthday party."

"This is not a party, Mr Frost, I can assure you of that. Can you be available shortly – both of you if possible?"

"How shortly is shortly?" Amy asked.

There was a pause. "Ten minutes? There's a car on the way." He chuckled. "I think they got lost."

"Tell them to look for a much bigger wall than you'd expect and gateposts with owls on them," said Amy.

"Thank you, Miss Deerborn," said Addison. There was a silence, and I guessed that he was texting the driver. "Could be fifteen minutes – they've overshot by quite a long way."

"So what is this incident?" Amy asked as I put the baking ingredients back.

"I think it's related to that hard-light vehicle business, but it isn't the same."

"Okay, where?"

"An army training camp near Newark." I heard the crunch of a car pulling up outside. Amy looked at me and frowned – it had been barely two minutes. I walked over to the kitchen window and looked out at the gravel.

"Mr Addison, what make of car did you send?"

"Er... it's a Mondeo, dark blue. Why?"

"A Vauxhall Vectra in grey has just pulled up outside our house. The driver is just sitting there." As I gave him the index it suddenly looked awfully familiar.

After ten seconds he was back. "Don't get into it – that car was reported stolen. Someone rented it on dodgy paperwork and didn't return it."

"And now it's sitting outside our house, just when we were expecting yours. Someone's listening to what's going on."

"Shit. They must have guessed we'd send a car for you..." He trailed off. "Do I have to say 'be careful'?"

"No." I looked at Amy. She'd already blocked the car in with *Armarria*. "He's still sitting there. It's a bloody trap, isn't it?"

"Of course it is. Who's driving?"

"Er... male, Caucasian, er, probably in his twenties, maybe early thirties, dark cropped hair, clean-shaven, dark blue jacket. Not someone I know." *Or would reliably be able to recognise again*, I thought.

"OK. Don't do anything – the pickup car is now only

four minutes out and I've sent a patrol car too. Stay where you are – you'll be fine, we'll get him."

The driver slammed the car into gear and, spraying gravel from the drive like machine-gun fire, shot off down the road. The *Armarria* appeared to have no effect.

I swore. "He's gone," I told Addison. "He legged it the moment you mentioned the patrol car."

"So we have to assume your landline is compromised."

"Or yours. Anyway, he's headed down towards Linby."

"Good – the patrol car's coming from that way and there's only one road. They can deal. The pickup car is nearly with you. Blue Mondeo." He gave me the index. "The driver is not an IC1 male and they have a password – the name of the next town along from where we first met."

"Understood," I replied as we slipped on our jackets and Amy grabbed her crutches. At that moment I realised that we hadn't actually agreed to go with them. Addison was a pretty good persuader.

The car purred into the yard and a few moments later the driver knocked on the door. She was slim, quite tall and of Asian heritage.

"Hello," she said. "Constable Ishka Perera. Er… Hendon."

"Thank you, Constable," I said, and we followed her towards the car. Without thinking I pulled the door shut behind us with a gesture, and her eyes widened.

"Interesting," she said. "Most people only have those on their garage, not their front door."

Amy fielded it beautifully. "I sometimes have to use a wheelchair," she said, lifting one of her crutches slightly, "so being able to do that is very useful."

Ishka nodded and ushered us into the car. Amy elected to sit in the front, citing leg room, but I guessed she was up to something.

The journey took about an hour, and to be honest I stared

blankly out of the window for most of the time. Ishka and Amy were talking in low tones, about what I don't know, but I clearly wasn't invited.

We turned off the main road and down a narrow track to the heavily fenced perimeter of a small military base. There was a guardhouse on the right, just beyond a red and white striped barricade that would have had trouble stopping a five-year-old on a tricycle. Behind that were rows of blocky brick buildings, a parade square edged with parked cars and lines of Nissen huts where the trainees slept, usually in significant discomfort. The base was built in 1941, but if you'd told me it was 1841 I wouldn't have been the least bit surprised. It certainly smelled like it.

There were three people waiting for us – Tony Addison, Nadia Hussain and a woman in an army uniform who looked like she hadn't slept for a week. I never found out her name because everyone just called her 'The Major' or 'Ma'am'. I gathered she was the base commander and was extremely unhappy about having a bunch of civvies littering up the place. How the hell Nadia had got there so fast I had no idea. She must have a magic carpet.

"These are your civilian 'experts', are they?" The Major sounded sceptical going on scornful. She had a face like a smacked arse which was twisted with disapproval.

"Yes," said Addison placidly. The Major harrumphed. Honestly, I don't think I've ever actually heard someone harrumph before. It's an unattractive noise, like a bulldog breaking wind in a lift.

I turned to Nadia. "This had better not be another thing like that rubbish at Russell Square," I said testily.

She sniffed, rubbing her nose on the sleeve of her heavy blue waterproof. "Ow. That was, yeah, well." She shrugged. "I don't know how you found that thing."

"Did you work out what it was?"

"Oh yeah. It was a static repulsor, World War II vintage."

"What's a static repulsor when it's at home?" Amy asked as we walked slowly around the cracked roadway that circled the camp.

"They were deployed in places that were likely to get bombed. The mages of the time found that places of power put up a natural repulsion field – that's why St Paul's wasn't destroyed during the bombing – so they tried to make artificial ones. That was about as big as they could manage back then."

"But in a Tube station?"

"Russell Square is one of the deepest stations on the whole network, and lots of people sheltered there during the Blitz, even though they were initially told that they weren't allowed to. They were trying to stop it getting bombed."

"Did it work?"

"Yes. Sadly, some of the other repulsors didn't."

"So why was that one still there? Are there others still lurking around the Tube network?"

"They were supposed to have been collected after the war, but they obviously missed one."

"So why didn't anyone notice it before? That station has about 13 million passengers through it every year."

"Not sure."

"Why did it go off like that? What triggered it?"

"Don't know. Last surge before the spell faded I suppose." She didn't seem concerned.

"If we could get on," growled The Major. She wore her uniform like a costume, unlike the sergeant who walked mutely behind us, who had probably worn camouflage nappies.

The damage was to what The Major called 'the ablutions', a single block in the top right corner of the camp, pretty much backing onto the small assault course. The roof had gone, as in vanished completely. They'd found it, in fragments, two fields away, which suggested that whatever had hit the building had been fired from low down and had been aimed upwards. The walls had collapsed inwards, revealing lines of toilet stalls in one half of the building, and shattered sinks and tiled showers in the other. Water soaked the ground, but thankfully by the time we arrived the mains had been switched off. It was a mess, and would be much easier to rebuild than repair.

Viewed magically, the whole place glowed like a sunset, and I could see a furrow across the assault course grass that showed that whatever had done this had been 'fired' from the road beyond the main gate.

Nadia looked at me. "Hard-light?" For some reason we were now considered experts on all things hard-light, even though the spell was well beyond any of us.

"No," I said after a moment. I walked over to the debris and waved my hand above it, all the while being watched by curious soldiers who stood around, openly staring. God only knows what they thought we were doing.

I could feel the energy still humming in the burning hot bricks, the residuum of an abrupt, large-scale and apparently uncontrolled expenditure of spell power. It lacked any *esku*, the signature of the specific person who cast it, which was odd.

I thought about what Nadia had said about the power of a place. That was what this felt like, but with a taint of anger too. "I think this was *kemen*, raw spell power used as a weapon."

"I knew it," said Nadia under her breath.

"Is this a terrorist action?" The Major asked.

"No," I replied, my mind far away in the twists and subtleties of what was a very complex, if not complicated, use of magical energy.

"No, *ma'am*," she replied. I didn't respond to that, so she stepped closer. "I am in command of this base, and you will address me in the appropriate manner."

I had neither the attention, or the intention, to be bothered with it, or her.

"Why here?" Addison asked, ignoring the exchange. "Isolation?"

"Lots of places are isolated," said Nadia, "but most of them don't have armed guards wandering around the place twenty-four hours a day."

"Contamination," suggested Amy, who had been looking vaguely into the distance while I had been talking.

The Major, who had been equally blank, perked up. "Is this area contaminated? Do we need to evacuate?"

"No," said Amy, leaning heavily on her crutches. "It's not that kind of contamination." She looked a bit pale, which concerned me.

PC Perera walked across the parade square to reach us, pulling a great many eyes towards her. Most police officers don't look that good in uniform.

"There are no other sources of, er, that sort of power in this area, are there?" Amy asked.

Nadia paused. "Not that I know of."

"I think he wanted to test this thing, see if it worked, and to do that he needed somewhere where there would be no interference from other sources, and he was unlikely to be interrupted by anyone," she said thoughtfully. "God alone knows how much damage he would have done if it had worked properly. I think he burned it out doing this, because in the last bits of the energy transfer the wavelengths are all over the place." Nadia nodded, as if this just confirmed her perceptions.

The Major, who obviously didn't like being excluded from things, even when she had no idea what was going on, pushed her way forward. "What are you talking about?"

I looked out across the sturdy wooden assault course and the flat grey-green fields that surrounded the base. "I think the person who did this was test firing some kind of weapon. He needed to do it where he could hit a substantial building, but wouldn't be observed. There also had to be no interference with the way the weapon works; your own security kept other people away, and that gave him the isolation he needed to attack you."

"Right. And the contamination?"

I paused, trying to work out how to explain something this complicated in a way that she could understand. "It's the energy that's left after the weapon has been discharged. It will fade over time, and in the meanwhile represents no danger to anyone. It's like the… lingering smell of smoke, long after a fire has gone out."

"Left over energy?"

"Yes. It's in the debris."

"Show me," said The Major abruptly.

"How long ago did this happen?" Amy asked.

The Major glowered. "04.00 or thereabouts."

Amy lifted her hand and slowly – deliberately slowly – floated a brick from the rubble toward them. "That was more than six hours ago, and yet…" she indicated the brick.

The Major, with the strangest look on her face, reached out and grabbed it. We'd all noticed that the bricks were still almost red hot, but she seemed to have been too cross to do the same.

She dropped it immediately, muttering words that could be considered most unladylike, but seemed to be soldier-normal vocabulary. She shook her hand violently, staring at the deep burn across her palm. "Why didn't you warn me?"

"Didn't you wonder why I didn't pick it up myself?" Amy asked sweetly.

"You people are just fucking weird. Inspector?" Addison looked at her. "Do you need anything more?"

"No, thank you. I recommend you leave the rubble to cool down for a couple of days before you get it shifted. We'll look at the firing site when we leave."

"Right. Sergeant, please escort these people back to their vehicles. I'm going to see the MO."

"Yes, ma'am."

"You won't need the medical officer," I said. Although she had annoyed the fuck out of me, and I was pissed off enough to want some respect for what I could do, I still took her hand. The burns, deep and angry, were already weeping lymph and must have been agonising. Certainly her fortitude deserved some respect, if not her tact or manners. I hovered my hand over hers and poured on all the Healing energy I could. I am not a Healer, but the higher up the grades you get, the more of everything you can do. I thought I felt Nadia add some power to what I was doing, and when I removed my hand the burns were gone, the skin undamaged and flawless.

"It'll be sore for a while, and stiff for a few days, but otherwise you'll be fine."

She stared at her hand, opening and closing it slowly. "Right." She seemed to shake herself. "I must ask you to leave now."

"Of course," said Addison smoothly as she stalked off.

We found the firing site – an empty lay-by – and the shredded hedge that the energy had passed through. The uneven damage and the deep burnt gouges in the ground confirmed our suspicions that someone had managed to build a system for storing spell power, but that something had gone seriously wrong when they used it. Previously control had been stolen from the conduits, which had killed them – this was an attempt without a conduit, and it had gone badly wrong.

If they could make it work they would be a magical

superstar and, incidentally, very rich. Ishka took us home. There didn't seem to be anything else that we could do.

*

Amy and I were at home the next morning when we felt the looming and unexpected arrival of several mages. I had put up the usual shields, but they came straight through them. Fortunately, one of them was Professor Gowan, so I opened the door and invited them in. Professors Wicks was there too, plus a man I thought I vaguely recognised.

"Thank you," said Gowan, looking around with unabashed curiosity. The house, a u-shape, was essentially one huge room on this floor, partially screened at one end to make a kitchen, with toilet, utility, woodstore, garden room, larder, et cetera, built onto the back as an aesthetically clumsy afterthought. Three bedrooms, a bathroom and an office upstairs, with mostly smallish windows, thick walls and a wide, shallow staircase. I loved it, and it felt at home from the first time we came here. The longer we lived here the more interesting it became.

Amy's archaeological curiosity had kicked in quite quickly. Although she's mostly a marine archaeologist now, she started off doing everything, so she'd managed to work out some of the history of our home. It had started as a byre house over 400 years ago and had been expanded with the addition of a cob gable end, which was then replaced with stone around 200 years later. It was converted to its current configuration in the early 2000s.

Sometimes, when it's very quiet, you can almost hear the former occupants trying to be heard, trying to tell the stories of the lives that had soaked into the stones. We haven't seen any ghosts, but the whole hill is a prime site – I doubt his Earlishness, or whoever lived in the big house at the top, was too kindly a soul. He may have been, but that would have been unusual, so lots of powerful memories would have been created here. Negative memories are always harder to step away from than positive ones; there are whole family groups in the Ozark Mountains who are still offended by what Grandad Obadiah said to Cousin Jed one drunken night in 1847.

"This is nice," said Gowan, looking at the laden bookcases.

"Thank you," said Amy, easing into her special high-seated chair. We had decorated the house – well, I had, while Amy pointed out the bits I'd missed – to make it soft and warm, like a nest, a refuge. A cuddle with windows.

"To what do we owe the pleasure of this visit?" Amy asked. Nobody introduced the unknown male, so I ignored him, knowing Amy would be doing her best to work out what he was.

"The usual," said Wicks wearily. I had never seen her look so tired, almost hollowed out. Her energy levels were so low I wondered if she were ill and if I should offer her some *Indar*. I knew her *erdikide* wasn't in regular contact with her any more, so that source of support wasn't available. "We got some news about the attacks."

Amy stirred as the timer pinged and she pressed the plunger on the cafetiere. "And you couldn't have said this to us a few hours ago, when were all together at college?"

"No. We had to wait for someone to arrive." She glanced at the man. He was stocky, not very muscular, with dark sandy hair, stubble almost heavy enough to call a beard and clothing that just had to have been chosen to be nondescript. "We still got no idea why the hard-light vehicles happened, but we're certain that the residuum of the parasite in your *gogoan* contains something that will allow us to identify the attacker."

"You said this before." Several times in fact.

"No. We *thought* this before," said Wicks, "but now it's certain."

"Fine. Now what?"

"You have to learn some new spells, and we also need to have another look at that thing in your head," said Gowan.

"More? What happens if it isn't a magical attack? What if he just tries to run me over?"

Amy didn't slam the drinks on the table because that might damage the wood, but I could see the temptation. "So what are you going to do?"

"Well," said Wicks, wrapping her fingers around the mug as if to warm them. "Y'all know we set up extra defensive shields around the college, so's you'll be safe there."

"And here?"

"We're gonna do it here as well, to make your home safe."

"*Armarria*? He went straight through it."

"No. *Harrise*." I looked blank, as did Amy. By the time you get to our level you've heard of most of the spells in the repertoire, even though you can't do most of them. "It means 'stone wall'. Don't nothing get through that."

"So how do we get out of the house? Or breathe, for that matter?"

"We'll set it up so you and Amy got free passage all the time, plus Sam and Clara of course. We'll also make sure it don't block the passage of air, electricity, gas for your cooker and so on. You can make it open for others, either permanently or at need, so when you got visitors like family, they can pass through without knowing it's there." She indicated the silent man. "He's been working with Professor Weaver to create this version."

"And who is he?" Amy asked in her best supercilious and arch voice.

"You can call him Jan," said Gowan. She pronounced it 'Yan'.

"Why?"

"Because that's his name," the man replied. "Jan Cherekov, defence specialist."

I nodded, wondering if this was Central setting us up as bait again. "So what happens now?"

Amy had been listening intently while plaiting her hair. It was now as white as snow never is, so she had let it grow, hoping that the old colour would return. But it hadn't, so she wove it into ponytails and plaits and all sorts. She thought it made her look old. I thought it made her look striking. I noticed that she had gone back to her wheelchair after serving the coffee, a sure sign that she was tired or in pain.

Gowan looked at me for a moment, then her eyes flicked to Amy, registered the wheelchair and the strain on her face, and nodded faintly. "Aye, well, let's get on then. Jan here is going to put a tracery around your property and then Terry-Anne will put in the *Harrise*. Meanwhile I'll teach you – both of you – the control modifier so you can adjust it as necessary. I suggest you fully seal it around the house at all times, but leave the area directly above the house clear so you can breathe. Leave the alert version on the boundary layer."

"Alert version?"

"Sorry, should have explained," Jan apologised, without sounding the least bit apologetic. "We're going to be putting two sets of shields around the house. The inner one, just outside the walls, will be a straightforward barrier. The outer one, which I'll set at around about the distance of your gate, will have an alarm function as well. If anyone comes through it an alarm goes off and the shield immediately around the house closes fully and goes completely solid. You can release it whenever you want, of course."

I looked out of the big window at the open countryside. I felt obscurely sad that we would be actively separated from one of the main reasons that we moved here.

"Very well. Carry on."

It took hours, and I mean hours, so I had to work up lunch for everybody without any notice. The meal was surprisingly congenial, partly because eating together tends to relax people, and partly because Terry-Anne used her power to give Amy a huge jolt of a painkiller that didn't make her sleepy. This allowed her to move with comfort for the first time in weeks.

We have no illusions about this. Removing the pain does not resolve the problem, it just means you can't feel it for a while. Amy gets better day by day, a little and a little, but we suspect that short of a full bilateral hip replacement she'll still need a stick most of the time. She insists it's going to be a sword stick, but when I suggested that she should conceal a wand inside it, like Lucius Malfoy, she tickled me until I couldn't breathe properly, so I stopped.

Gowan taught me to operate the spell and, possibly without realising, how to cast it as well. After they had left I put it around the barbecue, lit it and then closed the spell. The fire died within a minute, starved of oxygen. It seemed quite effective to me.

*

Our feeling of being on high alert faded once the shields were in, which probably wasn't a very good idea, but this was when Amy and I really got to know each other. The initial excitement of being together, the careful lust that took us to our bed at the slightest hint and the unexpected joy of just doing things with your other half, sort of faded over time. It didn't vanish, but some of the urgency went out of it as the realities of a shared life overbore the unreasonable expectations.

To be a bit soppy and purple, this is when we stopped being in lust and started being in love. I'm sorry, but that's how it is. Ordinary life, with all its mundanities, irritations and routines, takes over. We found what we could compromise about, and what we wouldn't, and worked out how to live with the dissonance.

The relentless domesticity also drove back most of the worry, because nothing untoward happened to us or anyone else we knew. Well, not that's related to the hard-light vehicles anyway. Plenty of other untowardness occurred of course, including Ambrose and his brother Gideon being pulled over by the police near Haggerston Park for 'Driving under the Influence of Burundi Beat' – at least that's Ambrose's version.

Mum and dad invited us for Sunday lunch, and because Simon was at Idris' house it was very civilised – i.e. dad and I cleared up after the meal while mum and Amy gossiped in the other room.

We had a glass of port and settled down with Vivaldi and the comfy chairs.

"So, any progress on those crashes?" Dad asked as the dishwasher churned.

"None that I know of. The police haven't shut the case, but I've been in contact with one of them and he said they've given it to a small unit whose job is solving unsolvable cases, or losing them in the paperwork."

"I'd almost forgotten about them until you got that medal," said dad. "I wondered, why use vehicles at all? Why not tornadoes or sharks or giant versions of Z-list celebrities that nobody ever recognises?"

"Yes, I wondered about that myself. I mean," I went on, making a gesture so expansive that I had to throw out a quick spell to avoid spilling port on the carpet. "I mean, if he was a real train spotter he would have used a Peppercorn locomotive, or *Mallard* or *The Flying Dutchman*."

"Scotsman. Not Dutchman, Scotsman. Dutchman's an opera, or something equally noisy."

"Scotsman then. Isn't that a newspaper? Anyway, I can't think why vehicles either."

Dad paused for a moment, and I decided that coffee might be preferable to more port. Amy nudged me that she was going to lie down for a bit and no, that wasn't an invitation.

"Could it be because that was the environment that they should be in?"

"As in?"

"The train was on a railway track; the boat was on a river and so forth."

"Okay, I can see that. And?"

"Did anyone ever find out how far away they were when they first appeared?"

"I don't know."

"I just wondered if they had to pass through somewhere before they crashed. A ship on a railway line would cause alarm and consternation, but a train would go unnoticed, or at least uncommented upon, and that would give whoever made it more of a chance to get away with something like that."

"That is either an amazingly cogent observation, or so obvious that someone else must've thought of it already."

"I'll leave that with you." He smiled. "You and Amy getting on all right?"

"Very good."

"Splendid. I do like your house – what's it called again?"

"Whin Hill Farm. We love it."

"Do you plan to make it your permanent home?"

"We want to, but it depends – Amy's unlikely to find work as a marine archaeologist around here, but the uni has been making noises about getting her a job where she teaches specific courses on the subject at various universities – even before she's finished her Masters."

"Well, that's good. A university lecturer at her age. How old is she?"

"Twenty-three, near enough."

"Good." He paused. "What about you?"

"Well, I could be a kept man I suppose…"

"Hardly," he chuckled.

I smiled. "Well, you know I just had this sudden… promotion?"

"Yes. Startling, I think you said."

"Astonishing would be a better word. Fucking amazing barely covers it."

"Language."

"Sorry." *Great*, I thought, *I'm a senior mage, although I still feel like a kid with his hand in a box of fireworks, and he tells me off like I'm six years old, and I still take it.*

"So what actually happens now?"

"Well, I have to do an awful lot to be able to do everything properly."

"Properly?"

"It's like I'm juggling axes but I haven't learned how to stop. If I get it wrong, messy ain't going to be the half of it."

"A painful experience?"

"Blood and snot everywhere."

"Sometimes your terminology is a little distasteful," he grunted.

I bit my tongue. "So I'm going to be – like Amy – a senior practitioner, which is a bit like doing postgraduate studies – plus doing my MSc, of course."

"And what will you be studying, exactly?"

"The MSc's to do with how rocks and soils influence the environment, so it's got a lot of geology in it. The other thing… it's mostly going to be the same stuff but at a much higher level. Some new things of course, but…" I shrugged. We let the warmth and the music, and the port, soothe us. Five minutes later I got nudged again and eased myself out of the chair.

"Everything all right?" Dad asked, half asleep.

"Yes it's fine. Amy said she needed me."

"You know, it's rather unnerving when you do that."

"What?"

"Telepathy."

I carefully didn't laugh. "It isn't like that; you just get a feeling about what the other person is doing or thinking. There are no actual words." I stopped. I've listened to Professor Ngozi explain it to first years since I was a first year myself, and although it's been happening to me ever since I met Sam, her explanation still doesn't really explain anything. Instant transmission between two rooms in the same house is fine, but it's the same speed when Sam's in China and I'm here, which classic physics says isn't possible...

"Oh." That seemed to be the end of it, so I wandered into what had now become our room – what used to be Nonna's bedroom-cum-sitting room.

Amy was awake but horizontal, dressed in just a snug T-shirt and some skimpy knickers. Her left hip looked puffy and slightly red. And yes, I was looking at her hip. Mostly.

"How's things?"

She stretched out a hand, which pulled her T-shirt tighter across her chest and I felt a surge of desire. Okay, lust. She may not be my *erdikide* but she can still hear what I'm thinking. "Not right now."

"Okay." I sat next to her and gently rubbed her hip, but she asked me to stop until she turned on her right side, presenting me with a splendid view of her slender and lightly-clad bottom.

I put some heat into my hands and laid them on the inflamed area. As the warmth penetrated I added a little of the painkilling spell that Bev wasn't supposed to have taught me. Amy relaxed, sighing deeply as her shoulders unclenched.

"I'll give you several decades to stop doing that," she murmured.

"I love you," I said, without thinking about it.

"Good. I'd hate to think it was just me." I worked on her hip for a good ten minutes before she sighed again and rolled onto her back. "Is it going to be all right?"

"Your hip?"

"No. Us, what's happening to us, the attacks and everything."

"Nobody's gone anywhere near us for ages. We've got *Harrise* around the house, college and here. Terry-Anne has put up her own wards as well, and now they want me to go to Central again to see if they can get far enough into this thing in my *gogoan* to sort out what's happening." I don't know who I was trying to reassure.

"Will that work?"

"I have no idea. They keep thinking that they've got rid of it and then they haven't, so honestly, I don't think they do either. That may be why we've been left alone." I explained Jerry's theory. "It's a risk for whoever is going for me too – the more often they try, the greater the chances they'll be identified."

She pushed herself upright, wincing as her foot dragged against the bedding. "You understand how scary that is?"

I nodded. If I was right, it was very scary indeed. The only people who knew about the whole *gogoan* business were at Central and our college. If anyone from Central wanted to get me they'd had ample opportunity over the last several months, which meant it was almost certainly somebody at our college.

"Let's think the unthinkable," I said grimly, settling back. "It must be one of the professors – nobody else is advanced enough. Terry-Anne Wicks?"

"I don't think she's the most likely," said Amy, "but as nobody has worked out why the attacks happened, we can't rule her out."

"Gowan is more likely because of her frequent contact with me, but at the same time the least likely, because she could have killed me in all sorts of undetectable ways whenever she felt like it."

"Weaver the *kemen*?" Amy asked, drifting seamlessly into the rhetorical. "Ngozi the Flame, Denisov the Waterfall, Sigrún the Tornado? You've worked with all of them, and it almost has to be one of them. It couldn't be someone who left the college too long ago because getting into your head undetected must have been a slow and careful process." She sighed. "Plus Sigrún and Denisov are frequently away from college."

"The other conduits appeared to have been ambushed and had the parasite forced into them, but that didn't happen with me. I wonder why not?" Amy shrugged. "I'm not sure if we should go back to college at all," I said glumly, looking out at the lumpy rain that was hyphenating the view. "Maybe we should transfer to Newcastle, or Yellowknife."

"Oh, I see, fed up with me already and running after old girlfriends, is it?" I smiled. Only oblique references to ex's were allowed. "Come to bed," she said. "Just for a little while." I did, and we snoozed and cuddled until Simon came home, banged on the door and told us to stop doing whatever we were doing and come out for supper.

15

Nottingham in March isn't somewhere I'd recommend for a holiday, but I'm still quite fond of it. I am biased of course, because the city holds lots of firsts for me – first school, first kiss, first time I got beaten up, first time I caused an earth tremor because I was annoyed about something – you know, just the usual stuff.

I even like the Old Market Square, with those funny fountains and the sonorous clock and the trams humming and clanking by. I've watched archery and volleyball there, and even ridden the temporary Nottingham Eye. And today I saw a stranger get killed because of me.

I had come into town for some shopping and gone to the square simply for a break. By the time I'd done all the practical stuff and vacillated my way through several bookshops I fancied a sit down, so I perched on the lower side of the pedestrian area and looked around. People were strolling about, queueing for the trams and window shopping. I've never seen anyone buy a window because of doing that, but maybe I'm just not paying enough attention. It seemed like a normal day, an unremarkable day. I wasn't cold, or hungry. I just was, an unusual event in troubled times.

There was a disturbance off to my left, which I assumed

was a reluctant child, a drunken adult or a recalcitrant shopping trolley, and paid little attention to it. Then I heard the deep, rattily growl of a diesel engine at full chat, mashing through the gears. Heads turned, and people's glances went from curious to nervous to alarmed.

I stood up, because I knew that this wasn't what it appeared to be. The vehicle was one of those huge and pointless 4x4 Chelsea tractors, all very glossy with a radiator grille like chrome teeth. It was being massively overdriven as it bounced across the tracks, the wheels twisting and hissing, and avoided the Hucknall tram by inches. Then it mounted the pavement, heading straight for me.

I didn't put up a shield, use a spell to kill the engine or anything heroically sensible like that. Instead I froze for a moment and then legged it, just like everyone else, splashing diagonally through the fountain and heading uphill as quickly as I could.

The bloody thing followed me, crashing across the pavement, shedding bits of trim and parts of the exhaust as it went. Then one wheel caught on something architectural and I heard a metallic snap. The vehicle skidded as the driver tried to correct and failed, then spun on its front axle and set off with a jerk at 90° to the previous direction.

A few people, brave, stupid or overconfident, had stopped running and were recording the event on their phones. That meant they inevitably weren't paying attention to what was going on, so the 4x4 ploughed straight into them. One young man was still peering at the screen when the vehicle ran straight over him. He didn't make a sound, but there was a nasty crunch and suddenly the pavement was bright with blood and fragments of bone. There was no point trying to help him.

The vehicle clipped a couple of other people before bouncing to a sudden halt that had nothing to do with the brakes. Yes, that was me, finally.

The driver's door opened and an indistinct figure, probably male, jumped out and vanished from view. I don't mean he ran into the crowd – he faded away; I could sense the spell, loud and not well controlled. Then I felt another forming and threw *Harrise* around the vehicle. I was just in time.

The 4x4 caught fire, all of it, all at once. Everyone scattered but I kept the heat and the blast from the injured. Once the initial flash of fire had passed I used an earth spell to neutralise the fuel, one we normally employ to purify masses of polluted water very quickly.

The emergency services arrived, and I backed away from the scene. I was fighting the urge to scream and run until I was exhausted. I got grabbed by a copper who wanted a coherent statement from somebody with an IQ bigger than their shoe size, which I really didn't want to do.

It took fucking hours, but I was allowed to phone Amy and, during the interminable wait to tell my story to yet another person, to call Central and let them know what had happened. Once they were sure I was unhurt, all they said was 'thanks for letting us know'. Thanks for nothing.

Eventually I went home and drank rather a lot. The flashbacks were horrible, and bits of fire Talent stuff started to leak through as I lost concentration. I kept seeing Paddington and the face of the man as he died and feeling a wave of something emanating from him, being buffeted in a way I had been unaware of at the time.

I was exhausted, very frightened and barely in control, and it all conflated with the memories of Paddington until Amy had to call a doctor and I was sedated until the worst of it had passed.

*

I was called back to Central a few days later. I had spent the intervening time distracting myself by getting on with the adaptations to the house. The kitchen had to be completely rebuilt, something well beyond my meagre skills, so we had ample opportunity to check out the local pub. I can strongly recommend it.

By now Amy was pretty mobile and only needed her chair when she was very tired. We had gone for a longish walk, but that was a mistake, so she restricted herself to swimming.

Despite the improvement in Amy's health we decided between us that Clara should come and stay while Sam and I were in London. Amy would have been perfectly fine by herself, of course, but I think she wanted the company as much as anything else. Our nearest neighbours are on speed dial but, well, Clara is her *erdikide*.

I know that I sounds like I'm trying to justify not taking Amy with me; or trying to convince myself that I didn't abandon her or leave her vulnerable. It only works sometimes.

I thought that going to Central would be another great waste of time. It wasn't, if you consider giving me a headache you could break rocks with a successful outcome. Sam, who perforce had come with me, was unimpressed. "Why we come here again? You got better things to do."

"I have?" We were in the common room and the bright, interested chatter around me felt like an admonition for my lack of progress.

"Sure. Should be home shagging Amy." She laughed. So did Nadia.

I smiled, wishing that I was there with her. I missed her and all the daft little things that made her who she was. What chilled me then was the idea that because of this whole stupid business I might actually lose her.

I didn't think she would leave me, because she isn't

the type to give up without a fight, but there might come a time when the only sensible thing might be for her to be somewhere else. I might give up my life to save her, but I don't think she'd be that stupid.

It's a difficult thing to live with, knowing that someone is planning to kill you, even if the attacks are intermittent and oddly desultory. Normal life becomes a facade, unless you have a place you know is safe, and that becomes a bastion, a refuge, from the whole world. And if that fails, then you are adrift and in danger of sinking. Just the idea of being like that frightened me. I don't think I had really recovered from the thing in the town square.

Whin Hill Farm was my refuge, and although I'm not one to run away from things, all I felt at that moment was the burning desire to go home. To hide? Perhaps, but only perhaps, because half of what was screwing me up was inside my own head. And it wasn't PTSD this time.

"So, now what?"

"We are letting it be known that we have made no progress in finding any information about the fragment in your *gogoan*," said Nadia, "and that it is, in fact, slowly withering away."

"It isn't."

She sighed. "We know, that's just what we're saying."

"Fine."

"We hope that the perpetrator will think he's safe from being identified and will leave you alone," she added.

"Hope?"

Nadia shrugged. "What else is there but hope? You can't force somebody to do something if you've no idea who they are."

"Indeed." I was calming down now, and Sam let go of my hand. Then I got a nudge from Amy and a flood of love came over me, all hot.

As predicted Amy was becoming *erdikide* to my fire Talent, so my head was getting even more crowded, what with Sam and the parasite being in there as well. I sometimes felt like taking a step back and letting them operate me for a while. Mind you, I couldn't imagine Sam wanting to have sex with Amy, so maybe not. Unless I can watch. Sorry.

*

We left London the next morning, and I texted Amy to collect us from Newstead station at around 11.30. Sam was staying with us for a couple of days, because they'd been messing around with my synapses again and I'd warned Amy that Sam would be there for lunch. I wasn't the least bit surprised to discover that she'd anticipated this and that Clara intended to make something for us all. The train journey home took too long.

It was raining when we got to Newstead, but Amy wasn't there. Neither was Clara. We eventually found a taxi which dropped us by the owls. As soon as we got out I knew something was very wrong because I couldn't detect the outer *Harrise* field. I didn't know how that could be, because Cherekov and Wicks had embedded it into the fabric of the stones around the house. It wasn't just breached – it had vanished. We dumped our bags and ran.

Without finding any more shields we reached the house. It was deathly quiet; even the birds had stopped singing. The front door was ajar and I could smell something like burning meat. It took everything I had to not just charge in, calling Amy's name. I looked around to steady myself, then created *Harrise* and wrapped it around Sam. She looked startled but she took it over and poured power into it until she looked like she was embedded in ice. I beefed my own up as far as I could and then walked, as quietly as possible, up to the side of the door.

I was wrong, there was sound inside the house. Over the insistent shuffle of the wind I could hear a sort of grunting noise. The burning smell was stronger here, but even though I opened all my senses I had no feeling that the building was on fire.

Lacking the imagination to think what else I could do, I pushed open the door and walked inside.

The room was untidy, but it didn't look like it had been ransacked. I spotted a pan burning dry on the Aga and quickly lifted it off. The grunting noise changed to a snort and I turned to find Sam crouching down behind the couch. She was helping Clara, who had been lying on the floor in front of the bookcase opposite the big window. Her hair was glossy with blood.

I ran upstairs but the house was empty, as I'd known it was before I set foot in it. I walked back to the living room with leaden feet and knelt by Clara. "What happened?"

She blinked at me. "He took her."

"Who?"

"Amy."

"Yeah, I got that. Who took her?" I don't know how I remained so controlled. Paddington calm again.

"No idea." Clara lifted her hand away from the back of her head, and stared at the bright, sticky blood that coated her fingers. Sam got a clean cloth and replaced her hand on the wound.

"But it was a man," I said.

"How did you…?"

"You said 'he took her'. How long ago?"

She blinked a few times. "Um, what time is it?"

Sam glanced at the clock above the fire. "Twelve o'clock."

"I was just starting lunch so, er… quarter of an hour or

so." She was much more alert now, and the cloth that she was holding to her scalp wound had stemmed most of the bleeding. "I'm sorry, Mike, I tried, but it was like picking a fight with a bulldozer."

"Which Talent was he?"

"*Kemen*, I think. *Jaun* level." She closed her eyes.

I lowered my shield and Sam followed suit. The silence was eerie. "Call an ambulance, and the police." Sam nodded. "Clara," I held her hand, "can you still feel her?" I didn't want to ask 'is she still alive?'

"Yes, but she's very deeply asleep."

"*Lo?*"

"I don't think so. Not even *Loaren*. It feels more like anaesthesia than sleep, so more like she's been drugged." She blinked a few times. "He walked into the house…"

"Didn't the alarms go off?"

"No. They did when the postman came, so they were definitely… working." She winced. "He just… walked through the barriers like they… didn't exist."

"Then?"

"Oh, my head." She took a slow breath. "He knocked… I opened it… I was thrown back across the room. I don't think he even spoke." She paused. "Amy was in her chair – she was aching a bit – and he did something and she just slumped. I felt the spell, but it wasn't one I recognised. Then I passed out for a bit," said Clara with a huge sigh. "When I came to he was carrying her out of the door."

"Over his shoulder?"

"No, he was too skinny. He was floating her. He saw me trying to stand and grabbed that karate award of yours from the bookcase and hit me with it." She closed her eyes. "Maybe they can get fingerprints."

"Maybe." I'd been carefully not touching anything.

"Why can't I see his face?" Clara asked vaguely. I shrugged.

"He blocking you," said Sam, helping her into one of the kitchen chairs and fetching a glass of water. I looked around the room – nothing contradicted her account. I felt heat and anger rise in me, and realised that I could also feel Amy in nearly the same way that Clara does.

Her eyes flew open. "How the hell are you doing that?"

"I don't know." We'd discussed the second *erdikide* thing before. "I need to see him."

She closed her eyes and I leant into her mind. The spell *Mail-Memoria* is extremely complicated and is closely related to *Mail-Beg*, but it involves memory rather than vision. It was fuzzy, but Clara did her best to bring it into focus with me. There was no sound, but the pictures were clear enough and the *esku* was unmistakable. We broke contact just as the ambulance pulled up outside the house. Sam looked at me.

"It was Professor Weaver."

"*Shénme juéduì de húndàn. Wǒ yào sī kāi tā de xióng, bǎ tāmen wèi gěi xióngmāo.*" This was very rude about his ancestry and habits, and I couldn't have put it better myself.

16

The police arrived very quickly once they'd understood that this was a kidnapping – especially as Amy's disability makes her a vulnerable person. Only three officers came to the house, but Amy's details, including a recent photograph, had been sent to half the universe within fifteen minutes, and they attached Weaver's details as a 'person of interest'.

I don't think they felt they could rely on my viewing of Clara's memory as proof that would stand up in court, even though we told them that she'd remembered it. They took the karate award away for forensics to ponder over. I wondered if I'd ever get it back.

As is normal, we were given a family liaison officer, Detective Constable David Halsted. He gently asked a lot of questions, but not until he had reassured us that his colleagues were already searching, and that his being here was no impediment to that. I immediately liked him, a tall dark-haired man in his fifties with extremely sensible glasses and a slight Yorkshire accent. I got the idea that he believed what we told him, but knew we weren't telling him everything.

"Right then, Mr Frost, I get it. You and Miss Lee were in

London and Miss Downing was here with Miss Deerborn, keeping her company." I nodded. "And you're all students of one kind or another."

"That's right."

He was sitting at the rough oak slab that is our dining/kitchen table. He drummed his fingers for a moment. "Mr Frost, you'll not know this, but your name, and Miss Lee's, are on the police computer with a thing called a flag."

"The Blue Peter? White Ensign?"

"Jolly Roger?" Sam offered.

"The flag says to call Chief Inspector Addison in Special Operations and believe whatever he tells you, however mad it sounds."

"Right. So, you understand…" I balanced a ball of light on the tip of my finger. Although it was only the size of a sugar cube it glowed like molten glass. Anger is a form of energy, and I had a lot of it just then.

"Aye, that sort of thing. So, are you all…?"

"Mages? Yes. You can use the word 'practitioner', if it makes it easier."

"Happen I shall, Mr Frost. So, Miss Deerborn is too?"

"Yes, she's a water Talent." I had to stop at that point to explain about the Talents. Halsted's face didn't change, apart from growing slightly craggy.

"You got any idea why he took her?"

"I don't care," I replied.

"It could help to know. Might change what he does wi' her," Halsted replied. "I know about the crashes – could he just be stopping her investigating them?"

"Wouldn't help him," said Sam. "Lots of other people working on it."

"Was he trying to frighten you off? Terrorist tactics?"

"More likely," Sam replied. "He not kill Clara, maybe he can't kill."

"People died in those crashes, lots of them," Halsted pointed out.

"But he didn't kill them personally," I said. "Killing at one remove is much easier – ask the people who plant bombs and then run away."

Halsted sighed. "Anyway, can you use this… practitioner stuff to find out where she is?"

"I'd hardly be sitting here if I could, would I?" I replied without heat. "If we do a 'locator'," I carefully omitted the word 'spell' because it obviously made him uncomfortable, "then the… practitioner who has her will know we're doing it, which would be… unwise."

"Aye, fair point."

"You know who's taken her, so I presume that you're investigating his known locations?" I don't know how I remained so calm – I suspect I was nearer to numb. 'Paddington Calm', you might call it. I knew the police were far more likely to find her than I was.

As for magic, well, I couldn't think of a safe way to use it. I'd be suggesting ley lines next, something that archaeologists and mages alike are rightfully scornful of. You can get longer and more precise alignments using telephone boxes and pubs called The Red Lion, Amy told me. The thought made tears prick the corners of my eyes.

Halsted glanced at his tablet, and sighed at the frankly glacial speed of the Wi-Fi connection in the house. "Aye. Your Professor Wicks has been very helpful. Nothing so far."

The front door opened and Clara walked slowly back in. She had a big dressing on her head that made her look like a half-done mummy. She sat at the table and I squeezed her hand.

"How are you?" Halsted asked her softly. He spoke quietly most of the time, but I guessed he had a pretty good shout in there somewhere too.

"Slight concussion, nasty gash, saturating headache and a powerful urge for strong drink, which I can't have. Could I have some tea, please?"

I made tea, slowly, as the light drained from the sky. Halsted declined to stay for dinner, which was good because I would rather have stabbed myself in the foot than cook anything.

Mum came to the rescue. We had told them what had happened, so without being asked, she turned up with a chicken casserole with baked potatoes and sticky toffee pudding. I could have cried. I may well have done.

*

The next day was no better. Weaver didn't make contact, not a sound, so we… waited, while the police ran around like, well, any simile you care to think of.

I brooded, or at least that's what the police thought I was doing. Or they believed I was numb, or pissed. I didn't care. But I wasn't brooding – I was thinking.

I was thinking about what a bastard Weaver was. I was thinking about what I would like to do to him when I caught up with him. I was thinking that him behind all this didn't explain almost anything that had happened.

I was wondering where he'd taken Amy. I was wondering *why* he'd taken Amy, and if he had hurt her. After about ten seconds, I knew why he'd taken her. He'd done it so he could get to me, because he knew I was the sort of dumb fuck who would sacrifice himself to save a person he loved. Not that I intended to, of course. On the whole, I thought, if anyone was going to get killed, it was going to be Weaver.

Once I'd started thinking a bit more clearly it took me less than a minute to realise that really didn't make sense as a motive – in fact almost none of it made sense, least of all why he would expose himself now.

Weaver had organised the hard-light attacks, for God alone knows what reason. Because of what he thought was the power I was getting from Sam, he'd used me three times without managing to kill me. But, by malign coincidence, Richard Slater had managed to seal his nasty little parasite in my *gogoan*.

Fearing that it could reveal his identity he had tried to kill me again, twice, but the attempts had seemed unconvincing, half-hearted even. Maybe he only did it when he thought we were getting close to finding out. That was another question I was going to ask him, just before I ripped his heart out.

Then he took Amy, but in a way that almost guaranteed that he would be identified. That didn't make sense either. Only killing Clara would have prevented it, but maybe he hadn't known she was there, or hadn't had the guts to kill her when he found out. Maybe the blow to the head was supposed to finish her off, although why he didn't stop to make sure… or maybe I just had no fucking clue what was going on. I was getting a headache again.

"Him *húndàn*," – a bastard – was Sam's considered opinion. "We find him."

"He can wait – we find Amy first."

"Find Amy, find him."

"Probably not. He'll know we'll have lots of help. My guess is that he'll stash her somewhere and then leave, so even if we do manage to find her, we won't find him."

"Sounds reasonable," said Clara. She looked thoughtful for a moment. "So we have to focus on finding Amy. I have a slight idea about that – let me think about it for a bit." Sam and I had done some amateurish Healing on her head wound, and she was looking much better.

"OK. We know Amy won't be lying around waiting to be

rescued either. If she can't get herself free she'll be doing her best to make it easier for us to find her."

"How you think she do that?"

"Well, anything from sending out a beacon in *kemen*, making the building glow in the dark, setting it on fire or, knowing her, knocking it down with a wall of water."

"If she's conscious," Clara said carefully. "I'd know if she... wasn't with us anymore, but even though I can feel her, I get absolutely no response."

"Shielded or unconscious?"

"Unconscious, very, very far down, much further than just sleeping. If I had to put a word to it, I would say comatose."

"Shit." I remembered Melita and her chums talking about the person who was trying to find us in Malta. "Clara, can you do a track and trace and get a rough direction for her?"

"No problem."

Sam got out a large-scale OS map. Clara turned slowly on the spot, her hand extended. The pirouette was more mechanical than balletic, and I was glad that Halsted and PC Perera, who was the other family liaison officer, had absented themselves. It being a Sunday, the DCI in charge had been making noises about the overtime bill.

As she was looking for her *erdikide*, I had hoped that Clara would be able to do more than an ordinary 'track and trace' and give us an exact location, but she couldn't. It's a bit like the military – the higher the rank, the bigger the pointer they use: a General will indicate a battlefront with a sweep of his hand; a Major will use the blunt end of a pencil to specify a line of attack; a Lieutenant will show which side of the trees to go around with the tip of a blade of grass. By that standard Clara was at least a Colonel.

That said, it was solidly south-south-east, heading in the direction of eastern Leicestershire. Or Corby, or Bedford, or possibly even Milton Keynes. And at a stretch it could even be Ilford or Hastings. I hoped that it didn't cross the Channel, because by then the width of the arc she was indicating was well over a thousand miles and probably contained more than ten million people.

Sam quickly marked the wedge on the map. We are taught to do this from the middle of the second year at college – 'track and trace' is a big part of what we do in the public domain, even though you've probably never heard of it. We stared at it.

"We'd have to go to bloody Plymouth to triangulate on that," said Clara, "and we'd still have an area the size of Derbyshire to search – even if he doesn't move her in the meantime. I really can't get close enough." She went on. "We need some help."

She looked at the map, tracing the countryside with her finger and stopping not far from Corby. She looked away, one of those distant moments when you know that somebody is making a really, really big decision that you know nothing about. "I should have done this a long time ago. We need to go to Rockingham."

*

We had been in the car for nearly half an hour before Clara would tell us even vaguely why she had made what was, apparently, a very important decision. "Have you visited the castle at Rockingham?"

"No." I glanced at her. She's normally quite lively, and prone to a big white smile in a dark face, but now she looked like she was carved from obsidian.

"There's power at the castle like you wouldn't believe. The people who can see spirit animals say it's a dragon – funny how they always see eagles and tigers and never stuff like slugs or weasels. Anyway, aura readers see the entire castle pouring out golden light like a volcano. Some days birds will change direction rather than fly over it. I've seen clouds change direction rather than fly over it." She paused. "You told me what that place in York was like, how strong it made you feel. Rockingham Castle makes that look like a firefly in a jam jar."

"Then why don't we all know about this? Why aren't we taught about it?"

"Some people get nothing when they go there. In the big serious ones, like St Paul's and that one in York, everyone gets a boost. In places like this, fire Talents and earth Talents get it in spades, *kemen* get a little but otherwise – nothing. So they call it an 'unreliable source'."

I nodded. "Those I've heard of." We wound through the countryside on a steady switchback of a road. "So how do you know about it?"

"We came to this country when I was not quite three, and I was brought up in Corby." Her mum is the head of radiology at the local hospital. "I used to have a summer job in the teashop at the castle. One day I was clearing up after we'd closed and I felt the need to go outside. There's this little sward just beyond the entrance and I kept walking until I was standing on it. No idea why. When the power hit me I was literally pulled to the ground. I was about sixteen and I'd never heard of magic outside of Hogwarts and Narnia. I woke up half an hour later when one of the groundsmen found me. He thought I'd been attacked. Then some other person, a woman, came over, said that she understood what had happened to me and that she would send someone to see me."

"Who was she?"

"I never found out, but the groundsman didn't know her. The college contacted me three days later. It was Professor Ngozi who came – mum was well impressed that

I warranted a professor." She fell silent and her eyes came back to the present.

We drove on in peace until we crossed the long causeway over the River Welland from Caldecott to Rockingham, then climbed steeply through the village to the castle entrance. It was closed to the public that day, but we pulled off the road into the drive anyway. In the medium distance the castle sat nestled in the landscape, a broad, not very high and extremely old building of pale stone set amidst impressive grounds that dropped sharply towards the river valley. It looked beautiful and I was sure that Amy, with her archaeological head on, would have been fascinated. I decided I would bring her here as soon as I could. I felt that there was power here, even when we climbed out of the car, but nothing like the great beast of a thing that Clara had suggested. Sam clearly felt nothing, but Clara was so silent, so absorbed, that it was hard to attract her attention.

"Can you feel it?" Her voice was soft and abstracted.

I couldn't, and I was about to say so when the Dragon came over for a look. Magic is not sentient any more than the wind is, but we all know the feeling that it gets stronger the moment you try to open a map or fold a picnic blanket. It was like that, in the same way that being hit by a snowball is like being hit by a hand grenade.

"Bloody hell," I said in a desperate whisper. It was all I could manage.

Clara laughed, a brittle sound that echoed inside my head like crystal glass shattering. "Amazing, isn't it?"

I couldn't reply. I didn't have the words to describe what was happening – it was like I'd stuck my finger into the mains socket for the universe. My vision blurred and pulsed. I sagged back against the side of the car and slid to the ground, struggling to take a breath. Clara laughed again. Sam looked anxious.

"You hurt?"

"He's fine," said Clara, lifting her hands towards the sky in a supplicant gesture.

"Why here?" Well, that's what I tried to say; it probably came out like the first line of the Magna Carta in Maori, or possibly hamster. Clara understood me anyway.

"There are places of extraordinary power like this, but only a few." She was almost purring. "Lindisfarne, one near Stirling, Southall, near Yeovil, Canterbury Cathedral."

I couldn't speak; I felt light-headed, like my brain was full of helium or I'd been smoking some seriously funny cigarettes. I felt we shouldn't be here; we were supposed to be searching for Amy and that bastard Weaver, but we'd come here instead. But there was no way that I could feel that this was wrong, that we shouldn't be doing it. It felt... extraordinary, exhilarating. I know that cars were passing us all the time and the air smelled of petrol fumes, but it was as if we were in a bubble.

This mattered, far more than anything else I could think of in the last, say, ten years. This is what it's like to be in full possession of your powers. This is why most people are frightened of mages, and are frightened of magic, and why we choose to hide. It is a terrifying beauty, and I revelled in it.

I felt my *gogoan* being ablated, and at the same time I was burning. Every nerve was firing, every synapse sparking, sensations so strong that they bordered on pain. I didn't ever want it to stop, but I wasn't sure how much longer it could go on, how much more I could bear.

And then it did stop. Just like that. The Dragon had turned away, and the chill spring air made me shiver. My trousers were cold and wet from where I'd been sitting on the ground, and I was shaking.

Sam helped me up. "You okay? You not look okay. You look... I not know. Odd."

"I'm fine," I replied shakily, taking her hand. Something of it passed to her in that moment, because she clenched my fingers and stared at me, wide-eyed. I felt alive, alert and hard enough to spit nails through a wall. "Clara, did you know this would happen?"

"What?" I think she was still communing with the Dragon, because she seemed very distracted.

"Did you know that this would happen to me?"

She seemed to focus slightly. "No. I did wonder, but you're a big boy, so I thought you could cope."

"Thanks. You know what it's done, but it's also opened the parasite a bit. I know why we couldn't make sense of how Weaver was doing all this."

"How?"

"Because he hasn't been working alone. The *esku* of the person who went for me in London isn't Weaver's. He may have set the parasite, but someone else carried out the attacks. I don't know who."

Clara nodded, but she wasn't really listening.

"I found her," she said matter-of-factly. "I needed the boost from the Dragon to be able to do it properly." She giggled. "A locator without using the spell."

"How?"

"I set the earth searching for her."

I digested that for a moment. "Where is she?"

"Near Burrough Hill. It's a multivallate Iron Age promontory fort on the edge of Rutland."

"Another place of power?"

"Nah, it's just a sodding great hill."

We left, stopping only once on the twenty-mile journey to fill up with petrol – a mage can make an awful lot of things, but not miracle-powered cars.

*

236

We called Nadia and Dave Halsted as soon as we hit the road. We were more than capable of looking after ourselves, even if we did look like a poster for a diversity initiative, but we needed backup, so the police were the people to go to. There's being self-sufficient and heroic, and then there's being stupid about it. Clara got more accurate as we got closer; Amy was no longer near Burrough Hill, she was now actually on it.

I made sure we got to the hill first. There is a soggy car park on a bend in the road, some wet grass, a toilet block and mud, lots and lots of sticky mud. Did Weaver know we'd find her this quickly?

We didn't care. If we were being decoyed here, why? Was it to put us where we could be attacked, or to get us away from somewhere else? Flip a coin. At that moment, I didn't give a flying fuck.

We ran past the farm up the half-mile-long, foot-sucking path to the hill fort. It stands out over the east Leicestershire countryside like a pointing finger, surrounded by at least two layers of bank and ditch, which are still huge, more than three metres high. The vertical drop to the plain below is the best part of thirty-five metres. On the ramparts you feel like you're flying.

Wrapped in *Harrise* I ran through the forty-five-metre-long entranceway and into the vast, empty interior as the others circled the ramparts. There was no sign of Amy on the rough, flat grass inside, but we didn't have to search the whole twelve acres because now even I could sense her. I pointed to the far side and Clara ran towards it. Once we joined up she and I walked forwards, closing in on the location. Sam came in from the other direction and we stepped down over the edge. The wind was swirling from the huge sky, a storm poised to strike, and I knew Sam was stopping it, at least for now. The furze grabbed, but we ignored it. I'm sure the views were magnificent, but I didn't see them.

We found her bundled up in the bottom of one of the folds of ground that make up the outer edge of the rampart. She was wrapped in a stained and torn blanket that had a distinctive and particular odour to it. She was unconscious and unresponsive, deathly cold, still dressed in the jeans and shirt that she had been wearing three days earlier.

Sam called Halsted again as Clara pumped *Indar* into her and I warmed her up and wrapped her in my jacket. I was near to tears, but lack of visible injury, the regularity of her pulse and the evenness of her breathing gave me hope.

Then the police arrived with first aid and thermal blankets, and less than fifteen minutes after that there was the glorious sight of the air ambulance. The blue and yellow miracle workers landed in the centre of the fort and disgorged a doctor, a stretcher and heat packs. They said that Amy hadn't been here very long, which suggested that Weaver had somehow detected Clara locating her. And that meant we had been lured here. Clara went in the helicopter and Sam drove while I made lots of phone calls.

*

The hospital was just another hospital, full of people who needed help and people dedicated to helping them, whatever shit they got handed by governments or managers or any other fucker who knows all about performance targets and penny-pinching and doesn't give a damn about the scared, the sick, the desperate and the dying.

Amy was asleep when we arrived, with Clara dozing next to her. She stirred when we came into the room, blinking at us, and then smiled.

"She'll be fine. Mild exposure and slight dehydration. They

238

don't think she'd been there very long – possibly only a couple of hours. They said she was drugged when she was taken, and they think she's just coming out of it now. She wasn't drugged," she added. "I called Nadia. She said it was probably a spell that Healers use called *Lasai*, which reduces neural activity to maintenance functions only while it's active. Very advanced and quite obscure, but well within Weaver's abilities."

"Was she hurt…" I swallowed. This was a difficult question, "… in any way?"

"One injury, but otherwise no."

"Injury?"

"She's partially dislocated her right hip."

"Oh shit, not again." I unclenched my teeth. That was not nice, but it was at least familiar territory.

"I suspect it happened when he took her," said Clara. "I don't suppose he supported her fully when he started to float her out of the house."

I sat next to Amy and took her hand. Her skin was cold and dry and a little rough, and I knew that I would have to bring some of her hand cream from home on my next visit. Or get sent to the hospital shop to buy some when I forgot. I'm good at that.

I felt her hand move slightly and then tighten the tiniest fraction on mine. She was only just waking up so she didn't open her eyes, but I think she knew I was there. Sam and Clara left, and I stayed for an hour. Amy became a little more alert as each minute passed.

Clara, influenced by Amy's condition and exhausted by her encounter with the Dragon, had been sent home to sleep, so Sam had driven her. Amy was not expected to wake fully for several hours so I was told that I should go too, but I couldn't. They insisted that I leave the room when they had to do something medical and aimed me at the restaurant.

I headed that way but, when I reached the distant

reception area, I found that Dave Halsted had been waiting for me. I sat next to him on the ragged benches, but we didn't speak for some moments.

Eventually I told him of my belief that Weaver hadn't been working alone, and he passed it on to Addison. I shifted in my seat and he looked at me anxiously. I suddenly felt another Talent in the area. Then I saw Jan Cherekov, the person who had helped Professor Wicks to put up the barriers on our house, presumably here to take up bodyguard duties on Amy. I relaxed a tiny bit.

"At least she's safe," said Halsted as Cherekov circled the crowded car park outside, looking for a parking space.

"For now."

"Aye. We checked your house, by the by. Nobody's got into it, or even tried, as far as we could see. Happen you'll have some special way of looking?"

"We do. I'll see what it comes up with. Any sign of Weaver?"

"No. He's upped and vanished. We're doing all the usual things to confirm he did it – might be handy when it comes to court."

I grunted. This going to court was only a remote possibility, and wasn't something that I was especially concerned about. "But no clue yet."

He shrugged. "None of your colleagues in Nottingham has any idea and they're sending a specialist up from London to help with the search."

"Who did you speak to?"

"A Miss Hussain. She any good?" I explained just exactly who and what Nadia was. "My word," said David. "To think we had all this going on and I never knew about it." He shook his head.

I smiled. "Are you aware of the existence of the Hammond Organ Appreciation Society? That there is a Pencil Museum in Cumbria, a Pen Museum in Birmingham and a Shell

Grotto in Margate, which is lined with 4.5 million seashells, but nobody knows who made it or when?"

"Well: no, thank God; yes, I've been there, no and really? in that order." He chuckled. "I suspect the difference is that they couldn't set fire to my shoelaces just by thinking about it." By now Cherekov had found a distant parking space and, raising his hand to us, walked into the building.

There was a placidity about Halsted that couldn't help but calm things down, yet I was still anxious. "Are you sure she's safe?"

He shrugged. "She's on a closed ward with restricted access, in a side room, with a nurse monitoring her and a bodyguard outside the door," he gestured at Cherekov's retreating back. "What?"

I went cold. "Did you ask for a bodyguard for her?"

"No."

"Mr Halsted, do you think you could go and stand outside Amy's door for a moment?"

He stood up. "Yes, of course. Why?"

"I'm not sure about a bodyguard – nobody told me she was to have one."

He went, moving with surprising speed for someone of his comfortable bulk. I grabbed my phone and called Wicks. Professor Ngozi was there too, so she put in on speaker.

"What's wrong?" They asked in virtual unison.

"Amy's in hospital and is going to be fine. I need to know if you've sent someone to watch her, like a bodyguard or something."

"I ain't sent anyone yet, Mike," said Wicks. "I guessed you'd be staying with her a while, and I'd send someone along when you needed to leave. Who's there?"

"Jan Cherekov. He just walked into the hospital and headed for Amy's room." I started towards the ward entrance.

"She okay?"

"I sent a policeman down there. Who the hell is Cherekov, anyway?"

"No idea," said Wicks.

"Please give me a moment and I'll check the database," said Ngozi. I could hear her typing rapidly in the background as I waited impatiently for the lift.

"Weaver brought him in," said Wicks, her voice grey and cold. "To help with the security on your house and the college."

"I remember. Do you know where Weaver found him?"

"I assumed he already knew him from someplace – least, that's how it seemed; they were talking like they'd known each other for a real long time."

"That was before we knew Weaver was behind all this shit."

"Yeah." Wicks had no reason to sound embarrassed, but she still did. "Nobody thought to question it – Weaver's been here for ages and we ain't never had the least hint of him being untruthful or anything else."

"Nicely hidden in plain sight. I wonder what their connection actually is?"

"*Erdikide*," said Ngozi suddenly. "They're *erdikide*."

"Ah shit," said Wicks. "So this is a joint project."

"I have to go," I said hurriedly, reaching the ward entrance. A nurse frowned and pointed to a 'no mobile phones' sign. I nodded. "I just have to make sure that Amy and the policeman are safe." I killed the call and started to sprint.

Why the hell am I doing this? I thought. *Why is it me that's having to do this? Why aren't there magic policemen with batons a mile long and remotely castable handcuffs?*

OK, not the most coherent thoughts but when someone you love is in danger you don't really think all that clearly. Well, maybe if you're a Vulcan or something, but not me. I skidded on the nicely polished floor, earning a glare from several people, then headed towards Amy's room.

I wish I could say I had a premonition of trouble, but I didn't. It was just plain ordinary fear, fear that became horribly real when I saw a pair of legs on the floor that could only belong to DC Halsted. Fortunately, they were still attached.

He was lying across the open door. I didn't stop to check him but leapt over him and into the room. I had no idea what I'd see, how Cherekov had killed Amy – because I was sickeningly certain that was what I would find.

Amy was, however, awake and sitting up, her face drawn in lines of effort, and I could see she was heavily favouring her right side.

"Where is he?"

She pointed to the floor beyond the bed. Cherekov was kneeling there, choking, surrounded by blood-tinged liquid. He would vomit up a huge quantity of water, gasp in a couple of breaths, and then the water would start to trickle from his mouth again. I looked at Amy, nodded, and the purple glow faded as she stopped pouring water into his windpipe. He was bent over, still on his knees, and heaved water onto the floor, gasping like a man drowning.

No longer fighting for air, he turned to Amy and raised his hand, so I stepped around the bed and hit him.

I've been doing karate since I was eight. Although I rarely win competitions and I have more respect for my hands than to even try breaking bricks, I can punch. I hit him on the side of the neck with all the force that my anger and fear could create. My technique wasn't perfect but my fist landed just on the corner of his jaw. His head snapped sideways and slammed into the radiator, leaving a trail of blood as he slumped. It would be unheroic to mention just how much my hand hurt, but it was a lot.

I wondered for a second if I'd killed him, decided after another second that I didn't give a toss if I had, and stepped over to Amy.

"OK?"

"Better now."

I looked at Cherekov, lying inert on the floor. "I have to…" I gestured to Halsted. She nodded and reached for the emergency bell.

I bent over him and was relieved to find him breathing. I checked him for visible blood and had just decided not to do anything more, seeing as how we were in a building stuffed to the gunwales with medical professionals, when I heard a noise behind me.

I glanced over my shoulder to see Cherekov, who seemed to have extraordinary stamina, lurch to his knees and raise his hand towards me. I could see trickles of lightning flashing between his fingers, like the Emperor in Star Wars. I thought that *Harrise* might stop the first bolt from killing me straight away, but beyond that I had no idea. He gathered a ball of power in his hand, drew his arm back and made to throw it at me.

I tried to counter with a stun, but at that moment Amy, standing on her good leg and displaying a swing that would have made the average baseball coach weep with joy, hit him with one of her crutches.

I heard the noise of his cheekbone breaking from across the room, and watched him crumple to the floor as if she'd removed all his bones at once.

"Nice shot," I said, then turned back to the running medical feet. I looked at the doctor who was leading the posse and I pointed to Dave Halsted. "This man is breathing but unconscious. No obvious injury, don't know how he came to be knocked out, but he's been out for around three minutes." The doctor nodded. I pointed to Cherekov, who looked angry even when unconscious with half his face broken.

"He attacked this police officer, and then my fiancée."

This came from nowhere and still holds the Nottingham college's award for the Most Bizarre Marriage Proposal Ever Recorded.

"He's been punched on the side of the head," I indicated the corner of my jaw, "and then hit in the face with a crutch. He's dangerous and wanted by the authorities, even before he tried to kill Amy."

The doctor blinked. "Thank you." He turned to Amy. "And how are you?" I flushed. I hadn't thought to ask. Amy is all right because I've saved her.

"I think my bloody hip's gone again," she said, and two nurses helped her back onto the bed. She was looking quite grey by this point.

"Thank you for your help; you can leave it with us now," said the doctor. Someone more switched on than me had already called for help in detail, and soon there were gurneys for Cherekov and Halsted, police officers with guns for the former and another officer – PC Perera, who somehow always seemed to be around – with the latter.

Amy vanished with the doctor and a couple of nurses, and I was left standing in the room, alone apart from one nurse who was watching me massage my hand – which still hurt like fuck – and a familiar face: Chief Inspector Addison, Special Investigations, Very Senior Officer and nascent mage.

"Let me look at that," said the nurse. I'm clearly not up on medical jargon because I hadn't realised that 'let me look at that' means 'allow me to practise my torture techniques on you'. I promise I didn't swear, well, not out loud anyway. "X-ray," said the nurse firmly. "You can speak to him later," she said to Addison.

"I'll wait," he said as we vanished down the corridor.

17

He did wait, and in fact he waited two days before I could be bothered to talk to him. Amy was supposed to have been under his protection, and the only reason she was still alive was because of the things we did ourselves.

During that time she also quietly moved her ring onto her left hand. It may have been a very strange way to make it happen, but we were engaged and that, at least, made me smile.

We ended up sitting in another meeting room, thankfully in Nottingham this time. It was frustrating listening to Nadia telling me what we'd done. With difficulty I refrained from tersely pointing out that I knew all about it because I'd been there.

"As a defensive strategy it was very effective," she said. "He couldn't cast because he was on the edge of drowning, and when that stopped he was all geared up for another attack and you hit him. Inspired." I nodded. My hand wasn't broken, but it still bloody hurt. "And then you," she nodded to Amy, "administered the *coup de grâce*."

"All of which has been deemed as self-defence," said Addison.

"So what is Cherekov saying?" Amy asked. She was in

pain, and in her wheelchair again, and looking mightily pissed off, despite large quantities of industrial strength analgesia.

"Nothing. Not a single word in fact. You hit him… rather hard," Addison said drily.

"I do apologise," said Amy, with a smile that would have unnerved a Great White Shark. "Next time I'm preventing my fiancé getting killed I'll display more consideration. Hitting a murderer with a metal pole while standing on one leg is not as exact a science as you seem to think."

"Any more clues about the whole thing?" I asked hastily, before Amy could go off on one. Pain can make anyone tetchy.

"No," said Nadia, "although I do believe that Mr Addison might be able to help on that front."

"Yes, indeed I might," he replied. "We've been looking at the mute Mr Cherekov and what he's been up to. It's been quite illustrative. Fire Talent, *Jaun* 3, stopped active training ten years ago, went to eastern Germany and vanished. He left there three years ago and came back to the UK – the passport office confirmed that. We've found no record of any gainful employment, bank account or social security claim, but we know that he lived less than five miles from your Professor Weaver." He paused. "We have *unofficially* noticed that Weaver's bank account had significantly larger monthly withdrawals after Cherekov came back, so we surmise that Weaver must have been financing him."

"Makes sense," said Nadia. She made to say something else, but Addison, with the courage of the ignorant, talked right over her.

"Now it comes down to what these two have actually been doing."

"Weaver's been teaching and doing research at the college," said Wicks. She sounded puzzled.

"Full-time?"

"Not really. Ain't nobody really full-time. We all teach, but we also do a whole lot of research. That often requires us to be someplace else. Unless it's real important, or has an impact on what they're doing at the college, we don't ask for details. Their business."

"Not even by way of conversation?"

"Oh yeah, in a general sense, of course, chatting over lunch," Terry-Anne shrugged. "But success ain't no way guaranteed, so folk tend to be a mite vague, leastways until they're sure whatever it is has worked. We're just as prone to embarrassing foul-ups as everybody else."

"Hmm. Anyway, Professor Weaver becoming of interest has obliged us to circumvent the metaphysical and look at the extremely mundane, like ANPR." That's Automatic Number Plate Recognition, in case you were wondering. "And because he's implicated in all these crashes I now have Superintendents and Chief Constables watching and making... helpful suggestions," he finished wryly.

"How delightful for you," said Amy, deadpan.

Addison chuckled. "The upside of all the scrutiny is that I do have a lot more resources available now." He indicated the playing-card fan of papers on the big shiny table we were all sitting around.

"And stripped of the narrative and the implied smugness?" Amy again.

"We know where he's been going. And we have good reason to suspect that Cherekov's been there too."

"Where?"

"One moment. Have any of you checked to see if any of your – our – people were caught up in these crashes?"

Nadia and Terry-Anne looked at each other. "Of course."

"All of them?"

"Oh," said Nadia. "Not all of them, no." She turned to Wicks. "No."

"Thought not."

"You're doing smug again," warned Amy.

"Sorry," said Addison, without the least sign of sorrow. "There was at least one *Jaun*-level *kemen* Talent killed in each crash." He handed his pad over to Nadia.

We looked at the list – one at Paddington, one in York, one in Bristol, a couple on the Isle of Wight ferry, fuck knows how many in Sussex.

"Oh." She glared at Addison. "How did you know? Have you hacked our records?"

"Wouldn't know how."

Oh, yes you would, I thought. While he'd been looking at crashes, I'd been looking at him. Psychology graduate, probation in Manchester, CID immediately, rose to Chief Inspector indecently fast. Addison was the sort of bloke who just got stuff done without making any fuss about it, despite being a bit of a plonker. This makes him good as an ally, but a nightmare as an enemy.

"I found out by asking the people they worked with. Once I'd done the light trick that Mr Frost so helpfully showed me, they had no hesitation in discussing things with me. But this is as far as I can get, as I don't have access to their work."

"Fine," said Nadia impatiently, "we'll find the connection. Where have Weaver and Cherekov been working?"

"Ever heard of Somerby Court?" They looked blank.

"I have," I said. "It's a light industrial and office site about a mile from where we found Amy."

"Correct. He's been working in one of the units there. I suspect that's where he er… kept you."

"I don't suppose there's any chance he's there now?" Amy asked.

"No. We've had the unit under surveillance since we identified it, and it's dark and there's no heating on, plus there's no record of any movement." I thought about

Central and the illusion of the BT office that it presented to the world, but I kept it to myself.

"So we'll keep on searching," said Addison, "while you involve yourselves in finding out the connection between Weaver and these others. Do you have any questions I can help you with?"

"Yes," I said, abruptly, remembering something. The others looked at me with surprise. "With all the hard-light vehicles, did you find out where they first appeared?"

"First appeared?"

"The train at Paddington didn't flash into existence ten feet before the buffers, did it? So, it must've been created somewhere further up the line, mustn't it?"

"Yes," he replied, drawling cautiously.

"Same with the boats and stuff, right?" I paused. "So if we can find out where they were created, then maybe we can gain some more information about them."

"But we know who did it," Wicks protested.

"But not why. Ask yourself this – how were they able to ensure that me and the other poor bastards they used as conduits were in the right place to spawn the attacks? It's not an issue if they were on home turf, like me and the truck in Leicester, but the next time I was in York. So how did Weaver make sure the person he wanted to use was in the right place to get caught?"

"He's gotta be setting them up," said Wicks. "Now that's just plain nasty."

"What was the inducement to the *kemen* who died? How did he persuade them, or compel them, and then prevent them from knowing that the attack was coming? Because trust me, you can't half feel it when one of these buggers starts up. It's like having ice tipped down your neck."

"Questions I would very much like to ask him," said Addison smoothly.

"Is that before or after he's been through *Zikiratu* and been charged with kidnapping Amy?" I asked, looking at Nadia.

"*Zikiratu*? What's that?" Addison said.

"That would be a bit much, Mike," said Nadia cautiously. Her voice was oddly soft and utterly devoid of expression, something I'd never heard before. "I'm not even sure how you know about it."

"Neither am I."

"What are you talking about?" Addison pressed.

"*Zikiratu* means 'neuter'," said Nadia, in her flat voice. "We can kill the tiny part of a mage's mind called the *gogoan*. That means they would no longer be able to do any magic at all. It's the equivalent of destroying the speech centre in your brain so you can never talk again." Nadia looked grim. Sam looked shocked. Terry-Anne was glaring at me – I was sure I'd find out why later, probably at quite high volume.

"Can anyone do that?" Amy asked, obviously shocked.

"No. There are only three people in Britain – no, four – who can."

"Let me guess; it's you, Mr Slater and Mrs Collister?" She nodded. "Who's the fourth?"

"Angela Drew, the most senior mage this country has produced in the last century." I was, frankly, astonished. Angela Drew is one of those semi-mythical characters in British magic, unlike Merlin, who actually *is* mythical, and Harry Potter and his chums, who are fictitious. No, really, they are – you can look it up somewhere.

"She's beyond normal ratings – beyond Quad Talent, almost *euste*, so she'd be like *Jaun* 15 or something. But she's over ninety and lives in a fog of dementia in a nursing home near Exeter. We have Healers and senior *kemen* specialists on duty there, and the whole place is under a dampening field so strong that most practitioners wouldn't be able to light a match, let alone do anything else."

I had no idea that such prodigious Talents existed anywhere. Suddenly being a Dual Talent *Jaun* 2 didn't seem so much. Two years ago it was a fantasy of achievement, but now it felt like my progress report should read 'must try harder'.

"Do you have to catch him to do that?" Addison asked.

"Yes."

"So," I interjected into the silence, "what happens next?"

"Next," said Terry-Anne, "you, Amy and Sam will all go home. Mr Addison here – now officially an *Iksale* 10 air Talent, but without an *erdikide* yet – will look into the development points for the hard-light vehicles, while Nadia tries to find out what connects the victims to Weaver, and to each other."

"What will you do?"

She drummed her fingers on her table. "I thought I'd sit here and worry a whole lot – save everyone else the effort."

*

We did go home, but not before we collected Clara. I dropped the ladies at the farm and then sped off to the supermarket. My credit card was begging for mercy by the time I'd finished, but I had enough of everything I could think of.

There was no suggestion that we were going to be besieged, but it felt right to be doing the 'me mighty hunter, me provide food for family' bit, even if it meant pushing a trolley around Sainsbury's rather than sticking a spear through an antelope or something equally messy.

The whole house was quiet when I got back. Amy was stretched out asleep on the couch by the fire, lying twisted – her hip was obviously still very painful, although you'd never know it when she was awake. Clara was snoring quietly in one of the big comfy chairs nearby, her runner's muscles smooth and relaxed. Sam was in the other, reading a book in Chinese, only half concentrating. She, our Warrior Princess, smiled at me when I came in and I had one of those 'this is what is precious to me' moments and felt manly tears getting in the way. She got out of her chair and padded over to me, nestled into the curve of my arms and gave me an unsarcastic hug, then stretched up and kissed me.

"We all love you too," she said softly. "Thank you for being you."

I hid my tears by unpacking the shopping very quietly. I felt utterly useless. I can't say that these women depended on me, because they didn't. They would be fine if I didn't exist – better, because none of this shit would be happening – but we had become an interdependent group and it troubled me that I couldn't protect them. 'Me mighty hunter' thinking of course, but at a brainstem level it still bloody hurt.

I think Sam understood most of it. "I make coffee," she said, kissed me again and rubbed my back in passing.

I blew my nose, not quite as quietly as I'd wanted to, and Clara stirred. "Now then," she said as the smell of coffee filtered through the room. "What's up?"

Amy turned her head towards me and smiled.

"I have enough supplies to feed a short regiment for a month, I've slung even more protections around us and I now have the powerful urge to hide. Anyone want to join me?"

They all laughed as Clara helped Amy sit up. Her hip, she said, was simply sore, although it'd seemed to be more than that. She also said she now remembered Weaver bursting into our house, and that everything after that was a complete blank until she woke up in hospital. I was so glad that she had not been distressed. Bloody annoyed yes, but I could live with that; it's almost her ground state when dealing with the halfwits that seem to inhabit, well, almost everywhere.

So that, at least for the next few hours, is what we did. Sam poured so much power into our shield that it shimmered like heat radiating off a hot car; Clara cooked something Caribbean and delicious that I swear took the enamel off my teeth, and Amy lorded it over us from the comfort of the couch.

In this quiet time, I stopped thinking that I *shouldn't* take them with me, and knew that I *couldn't* take them with me, because although they are all extremely capable mages and highly competent people, it wouldn't be fair to endanger them because of something that was my fault. Well, no, not my fault, I mean, I didn't make Weaver and his nasty little friend use me, but I did feel responsible, or something. Oh, I don't bloody know. I just couldn't expect them to be involved.

But I know better than to rush things like this, especially when planning stuff that involves people who can damn near read your mind. It's like wanting to do something that you know your parents would disapprove of, and trying to think of all the ways you'll get found out – apart, obviously, from the one they actually use. Because however smart kids are, they often miss the extremely bleeding obvious, as in 'why does your vomit smell of whisky?'. I hadn't even tried to explain that one away, because I knew it was a waste of time. I swear I can still hear Simon sniggering.

When I came down the next morning, grateful that the house didn't creak as I walked, the view from the big window stopped me. Not the actual view, which was not quite familiar enough to ignore yet, but the sullen openness. A heavy cloud had settled by us, and our house was just level with the cloud base. It looked like someone had put a lid on the world and nothing could escape again.

Magic has been around since forever, and I couldn't help but wonder how much of this little world in a box had been made by it. There are any number of things that people struggle to explain, like the Coelacanth reappearing and Donald Trump getting elected, but many of them could just be uncontrolled magic surging around the place.

No, it wasn't magic that made the dinosaurs go extinct, nor is it responsible for ice ages, isostatic readjustment or climate change. However, Moses parting the waters could easily have been an untrained water Talent bursting out in a time of desperation. Then there's the Spanish Armada, oh so conveniently decimated by storms, and the exceptional winters that saved Russia from Hitler and Napoleon. Even the period that the Australian natives call The Dreaming may be a result of a natural outburst of *kemen* – although there is argument about that.

It kind of made me feel small but not insignificant – a mage is connected to other mages in a way that creates a sort of network across the country – and although nodes go dark when people die or become *lotar* or whatever, the network persists. To be a mage is to be inescapably part of something bigger than you.

It can make you feel a nagging sense of responsibility for something that you have no part in, but it can also make you aware that what you do has an impact on other people who are not connected to you. It's not always comfortable, and it can be hard to live with. But that's the cost of being a mage, one that you have to accept.

It left me in an odd mood which lingered until too much domestic ordinariness was piled on top of it and it was lost, like tears in rain.

*

It was mid-morning when the phone rang. It was Tony Addison, complaining that he couldn't get through our protection and could he please come in. Sam made a car-shaped hole in the field. I was cautious when I heard two sets of feet on the path, but then smiled when I realised the second person was Dave Halsted.

"One minute I'm standing there wondering what's going on and then I'm in a hospital bed, not a hospital doorway." He shrugged. "Weird."

"You shouted," said Amy. "That's what woke me. You saved my life. Thank you."

"You're welcome," said Halsted simply. "Some people are worth putting yourself in danger for."

Amy flushed at the implied compliment. Addison broke the moment. "David here asked about being transferred to my unit. As he's familiar with the teetering catastrophe that counts as a normal life for you people, I was happy to accept him."

"That's good," said Amy. "But you could have told us on the telephone that he'd recovered from a stun, and about his transfer, so, and please don't misunderstand this, why are you here?" She smiled at Halsted. "Not that we aren't pleased to see you."

"Fair comment," said Addison. "I need to talk to you about Cherekov."

"Is he talking?"

"No, but we've been finding things out."

"Presumably you've told Nadia all this?"

"Of course," rumbled Halsted. "I now understand why she frightens the Chief Inspector half to death," he added, which was brave for a DC.

Addison grunted. "Anyway, Cherekov. According to Miss Hussain, he and Weaver had been working on a device which can be used to exploit the changes in electron shell energies to generate power with magical potential which can be imbued into a non-static object by means of a non-cyclic wavelength shift."

Amy looked at him. "At which point in that sentence did you stop understanding it?"

"Around 'shell energies'," he replied with a slight grin. "I had an image of whelks doing press-ups."

"They've been trying to create a portable energy source, like a battery," said Clara.

"A battery?" Halsted asked.

"Yes, but for magical energy, the power to er... power spells, to make them stronger without the caster having to exert themselves more. It's a big thing."

"I don't understand," said Halsted, which I suspect saved Addison from having to say it. Having discovered a nascent ability – an *Iksale* 10 air Talent like him is not much more powerful than a civilian – he seemed a touch too confident. I knew Amy was thinking the same thing.

Sam lifted a book from the table just by looking at it. Halsted blinked. "Lifting book need same energy if doing with spell or with hand. Sometime spell better, sometime not spell. If thing too heavy, need too much power, can't lift. All power come from inside, but this thing Weaver do, it is power from outside, so mage can direct energy to come from somewhere else – so like a battery."

"And this would be useful?"

"Very."

"And nobody has done this before?"

"No, although a very low power and unreliable system does exist," said Amy.

"So what's so special about this one?"

"It's to do with the availability of higher levels of power. There's a lot of power in the land and sea, for example, which earth and water Talents draw on all the time," I said. "This is an artificial source, so all the Talents could use it."

"Useful enough to kill for?"

I paused; we were now getting into the properly

complicated stuff. "That rather depends on what kind of spell you are planning to use it for."

Halsted frowned. "So, it's not really like electricity?"

"No. It's hard to explain simply. Let's say… fire control requires the ability to dissipate heat, move ignition sources, control oxygen levels and so forth. Water control is largely the ability to move an incoherent collection of molecules as if they were a fully coherent mass."

"Fine, I'm with you so far."

"So, if you make the energy right for moving water, with lots of binding forces in it, then it isn't much use for controlling fire."

"I understand. Could other people tell what you intend to do with it?"

"Not in detail, but they could make a pretty good guess," I said.

"Do you think that Weaver and Cherekov were working with these others, and when they found out they were doing something out of order, they killed them?"

I shrugged. I was just so bored of talking about this. I was bored of talking at all. I wanted something to happen, and happen soon. "How the hell would I know?" I said wearily. "You seem to forget that we're the victims here. You're treating us like witnesses or experts."

"Oh. Sorry."

"So, have you made any progress with finding Weaver?"

"No."

"Has he come back to the unit at Somerby Court?"

"No."

"ANPR?"

"Nothing."

"Is Cherekov talking?"

"No."

"Because he can't or because he won't?"

"Won't, probably."

"So you've made no progress." I ignored a calming gesture from Amy. "So what's the point of you being here? I mean, really? There's a mass murderer on the loose, one we know is intent on killing me; he's decoyed us away once and you have no idea why, and now you've come here to tell us… nothing." I suspect I may have been shouting at this point and while Halsted looked concerned, Addison was clearly shocked.

"We're doing our best," he protested. "I would have thought, that as a fellow mage…"

"Oh, do fuck off," I snapped. "That's like a probationary PCSO claiming fellowship with the Chief Constable. In the same job but not doing the same job."

"Well, not that different," he said, sounding grumpy.

I clapped my hands together and then drew them slowly apart, creating a giant ball of light between them that sparkled like a snow globe on steroids. I made a twisting motion which turned it into a tornado of fire that filled the ceiling space and rained fireflies over the whole room. Then they became multi-coloured, vanishing the instant before they touched anything and the temperature of the room dropped by 20°. They were, in truth, rather easy spells to do and although spectacular, they were more to do with petulance than power.

Halsted was smiling like a kid at Christmas, eyes alight with simple joy. "That's grand."

Addison was looking even more grumpy. He held up his hands in surrender and I killed the spells.

"Please leave," I said tightly as the room warmed up again. Sam was staring at me. "If you've anything to say, send an email or use the bloody telephone."

Halsted stood up. "You don't do birthday parties, do you?" I nearly exploded before I saw the twinkle in his eye, and I burst out laughing. Damn that man is good. "We'll be in contact," he added, almost pushing Addison out the door.

"Very pretty," said Amy, glaring at me. "And just what was *that* all about?"

"He annoyed me."

"Well, yes, and?" I shook my head, still pissed off but now also baffled. "Sam, is it?"

She nodded.

"What now?"

Amy sat me down in one of the comfy chairs. "Darling, you are usually the most even-tempered person in the world who isn't currently dead. You only get angry like this…"

"When someone pisses me off?"

"When something is happening to the parasite," she said flatly. "Bev warned us what to look for."

I needed to deny it, assert that the parasite was gone, or was dormant, or asleep or something. I didn't know if it was because of the still-active inhibition or just plain ordinary denial, but behind that conflict was the absolute certainty that Amy was right.

"Last time you do this, you collapse, you die," said Sam. "We don't want that happen again."

"What?"

"We get help, stop it happening."

I sighed. "How? Before I collapse again, I mean?"

Sam put a hand on my forehead, whilst Amy took my arm. "*Loaren.*"

I opened my mouth to say that I didn't want to sleep, but Sam put every ounce of her power into the spell, and that's a lot of ounces, believe me. The room first lost its lustre, then went into monochrome and then vanished like it had been dropped into a black hole. I felt myself lifted from the chair, but I have no memory of what happened after that.

18

I had expected to wake up at home, once the women had done whatever it was they had planned, but when I surfaced I was somewhere that could only be a dreamscape.

Or I hoped it was, because if it wasn't, I'd probably gone nuts. It didn't take me long to suspect that this was just a representation of my *gogoan*. Last time it was a theoretical landscape, as real as describing blue without comparing it to something (go on, try it). This was much more surreally-real, a landscape of angles and planes in shades of black and grey under a dimensionless, pearlescent sky. It looked like a very primitive video game; you would almost expect characters of stacked cubes, like in Minecraft or one of those things, to be stop-motioning across the ground.

They weren't. Nothing was moving, but there were several shinier parts and brightly coloured spots, catching the eye like distant campfires in the darkness.

I had no awareness of having a physical form, but somehow I could choose to move, so I went cautiously to look at one of them. I could see six, but then I became aware of the seventh of the strange things, which was me.

What they were like is similar to the way people describe

wines – flinty, hints of leather, aftertaste of coffee, fresh cut grass and, frequently, 'pretentious nonsense spouted by people who can't tell the difference between Tabasco and soap'. These were like that, but the primary impression was whether they were friendly or not.

One, a brilliant, adamantine white was friendly, but by no means cuddly. I guessed that was Sam. The next one was a rich golden brown, not so powerful but very deep, if you can do that with a colour. Unlike 'Sam', who perched on the landscape like a diamond on glass, this one was nestled into the ground, supported and surrounded by what it rested on. I noticed a faint purplish tinge on the edge of it, and guessed that this was Clara.

Not far away was a blue one that was calling to me. Despite being unmoving it seemed to be reaching out to me and while I could see threads connecting it with the deep gold one, there was also a haze drifting towards a more distant spot of colour. This could only be Amy. The distant thing was red and orange, like roiling lava on a yellow background, but tinged with white – no, it looked like it was superimposed on a white version of itself. It was achingly familiar and I knew it well. This was my fire Talent.

All of these entities, crystals, whatever you want to call them, were facing one way – which is a good trick with something that can't move and hasn't got a face. It was not one of the bright spots they were turned towards but a sullen glow of black on a black landscape.

I circled it, wary but not afraid. It had very little power but seemed to be shielded from being attacked. I probed it and was rewarded with a shower of sparks that scattered across the ground, now the familiar gritty black sand. This just had to be the damn parasite.

I wondered what was going on, whether I could do something or if I was just going to wander around in here, like a gamer who can't find the arrow keys, until I woke up, or possibly died.

I decided to stop, which didn't work, because the landscape kept moving, rearranging itself. To fight it was to invite seasickness or vertigo, so I left it alone and watched.

I was wrong. It wasn't rearranging itself; something very big was rearranging it, rolling the blocks around themselves to create an amphitheatre. The parasite didn't want to stay in its scope but it couldn't move.

When the enclosing walls were complete all movement stopped and a new thing came into view. It was larger than the others, apparently softer, and pale green, and I had no clue who or what it was.

It flowed over to me, and for the first time I felt fear. So far everything but the parasite had been benign; I thought I knew what everything was, but I didn't know this one. I was startled to find my fire Talent next to me. I shouldn't have been amazed – whoever or whatever this was was clearly very powerful. Then I felt another one of equal power come into view, deep red this time.

If these two were Weaver and Cherekov I was in serious shit. If they could trap my consciousness in here, then I would be classified as being in a fugue and I would wander this monochrome landscape until my physical body died. Fortunately, that would be quite quick, as nobody in a fugue state is ever put on life support.

But Sam and Amy weren't helping, and we had been trained how to intervene in things like this at *Iksale* 4 – that's when the heavy magic starts.

The Red Entity – I could give them names but calling something that looks like a branding iron 'Betsy' or 'Melvin' just doesn't seem right – circled behind me and seemed to hold me in place. It wasn't forcing me to do something; it was more like a steadying hand. The Green Entity bought the lava – my fire – to me and the Red and the Green wrapped themselves around me.

I finally got it, okay – these people are trying to make me complete. But Nadia had told me that it could kill me if I subsequently tried to break the inhibition on the parasite.

One person says one thing; another says something else. Who do you believe? I had no idea, but I had to trust. I didn't even try to understand, but cancelled all the barriers I had erected so that I could receive it. I could feel Sam and Amy willing it to work, which was reassuring, but the oddest part was Clara – she had a purple glow around her but wasn't doing anything. I did the equivalent of frowning distractedly and that was when it happened.

I was going to say 'it was like', but I've never experienced anything remotely like it. I was a jigsaw with the missing pieces finally put into place; a half full glass being filled to overflowing; an Apollo moon shot when the second-stage rockets kick in.

I was exhilarated, terrified, confused and totally and utterly out of control. The Talents were fighting for domination of me, trying to take over the other as well, to make me subordinate to them. After I have no idea how long, I won. Nobody could help, but Sam being there and and Amy reminding me why it mattered that I came out as myself, gave me the strength I needed to integrate them. When I thought it was over I realised that the white shape, which had an odd silvery tinge to it, had come in too – an air Talent, underdeveloped perhaps, but nonetheless real and significant. Triple Talent – I felt like the king of the fucking world.

Green and Red withdrew, a little shakily I thought, and then we turned our attention to the parasite. I knew that between us we could obliterate it, but we didn't want to do that – we needed to see inside it first. It knew it couldn't win, but it still resisted. A thing like this isn't alive anyway; it doesn't have sentience or intelligence *per se*, but is programmed to respond in a particular way and will carry on regardless of what's happening around it. It's like trying to negotiate with a traffic warden.

We all tried, singly and together, but nothing had any effect. It seemed like the more we pushed, the harder the shell became. I tried moving slowly, and then a sharp stab, then a wide area effect. Nothing. Trying to twist it made some difference but it seemed to be twisting me in the opposite direction with each turn. It appeared that Sir Isaac Newton had been right, even in a dreamscape, so I stopped.

I really didn't want to destroy it without finding out its secrets first, but I couldn't see any other way. Then the purple glow of Clara moved in closer, probing gently. I didn't intervene because I have enormous respect for Clara as a mage. She has an oddness about her magic, probably a result of the slightly different techniques they use in her homeland, that interested me. In that glow I realised that she'd been using her power to quash the inhibition so it couldn't harm me.

She enfolded the parasite and made the ground below it rise until it stood on a basalt pedestal. All was stillness, and then she summoned the Dragon.

I've never scared easily, and my new levels of power meant that I was even less likely to be, but I confess I did the metaphysical equivalent of crapping myself.

It was fucking huge, huge like planets and unexpected tax bills are huge. Luminous dark purple, it coiled around the amphitheatre in a spiral that filled the world. I suppose it was my subconscious that gave it a face and put scales on its body, but by the time it landed it was a classic Chinese dragon. I suspect Sam may have had a hand in that bit.

Clara stood up – actually Clara, dressed in robes of gold

that moved like oil on water, an exclamation of light against those darkly luminous coils. The Dragon bent its head to be stroked and then extended a wing towards each of us. We all touched it and were filled with raw power, almost to bursting point. Even Red and Green touched it and glowed more brightly than ever. I felt a layer like a clenched fist fall away from me and the relief was immense. The inhibition was finally gone.

Then it sinuously, gracefully, bent its head and looked at the tiny parasite. It touched it with its snout, the briefest brushing contact, and all its protective fields became dust that tumbled from the pillar like silent grey rain. Clara and the Dragon bowed to each other and then both vanished.

I shattered the basalt column and we clustered around the parasite. It seemed small and weak and defenceless – and because we all knew this was just another form of its protection, we tore it to pieces. It died with barely a whimper.

There should have been triumph, celebration, vindication, but there wasn't. It was a soggy anticlimax, this act of thin violence, as the moment after finishing something big so often is. The parasite was gone and my *gogoan* was finally my own again.

By this time you must be wondering just how hard I'd been hitting the recreational pharmaceuticals, but I promise that this utterly lame description is the best I can manage for something that totally unscrewed my brain.

*

I woke up at home, on the couch, to find people strewn all over the place: Amy, Sam, Bev of the Amazing Snogging, Richard Slater and Anne Collister. The only one not variously slumped around the room was Clara, who was dressed in her usual running clothes and making tea with all the energy of the ridiculously well rested. It looked like the morning after an unruly teenage sleepover.

She smiled at me, so I slowly got up from the couch and headed for the toilet. Suitably eased, I returned to find everyone else stirring.

"How long was I out?" I realised that I was starving.

"Most of a day." She handed me a banana. "Don't eat too fast, you'll make yourself sick." Our fingers touched as I took the fruit and I swear I felt a spark jump the gap. She looked at me. "Yes, it did happen. All of it." She raised her hand and there was a faint purple nimbus around it. "To do that needed a lot of power," she said, "more than any of us could hope to muster, even combined." I nodded. "So I had to get help. One effect of this is that I'm now permanently in contact with my big friend. It's slightly… odd."

"Thank you, my Lady Dragon." I bowed slightly.

"My Lord Triple Talent," she replied, echoing the bow.

"Aren't we clever clogs?"

We hugged in a far from perfunctory manner and the power hummed between us. "Yes, we are," she said, "but that won't brew the tea or make you smell any nicer." She pushed me gently away. "Go and have a shower."

"Yes, mum."

*

There was very little to discuss, because we all knew what had happened, so the conversation around the table was domestic and strangely muted, right up to the point when the doorbell rang and Chief Inspector Addison turned the whole fucking thing upside down again.

He didn't recognise Richard, Anne or Bev, so we just introduced them as colleagues. I had to reassure him that they were fully *au fait* with the case before he would open up at all. The others draped themselves around the big room as we sat at the table. "And how are you, Miss Deerborn? I know you've been subject to some fairly traumatic events lately – can we offer you counselling?"

"I'm fine." She was too. She had little memory of the kidnapping, and the fact that she'd beaten Cherekov meant that the whole thing had given her no more than a few troubled nights.

"Good, good." He stopped. I guessed he had something to tell us that he didn't want to. I let him squirm, and in my head I could hear Sam giggling. In the background, deeply buried, was a warm throaty chuckle that just had to be Clara. Amy hid a smile behind her mug.

The silence stretched like chewing gum reluctant to let go of a shoe, and Addison started to sweat. He took a deep breath. "I'm sorry to have to tell you this, but Jan Cherekov has escaped," he said in a rush.

I blew out a long breath, but Amy got there first. "How the hell did you let that happen, you fucking halfwit?"

"Miss Deerborn, I am a Chief Inspector," he protested.

"And also, apparently, an idiot. How did it happen?"

"We put him in a cell at the local nick until we could work out what to do with him. They looked in on a routine check and couldn't see him, so they opened the door." Slater rolled his eyes. "They couldn't find him anywhere."

"Presumably you've worked out what he actually did?" Slater rumbled.

"Hid using magic?"

"I'm sure he interfered with your cameras first," said Slater. I could feel him adding power to what he was saying and Addison's confidence was eroding in front of our eyes.

"But the cell was empty," he protested plaintively.

"No, it wasn't – he used a spell called *Adigabezia*, which makes you think that you've looked where he is when you actually haven't. Why didn't his detention have a special notification on it that meant someone who knew the score would be called if there was a problem?"

"It did. They called me." The sentence and its implications hung in the air for several seconds.

"When did this happen?" I asked, making a conscious effort to unlock my fists. Even though our house is always comfortably warm, I suddenly felt cold. Addison would doubtless suffer the consequences of his hubristic cock-up in due course, but my immediate concern was the now-resurrected threat to our well-being.

"Three hours ago."

"Why didn't you call us as soon as it happened?"

"Well, you've got all these defensive… screens… around the house, so I thought you'd be safe for a while."

"Which Weaver and Cherekov can walk straight through."

"Oh – wasn't that just Weaver?"

"No. If Weaver can, Cherekov can." Addison clearly didn't understand enough about magic to be let out unsupervised. "I presume you're trying to find him?"

"Of course." He didn't bother to say they hadn't got him yet. The gathering broke up not long afterwards, and soon we had the house to ourselves. We changed all the defences on the house, but Anne said that more protection would be arriving shortly.

*

With both of them on the loose I thought it was even more important that I left the others behind and hunted them. This is when I stepped out of my own shadow and… what a load of bollocks. I am not James Bond or Iron Man. I'm a fairly average bloke with a head full of untested Talents, which is like having a really big gun you aren't entirely sure how to use, and the only things stopping it blowing up in your face are luck and wishful thinking.

Determination will not stop you falling into a hole. The justice of your cause will not turn away bullets. Moral outrage makes no difference to an alligator and a funnel-web spider doesn't care which flag you are marching under. What I needed was knowledge (which I didn't have much of), experience (which I didn't have any of) and a shitload of luck (I could hope, couldn't I?).

But I knew people that did – the police. No, not Chief Inspector Oh-look-I-can-do-a-light-spell Addison; I was really regretting letting him out of his box now. No, I needed DC Halsted – former entry-team leader, POLSA (Police Search Advisor) and hostage negotiator. If anyone could help me get it right, it was Dave Halsted. Who was on sick leave for two days. Bugger.

"What now?" Amy asked as I closed Halsted's 'out of office' email.

I shrugged. "Damned if I know. For all we know they're in Poland, Patagonia or Pluto. Central is looking for them, so are the police. I'd like to say it's inevitable that they'll get picked up soon, but Ronnie Biggs was on the run for thirty-six years and he had the magical talent of a teaspoon."

Amy laughed and hugged me. "Oh I do love you," she said. "What now?"

"Bed."

"Bed? You've been asleep for nearly sixteen hours."

"Who said anything about sleeping?"

19

The next morning it occurred to me that we had heard nothing more about the investigations into Amy's kidnapping. So I called Addison, got Ishka Perera and waited at home, mostly making cakes and snogging, until he called us back.

Only he didn't – I suspect he was embarrassed after the farce with Cherekov – so we got Ishka again. "Hello, Chief Inspector Addison asked me to call you. How can I help?"

"Are you working for him now?"

"With him. Special Investigations is quite a small unit, so they bring in people as and when they need them."

"Where did he steal you from?"

"Traffic."

"Why from traffic? I mean, why does he need a traffic officer?"

She sighed. "He got me because I've got all the advanced driving certificates you can think of. He seems to endlessly need someone, most often Nadia Hussain, collecting from Tube stations in north London."

So Ishka was Nadia's magic carpet. Addison makes the call, Nadia walks up the road to Blackfriars Tube and heads north, where Ishka meets her and they head up the M1 like their trousers are full of wasps.

"So what you want to know?"

"Any news on the investigation into the kidnapping?"

"Not a damn thing."

"Nothing?"

"Not a single thing. The whole business was very carefully organised to leave no trace at all, anywhere."

"CCTV? ANPR?"

"You live in the middle of a field, Mike, where, oddly, there aren't an awful lot of cameras. It's also a bit tricky to track a vehicle when we don't know which one we are looking for."

"Fair enough."

"We can't find anybody who saw anything. Forensics are certain Amy was taken up to the hill less than two hours before she was found, but we have no idea where she was held in the meantime. It was probably Somerby Court, but we've no evidence of that. The blanket she was wrapped in is ancient, and had probably lived in the back of someone's car for at least ten years. Apart from some dusty oil and a funny smell, we got nothing from it." I could almost hear her shrug. "Whoever did this is either very subtle or very, very clever," she went on.

"Both, I suspect."

She sighed again. "I prefer obvious and stupid – makes our clear-up rate look better. I'll let you know if we get any more information. Well, any information."

"No sign of Weaver otherwise?"

"No. He's vanished."

"Thanks." I killed the call. Exactly as expected.

*

Sometimes, just sometimes, the universe is kind. Although Jan Cherekov is as unremarkable as one grape in a bunch, something about his face had lodged in the mind of a

PC who was on patrol near Stamford the next day. She noticed Cherekov sneaking through a red light on the A606 eastbound and reported both the fact and the index of his car. He was seen again on the outskirts of Oakham. This time the flag system worked and a new face responded – DS Bella Sorrell. She'd been attached to Special Investigations by a thoughtful superintendent, ostensibly because of the number of females in the case, but I suspected this was also Addison putting another layer of authority between us so that he didn't have to talk to us directly. Sorrell was, we gathered rather quickly, unhappy about the attachment, and profoundly sceptical about magic.

Naturally they lost Cherekov. He was last seen turning north-west towards Derby in a manoeuvre so obvious that it could only have been deliberate.

DC Halsted passed all this on while sitting in our kitchen. We'd got him a mug with his name on, which made him laugh like a hyena on nitrous oxide. "You know where he's going, do you?"

"Know? No. Educated guess – Somerby Court," I said.

"We were watching it – he's not gone there."

Amy sighed. "David, you're talking about a man who can convince three experienced police officers that a cell is empty even when he's standing in the middle of it. Do you seriously think you could see him if he didn't want you to?"

Halsted nodded glumly as the doorbell rang. It proved to be DS Sorrell. 'Cross' seemed to be her default state, and I wondered if this was because she was around mages. Some people are profoundly jealous of our abilities and this makes them... tetchy. Other people mistrust us just on general principles, and even more think we're con artists or stage magicians. This last group really dislikes the fact that it can't work out how we do stuff.

Bella Sorrell had a frown that put at least five years on

her face, just as placidity took some years off Dave Halsted's. She even dressed crossly, her jacket not sitting quite right on her and her shoes in need of a good polish. I have no doubt that she's a good copper, but I hope she's less grumpy when not dealing with magical types. She took one look at Halsted and jerked her thumb towards the door.

"Sling yer hook. The chief wants to talk to you." David nodded calmly, drained his mug and made his steady way back to the real world. I pointed to the coffee machine and it turned on, then I raised an eyebrow.

"No, I don't want any, and you can pack it in with them silly tricks. It may fool DC Halsted but it don't fool me." She hadn't moved from her rigid posture two paces into the room.

Amy looked at me. "No, all right? Just no."

"You're telling me? I was going to say that to you," I replied.

"You two finished?"

"I'm so terribly sorry to inconvenience you by having a brief conversation with my fiancé and fellow victim," Amy replied, smiling sweetly.

Sorrell grunted. "Anyway." She stopped as Amy pushed herself to her feet, slipped on her elbow crutches and walked carefully to her high–seat chair by the fire.

"So how can we help you, Detective Sergeant?"

"I've got a message."

"And I've got a telephone," Amy replied, echoing her tone. I felt like hiding.

"The chief asked me to come – said it was time I met you."

"And now you have." There was a long silence, I mean really long. Amy doesn't get uncomfortable with silences. Most people can survive less than twenty seconds; DS Sorrell managed nearly a minute.

"He said to tell you that Weaver was seen near Tixover yesterday. I hope that makes sense to you."

"Thank you, Detective Sergeant. Was there anything else?"

"Yes. We've found the point of origin for the vehicles that crashed. All of them appeared in a place where there's no cameras."

"Not a surprise," I added.

Sorrell glared at me. "There is no indication that anyone of interest was anywhere near those locations either."

"Do you have any idea how they were created?" Amy asked, which was a bit mean. She often winds up people who irritate her by asking innocent questions that they can't answer.

"Some kind of stupid trick, no doubt. Typical of the sort of bloody pathetic things you people do."

"Hell of a trick," I said, "making a steam train appear out of nowhere and do that much damage."

"Would have been if it had been a real steam train."

"It was," I replied darkly.

"Why are you so sure?" Sorrell snapped, transferring her glare to me.

"I was there. I saw it happen."

She shrugged, as if the ability to cast spells made me incapable of being a reliable witness. She folded her face together into a frown.

"Was there anything else?" Amy asked tightly.

"No." She glared at Amy, ignored me and walked out – well, 'stormed off' might be more accurate.

"So when are we going to Somerby Court?" Amy asked after a moment.

"Well, me and Dave Halsted are planning to go later today, just for a recce, a quick look around. I wasn't sure if you wanted to come along. Under the circumstances I thought that we shouldn't put you under undue strain before the real thing tomorrow, even if you are in a monitoring role."

You know that moment when you realise that you've said the wrong thing, big style, and you only said it because you meant well, but nothing you say is going to make it any better? Yeah, one of those.

It was our first proper row. We'd done the bickering thing of course, but she was so annoyed that I couldn't even get her to listen to an apology, let alone an explanation. Before she could assassinate more than just my character, habits and ancestry (sorry, mum) I grabbed some power and wrote 'I'm sorry' in big smoky letters in the air in front of her.

They didn't last very long, but it did the job and she wound down for long enough for me to explain what I had made a complete hash of saying before.

"Go on," she said dangerously.

"All I meant to say was that I don't want you to come in – as in into the actual building – tomorrow because I need you outside."

"Because I can't walk properly."

"No, because your defensive spells are stronger than mine, and I think we are really likely to need someone to cover a retreat."

"And because I can't walk properly."

"Oh God. Look, there are going to be stairs, so it does make it more... logical for it to be you on the outside, although," I added hastily, "were it not for that I would just happily take you in with me and leave Sam or Clara outside. I'm sorry I didn't explain it better the first time. I..."

"All right, you saved yourself from sleeping on the couch tonight. When are we gathering?"

"Tomorrow morning, 8.30 am, in the next village along the road."

"And who's coming?"

"You, me, Sam, Clara, Dave Halsted, Ishka and, sadly, I suspect we won't be able to get rid of DS Sorrell."

"Fine. And remind me, why are all those thugs who hang around Central not doing this?"

"Because they can't be certain he's there. They want to watch for longer, make sure he's there before they act, but every bit of longer they insist on puts us all in even more danger. They know that he can make himself invisible, even to them, but…"

"You sure? Have you spoken to Nadia?"

"Yes. She understands our position, but she can't authorise a team from Central without much more evidence, not even to piss off Richard Slater."

Amy shook ahead. "What is it with those two?" I didn't reply. "We need to get some sleep." We didn't get much, but only because we were worrying – she hadn't forgiven me that much.

*

We had packed everything the night before, so we headed off less than half an hour after we woke up. It was a grubby morning, with heavy clouds at treetop height and intermittent-wiper-grade drizzle. It's never like this in Hollywood action movies.

DS Sorrell was indeed there, in Amy's car, in plain clothes that were so officious that they might as well have had 'police' embroidered across the back. Dave Halsted was wearing what were destined to be gardening clothes next because, he wryly informed us, his wife would murder him if he ruined any more of his good stuff. Ishka was in jeans and a sweatshirt, and driving the second car.

"We are just looking today," insisted Sorrell, unaware that we had already done that. "If we find out that either of them is in there, we pull out and I call for backup. You do not go into the building. Clear?"

"Of course," said Clara, radiating 'yeah, right' so clearly that even Dave and Ishka picked it up.

"So we'll drive into the main car park and everyone except Miss Deerborn and I will get out. You'll then walk around to the unit, like you're just innocently visiting the site, and then on my signal, and only on my signal, you go in closer. Then you withdraw, either way, when you are certain of your... facts. Clear?"

We nodded.

"Good. I'm not sure why we need you people to carry out what is a straightforward police operation, but according to CI Addison it has to be you that does it." She shook her head. "I'm going to have to speak to the Chief Constable about this – can't have a Chief Inspector being so heavily influenced by..." she trailed off.

We all nodded dutifully and Amy rolled her eyes – she was the one who was going to get an earful from Sorrell when we didn't do anything like what she said.

*

Somerby Court is in two distinct areas – the part nearest the entrance is a beautifully appointed single-storey building wrapped around a lovely quadrangle, and mostly contains offices of various kinds. The second part, slightly further down the hill and screened by dense trees, is a series of middle-sized industrial units of the kind usually referred to as 'tin shed disease'. The unit we were interested in was off to the right-hand side, the last in a line of four that ended on a heavily wooded bank that dropped steeply downward to the road. It was, to nobody's surprise, the most isolated unit in the whole place. The police observers had withdrawn days earlier, convinced that the place was empty.

We drove through the gates at a sensible pace, straight past the main car park, which left Sorrell sputtering like a boiling kettle, down onto the concrete apron of the lower car park and into the sight cover provided by some untrimmed bushes in one corner. Finding places like that was why we taken the trouble to have a snout around the day before. We piled out in a rush that was so quiet that Sorrell just had to believe that the *Isila* (silence) spell I had cast was real, but still didn't.

Clara, Dave and Ishka went around the back, where the emergency exits led immediately into the deep and impenetrable cover of the undergrowth. Sam and I went to the front, wrapped in *Harrise* shields harder than a mountainside. The louring fog swirled about us; Dave was a pillar of darkness on quiet feet, while Clara had a slight purple nimbus around her that suggested she was strongly in contact with the Dragon. We lost sight of Ishka almost immediately. Clara and Sam shared a *Mail-Beg* so we could all see everything, even though at that moment there was nothing to see.

We opened ourselves to listen, to feel for any magical activity, but there was nothing but background noise. No, not quite nothing. Sam looked at me and held up two fingers, then wobbled her hand for 'maybe'. Amy signalled nothing seen. Clara reported nothing either and Ishka, observing unseen from a distance, said the same, whispering into her radio.

We approached the domestic-scale door that led into the unit – it opened into a small reception area with a large door into the factory floor and a staircase to the offices at the top.

I pushed the door gently – not with my hand, I'm not that stupid – and it moved freely. This was tricky, because Weaver or Cherekov could be waiting to drop a fireball down the stairs the moment we stepped into the reception area. So I sent in an *Iheki*, a copy of me – which was slightly unnerving – and guess what? Yup, fireball.

This was Weaver's work, and fire billowed out of the door with a loud bang, blackening the paint and startling

279

half a tree's worth of crows into a cackling panic. I sent another *Iheki* in and watched carefully. I didn't have to warn Amy or Clara about what was happening; Clara would tell Dave and Ishka and I didn't give a shit about Sorrell.

There wasn't another fireball, so we edged slowly towards the door. Sam, her shield at maximum, stepped inside; of course there was another trap – all the oxygen had now been removed from the stair well.

At that moment I felt Amy sending me an urgent alert – the magical equivalent of shouting 'look out'. I turned sharply towards her just as Cherekov stepped out of the supposedly empty unit next door, and launched a fireball straight at me.

I recognised the *esku* immediately – it had been Cherekov who had attacked me outside the pub in London. I hardened my *Harrise* and the fireball bounced off, ricocheted into the bushes near where the cars were parked and set an area of greenery the size of a bus ablaze.

I had time to see Sorrell scrambling for the door handle before Amy casually raised her hand and extinguished the entire thing with a mass of water that she'd sucked out of the clouds.

Cherekov launched another fireball and I changed the angle of my shield to send it straight back at him. He cancelled it as soon as it bounced, then tried to do the lightning bolt thing again. I had no idea if *Harrise* would work against that, so I ducked. It was a good job I did, because the bastard thing went straight through it.

It shot past me, past Sam who was just outside the doorway, and into the trees, where it went off with an explosion that was audible a mile away. I was down, hunched in the angle of the building and the concrete floor, and my shield was unstable. Cherekov closed in.

He created a sphere of power that looked like a plasma

globe filled with lava, raised it above his head and made to throw it at me. Then he paused, spat out a mouthful of water – he'd obviously found a solution to Amy's party trick – then threw it, full force, but all I got was wet. Amy had created globes of water around the fire which snuffed it out even as he cast it.

He swore in frustration as I surged to my feet, and then knocked me flying with a great big push spell. I rolled sideways, just avoiding another fireball, and tried to set up *Harrise* again. It was half formed when the next fireball hit, punched a hole straight through my shield and hit me in the leg.

Even in its depleted state the pain was appalling and scattered every thought, every spell, everything but the urge to scream and hide. Through the haze I saw his feral grin and an expression of joy as he created another for the *coup de grâce*. So much the fucking hero me.

I didn't close my eyes, which is why I saw him pushed hard backwards just as he launched it, sending the fireball into the trees. Power rolled over me like a soft steamroller, and I knew it was Sam. I had bought her enough time to get into the unit safely, and now she was free to help me.

Cherekov fired a scattering of low-power shots as suppressing fire, designed to make us duck, and Sam just waved them away. Then I felt the whole place go cold and saw that Amy had poured water all over him and then frozen it. He was now standing on, and in, ice. He slipped, a real banana-skin moment, and that gave me time to struggle to my feet. I slammed my leg full of magic morphine, the spell *Sorgortu*, and turned to face him. But once again, I wasn't needed.

Sorrell was out of the car and running toward us, only to be intercepted by Ishka who wisely kept her out of the firing line. Clara, floating in the trees beyond the end wall like the rage of angels, raised her hands towards Cherekov.

I have seen some things in my time, but nothing like this. She wrapped him in a dense purple light and then unleashed the Dragon. It dropped on him in vast fury and literally tore him to pieces; not like shattering an image or glass breaking, but like a piece of meat. There was blood and screams and some noises that I can still hear on bad nights, silenced only when his head was bitten off. The Dragon vanished; the body dropped and coils of purple wobbly bits slid onto the concrete like a decomposing snake. The smell was appalling.

I was unashamedly, violently, sick, and developed an instant if fleeting urge to become a vegetarian. I spat the taste from my mouth. "Fuck."

"*Tā mā de*," agreed Sam.

I tested my leg – the damage wasn't too severe and it held me up, and that was all I cared about just then. I had time to register that DS Sorrell was also being sick before Sam and I ran into the building.

I think I was too frightened to be nauseous any more. I noticed, with some interest, that Ishka didn't seem to be too troubled – seen too many motorway crashes, I supposed.

Amy was in the doorway behind us when we opened the wall into the downstairs workshop – on such occasions one does not trouble too much with doors. It was completely empty, home to dust, spiders and patches of dusty oil from long-gone machinery. There was also a distinctive and particular odour in the room.

"Go up," said Amy, leaning on her crutches, "I've got this." We left her spraying a fine mist over the floor that would show up any recent footprints.

We didn't use the stairs but rocketed up the short stairwell on a column of something Sam had got from the back pages of a spell catalogue. She provided the power but I had to control it at the top or we would have shot straight through the suspended ceiling into the roof space.

This was worse – offices, still fully equipped. A big central room with desks, side offices on all but the end wall and a well-equipped kitchen right by the door. This needed a squad of people dressed in black, carrying machine guns and shouting 'hut' or something, but we were all we had, so...

Then Ishka arrived, slapping out her extendable baton and pulling us away from standing directly in front of the doorway. "We need backup," she said softly.

"Like who?"

"Oh. See what you mean. Any idea where he is?"

The fireball came out of nowhere and hit her in the chest, throwing her through the plasterboard wall and into the stairwell. I didn't hear her land. I was briefly stunned, then full of fury.

Weaver was on the other side of the room, watching us. He still looked like badly dressed matchsticks, still coughed, and still had that weary, supercilious look that lecturers get after years of PowerPoint.

"You just had to interfere, didn't you?" he said coldly.

Sam and I moved in opposite directions. It wasn't much of a defence but it was better than huddling together. The smell of scorched paint filled the air and our feet crunched on fragments of plasterboard and broken crockery – the wall he had blasted Ishka through had been one end of the kitchen.

"So why are you doing this?" I asked. It might seem an inane question, but it was the only one that came to mind and, anyway, I really wanted to know.

He sneered. He had never been a good-looking man, too pinched and jowly, and this made his face just plain ugly. He also didn't answer.

Instead he raised one hand, pointed and collapsed the corner of the office on top of Sam. It was so sudden, so shocking, that all I felt was an overwhelming flash of fear from her, and then she was gone.

The death of my *erdikide* should have brought me to my knees, and I think Weaver expected it to. But Sam was *erdikide* to my earth Talent, so I let that withdraw and grieve while I allowed the fire to rage. I found Amy preoccupied but still very much with me, and Clara too.

He tried to do it to me, but I rebounded his spell – I had no idea how, but I suspect the Dragon was involved. His fireballs turned into damp squibs. Compulsions became suggestions. Fire died and I absorbed all the energy he poured at me, channelling it to Clara, who remained glued to the spot, guarded by Halsted; the Dragon fed and grew stronger, and I think it had cast its wings over us.

My head was singing with power – mine, Clara's, the Dragon, Amy and some more that I couldn't identify. I felt like Superman's big brother on the day his new batch of steroids arrived.

But Weaver had been a mage for decades and a total bastard for even longer. He knew he couldn't touch me now, but he could still reach the environment around me, so he pulled an internal wall down on top of me. It slid off my shield, but by the time the dust had cleared he'd vanished. I scanned but I couldn't find him – not that I'd expected to. Nor could I see him, so I cast *Biziagotu* (amplify) over the whole space. He hadn't used a silencing spell, so I could hear him creeping around behind me.

I spun on the spot – the turn was actually quite sluggish because of the power surrounding me – to find him standing between me and the shattered kitchen.

I was too numb to be frightened, too frightened to think, and too thoughtless to be careful, so I simply charged at him. Our shields met and exploded outwards in a cloud of light and fire.

There are no spells when you are fighting like this; no time to formulate, to structure or to plan. When you're facing a tiger it's survival, not strategy. This was like fighting two tigers and a puma with toothache.

It came down to a shoving contest, using forces so powerful and so fundamental that lightbulbs exploded and unpowered printers started running by themselves. Monitors began to smoke and the water-cooler bottle exploded as the contents sublimated to steam.

I won the shoving match, partially thanks to the Dragon and partially because Weaver was now visibly scared. He must've felt Cherekov – his *erdikide* – die, and realised that instead of trying to kill one lone, frightened *Iksale* he was now facing four *Jaun*-level mages who wanted him dead, plus the ineffectual might of the local police.

He also faced my fury. To kill Sam so casually made me more angry than I thought I was capable of. The rage burned as we struggled.

Then there was, in that little, still place in my mind, a tiny voice. It could have been something Amy had said, Sam's dying thought or something I'd heard on a game show, I didn't know. It just said 'magic isn't the only way'. So I did something that you learn in the martial arts – if you suddenly stop pushing back your opponent falls towards you because they are still pressing forwards.

He didn't fall, he twisted, so I reached out to the kitchen surface behind him, snatched up the first thing that came to hand – a heavy cleaver – and drove it straight down towards the top of his head.

I didn't think it would hit him – it was meant to be a distraction; I imagined it would bounce, or melt, or turn into a ferret or something. It didn't. It passed straight through his skull, only stopping when the handle was sticking out of his forehead like a horn. I stepped back as all of Weaver's magic exploded at once. I felt walls falling in; a stray electrical cable swung sparks across the room, the floor gave way, and then most of the building landed on top of me.

*

Waking up really fucking hurt. I mean really. My brain was rattled and I dipped in and out of consciousness like badly edited highlights. I could hear groans as the building twisted – and my own, occasionally – and smelled concrete dust and smoke. I had fallen all the way to the ground floor, most of which was covered by heavy debris and shattered desks. I felt like I'd been trapped in a washing machine full of rocks.

I couldn't feel Amy any more. That said, I couldn't really feel myself either. I turned slightly and found myself nose to nose with Weaver, an unappealing prospect at the best of times, but the bloody, V-shaped cleft in the top of his head made it doubly so.

I tried to move, to get out of the building, but it hurt too much. By 'it' I mean every bit of me. My toenails ached, my hair was sore and I was almost matching breaths with Weaver, who was quite distinctly dead.

At least that bit had worked – whatever Weaver and Cherekov had planned had been stopped and some recompense made for the lives they had taken. Cheats shall not prosper. I would have laughed but I had too many broken bones to even consider it. After that small moral triumph it all went a bit runny.

Sam was under tonnes of rubble, almost certainly crushed to death. Ishka had undoubtedly been killed by the fireball, and it seems likely that Amy had been caught in the last collapse. I felt tears tracking through the dust and dirt on my cheeks. That left only Clara, and God alone knew what damage that amount of magic being released in one go had done to someone so close to it. Like I had been at Paddington...

So probably it was just Dave Halsted and Bella Sorrell, who didn't believe in magic and didn't trust any of us anyway. She'd be on her mobile, calling for backup and ambulances, assuming that Clara was in a coma and that we were all dead in a gas explosion, on the all-electric site. Prognosis was not good. I drifted in and out of consciousness.

I started to feel warm, which didn't seem right. I knew I'd taken a lot of damage, but blood loss makes you feel cold. I think. Think. Thinking. I was hazy and inc… something. Incubator. No, incoherent. I lay immobile for some time, just being, not even thinking. It didn't hurt so much if I stayed completely still. I sent a mental apology and farewell to everyone. I became small, a tiny thing, just the infinitesimal presence that is the mage in his *gogoan*. Time doesn't exist in there.

I was revived by the increasing smell of smoke and forced my eyes open. The smoke was filling the high ceiling above me and I felt the heat from the far end of the building. *Oh, how fucking lovely*, I thought, with a surge of anger. *Now I can get burnt to death because I'm too close to death to be able to move.*

The world went grey – greyer – and I felt warmth on my outstretched hand. I was trying to work out how fast the fire must be travelling – it's like doing calculus in your head when you're pissed – when I realised that the warmth wasn't flames but a human hand.

"I found him," said a voice that couldn't exist.

"Sam?" I croaked.

"Lie still," she commanded, then coughed. She crawled into view through the debris, her clothes torn and filthy, a deep cut down the side of her face, and placed my hand on the bare skin over her heart. I felt her take a deep breath and then the power hit me. I was light-headed, like a balloon inflating, and I swear I heard bones creaking back into place. My fingers twitched and brushed the rise of her breast.

"You better then," she said drily, releasing my hand.

"Hardly."

"We go," she said, helping me carefully into a sitting position. I coughed in the dust, which hurt.

"Ow, ow… why?"

"Fire, and traps set up before."

"Traps? How can we… avoid them? I have no power. I'm not sure I can walk."

"They come get us."

"Who? We didn't…?"

With a huge noise a large section of the wall behind us was torn clean out and suddenly the smoke and sunlight changed places. I felt myself lifted and floated out of the building and onto an area of the car park that had been converted into a makeshift medical clearing station.

A dark-haired woman I didn't recognise gave me a quick assessment, sat me up with brutal kindness, gave me a drink of something revolting and after that a shot of Healing, which allowed the world to come back into focus. Ishka was sitting on a chair next to me with a large dressing on her chest, just visible under a strategically placed blanket, and her ruined stab vest on the floor beside her. Sam was on the other side of me, although I couldn't feel her at all.

Clara was motionless on another stretcher, the slow, heavy breathing of the profoundly unconscious. Dave Halsted was sitting with her, holding her hand. And next to her was Amy, white hair singed and several long bloody cuts down one arm, but awake. She looked at me and smiled.

Even DS Sorrell was there, being treated for burns and culture shock. I should have been surprised that one of the people attending to us was Bev, but I wasn't, nor that Richard Slater was in charge. It seemed Nadia and Anne Collister were still in the building, dealing with the traps

– hence the muffled thumps that periodically made the building sway. I drifted off.

I opened my eyes again to find Amy, now minus blood and grime, and with neat stitches in her arm, sitting next to me. "Hello, you," I whispered.

"Hello, you," she replied.

We gripped hands and I still couldn't feel her, but I knew I would soon.

"Marry me," I said. "I didn't do it properly last time."

She started to laugh. "I knew you would find an unusual way to propose, my love, but whatever I imagined it didn't include burning buildings and a dismembered assassin."

"So is that yes?" It seemed incredibly important.

"Yes." She leant down to kiss me as a fire engine and two ambulances arrived.

20

I have oddly little memory of waking up, other than knowing that I was back in hospital. Again. Everything should have hurt, but in truth nothing did. I was entirely and comprehensively numb and drifted in and out of consciousness for several years, or possibly weeks. It was actually a couple of days. I knew the Healers were there. I knew Sam was there. I knew Amy was there, and Clara, and them being there brought tears to my eyes. I found out later that mum and dad visited too. Simon didn't.

I was also aware of Weaver and that I'd killed him. I think that Bev had done something to numb that too – I felt a disquiet that I had taken his life, but not that he was dead. Is that a bit complicated? Well, nobody ever said morality was easy.

Mages take longer to recover from mental trauma like this because of the extra neurological complications of the *gogoan*. It's why the medical sections of the colleges are as large as they are.

The first people I clearly remember were the dark-haired Healer I didn't know and then Bev. I was surprised when someone called her 'Dr Hinch'. I mean, I knew she was a Healer and all that, but it turned out she's also a real proper medical doctor too, trained at St Thomas', and well on the way to becoming a consultant neurologist. And still incredibly hot. Don't tell Amy I said that.

"How do you feel?"

"I don't know. I don't really feel anything."

"OK, let's start with the basics. Are you in pain?"

"No."

"Are you hungry or thirsty?"

"No."

"Do you have anything restricting your movements?"

"Ribs."

She nodded. "I'm not surprised, you broke almost all of them. Can you feel Sam and Amy?"

I thought for a moment. "Yes. And Clara too, but the connections have changed."

"In what way?"

"They're – oh, I get it, it's like I'm in sixths – Sam is two parts…"

She nodded. "Earth Talent."

"Amy is two parts…"

"Fire Talent."

"And Clara is one part."

"Your air Talent, which none of us had a clue was there. It's unlikely to grow beyond about 50% power. Who is the last part?"

"I'm not sure." I was – it was the Dragon that Clara had released at Rockingham – it seemed that if you got Clara you got the Dragon too. "Why were you at Somerby Court?"

"Chief Inspector Addison called us."

"Tony Addison?"

"Relax – he's a much better copper than he will ever be a mage. DS Sorrell told him about her reconnaissance plan, but Dave Halsted had told him that you'd already done it. He guessed that you lot would do your usual bull in a china shop routine, so he called Nadia and sent PC Perera to make sure Sorrell didn't interfere."

"Oh. Does she work for him now?" Even as I said it I knew it was a stupid question.

"She always did – she's been his right hand all along. Now go to sleep."

"Is everyone else all right?"

"They will be; so will you. Clara and her... friend... protected everyone. It was the largest single release of magic that we have records for. That's a powerful friend to have." I meant to ask why or something, but instead I just fell asleep again.

*

It was a couple of weeks before Slater and his people pieced it all together, and they filled in the details over a long and wandering Sunday lunch at Whin Hill Farm in late April.

"It was one of those things that's easy enough to see in hindsight," said Richard, picking at the remains of the rather splendid roast beef that I'd done.

Nadia chuckled. "You always say that."

"Yes, and you always say *that*."

Anne Collister laughed as they glared at each other. "This is why we don't meet like this very often – these two have been bickering like this for years."

The penny dropped with a clang you could have heard in Blackpool. I looked between them. *"Erdikide?"*

"Yes," said Richard, sighing. "Sometimes magic is not very kind."

"You're telling me," replied Nadia. *Erdikide* are like family – you don't get to choose them and very occasionally people get paired with somebody they have difficulty getting along with.

"Now, now, children," said Anne. "Play nicely."

"Enough. Please, go on," said Amy. Richard, Nadia and Anne were still the demigods of British wizardry, but after all that we'd gone through Sam, Amy and I had been declared *Jaun* 4, while Clara had become level 5, because of her connection to the Dragon. We were no longer nervous students in the presence of our masters, although occasionally we had to be reminded that they were still the bosses.

"OK. Weaver had been working with a small group of less than morally reliable *kemen* Talents to create a system capable of storing spell power. This could have been…"

"Will be," Nadia interjected.

"… useful in all sorts of ways, but he had tailored its output to be destructive. Put simply, he was weaponising magic."

"As if it needs it," Anne muttered.

"You saw the effects at the army base. Anyway, there was a falling out. From the e-mails we found it was clear that some of them disagreed about the conversion to a weapon, and others that Weaver should have sole control over it. So he dreamed up…"

"Nightmared up…" said Nadia, laughing at Slater's expression.

"The plan was to use powerful *Iksale* as conduits for this damned thing. He wanted to draw on their capacity to control it, not power it, because he hadn't got the device working properly yet. Then he made sure all the others in his little cabal came within range, so he could dispose of anyone who opposed him. The last one was in the building in Sussex that he destroyed." Richard sighed. "Pretty obvious motive, but why he felt he had to kill the others…"

"Such a charming man," said Amy.

"An absolute sweetie," agreed Anne.

"So why didn't anyone spot him?"

"Because he's – was – very clever, and used Cherekov to

do his dirty work. They'd made sure we lost track of him so that Weaver could be alibied to within an inch of his life all the time, and then gave Cherekov a legitimate history so we would trust him."

"He just didn't count on Mike having a buried second Talent," said Nadia. "None of us did, and now he's got a third one... sheesh." She shook her head.

"And he would have gotten away with it, if it wasn't for you meddling kids," added Anne. "James Greylock asked me to say that. He said that Michael would understand."

I laughed, then stopped. I'd broken about twenty ribs at Somerby Court and although the bones were healed, the muscles and other squishy bits still objected to levity, like a Methodist grandmother being horrified by the thought that someone, somewhere, might actually be enjoying themselves.

"In the end it was quite simple – everything he did, including kidnapping Amy, were attempts at distraction, misdirection or to frighten you off," said Anne.

"Which, of course, was never going to work with you load of bolshie buggers," said Nadia. "I don't think he wanted to hurt you, at least not at the start. He just wanted you to leave him alone to get on with what he wanted to do. Same reason he went for the colleges, I guess, though we'll never know." If that was a dig at me for failing to keep him alive I chose to ignore it.

"Which is especially ironic as we didn't have a bloody clue what he was up to most of the time," Clara replied.

She was different now, starting with a luminous purple Dragon tattoo that stretched the whole length of her left arm, its head on the back of her hand. On her insistence, and with Amy's collusion, I had a much smaller, simpler one tattooed on my left forearm, which glows in the part of the spectrum that only mages can see whenever I call on the earth for power. And no, it isn't bloody Octarine. Clara designed both of them herself.

As I said, when you get Clara, you get the Dragon. And once you've got the Dragon, you'll never be rid of it. One day I'll give it a name, and it won't be Algernon or Jennifer.

The thing is, I still felt like me. I didn't feel like a very powerful mage, someone who is known at a national level and who gets asked to go to places to do what he does. It's a bit like when I got my driving licence – I was still me but I had this official skill. This felt the same, including the need to be bloody careful so I didn't run into/set fire to/blow up anything I didn't mean to.

Slater was still talking.

"We found the thing they'd been working on in the rubble of Somerby Court. It had been roughly repaired after the army base, but the collapse smashed it to fragments. Weaver was trying to use it on you when you fought, probably by drawing on all the power he'd managed to put into it. When he died, that power was released all in one go. That's why the damage was so extensive and you got hurt so much."

I nodded. "What's going to happen to Ishka and the others?"

"Halsted has been made a DS in Special Operations. He, Ishka and Addison have become our permanent liaison contacts. The hard-light deaths will have verdicts of 'unlawfully killed' put against them at an inquest, naming Weaver and Cherekov but being vague about what caused the deaths, if you see what I mean."

There was a silence, with wine and an easing of belts. "So what now?" I asked.

"Back to work," said Nadia with a shrug. "Your little gang has got some big things to sort out."

"Hardly my little gang," I protested. I wasn't in charge

of us – nobody really was. Sam is scary strong; Clara has a Dragon on speed dial and Amy is now so clever that I think I should stick to finger painting.

Nadia bit down on a smile. "You lot have become a '*laukote*', which literally means a 'quartet' – four mages of varied but significant abilities that work as a coherent and complementary group."

"Not too sure about the coherent bit," muttered Amy. I swear she didn't glance at me, but…

"Anyway, if you aren't careful you'll end up like we did." She gestured to the others.

"You a *laukote*? You only three." Sam said sharply.

Anne Collister shifted in her chair slightly, and lifted her chin. "Do you remember the last full Triple Talent? Ellie Hart?"

"I've heard of her, of course, but…"

"She was my *erdikide*," Anne went on quietly. Nadia gripped her hand. "When she died we stopped being *laukote* and became *hirko*, a trio."

"In a group like this everyone becomes *erdikide* to everyone else, at some level or other," said Richard. "I wondered if a three to one female–male ratio was just my bad luck, but it seems it's always three to one and in the last ten recorded groups – you get one every twenty years or so – only one has been male heavy."

"Any idea why?"

Richard looked at me and raised an eyebrow. "Because God is a feminist? Because one man is a match for any three women?" Nadia threw a roast potato at him. "Because dinosaurs had yellow toes and could hum the 'Marseillaise'?"

"So you don't know."

"Not a fucking clue." He stood up abruptly. "Excuse me for a moment." He headed for the toilet.

"Ellie was his girlfriend," said Anne softly. "They were living together and he was with her when she died. He stopped doing magic for nearly a year after that. It seemed to burn all the joy out of him."

That led to an introspective silence, broken by the sound of the toilet flushing. "So what happens now?"

"Well," said Nadia, "we've got a small problem."

"What, another one?"

"Yes, but this time it's not directly related to you." She let that hang for a moment, obviously hoping that my curiosity would get the better of me. I took a mouthful of wine and let it, which is always a mistake.

"Okay, so what is it?"

"We have found several objects that seem to be entirely resistant to the effects of magic. We were wondering if you would like to look into it? When your studies allow, of course. You seem very well suited to it."

Sam just sighed.